Buried Lies

JENNY O'BRIEN

ONE PLACE. MANY STORIES

HQ

An imprint of HarperCollins*Publishers* Ltd
1 London Bridge Street
London SE1 9GF

www.harpercollins.co.uk

HarperCollins*Publishers*
1st Floor, Watermarque Building, Ringsend Road
Dublin 4, Ireland

This paperback edition 2022

1

First published in Great Britain by
HQ, an imprint of HarperCollins*Publishers* Ltd 2021

ISBN: 9780008457075

MIX
Paper from
responsible sources
FSC™ C007454

This book is produced from independently certified FSC™ paper
to ensure responsible forest management.

For more information visit: www.harpercollins.co.uk/green

Printed and bound by CPI Group (UK) Ltd,
Croydon, CR0 4YY

Prai...

'Keeps you on the edge of your seat'

'A great crime procedural series!'

'An amazing thriller from beginning to end'

'Couldn't ask for a better read'

'This series just keeps getting better. I was hooked
from the first page'

'A five-star read, no question'

Born in Dublin, **JENNY O'BRIEN** moved to Wales and then Guernsey, where she tries to find time to both read and write in between working as a nurse and ferrying around three teenagers.

In her spare time she can be found frowning at her wonky cakes and even wonkier breads. You'll be pleased to note she won't be entering *Bake Off*. She's also an all-year-round sea swimmer.

Also by Jenny O'Brien

To Jean Russell, Roger Allsopp (OBE)
and the gang on table 3.

Chapter 1

Hannah

Saturday 22 August, 10.55 p.m. Ruthin

'I thought we'd try this next.' Milly placed the glasses carefully on the table before flopping down on the seat opposite. 'Blue Bottle Gin as recommended by the barman, no less.'

'I'm not sure I'd notice the difference, not after all that wine,' Hannah said, lifting up the glass and running her hand over the little blackberry etched onto the surface.

'It's award-winning apparently,' Milly went on. 'Good gin is like good coffee – one of life's essentials, and if we can't treat ourselves, it's unlikely anyone else will.' She raised her glass in a brief toast and took a long sip. 'Bloody divine, as is the barman by the way.'

'Ha. You can keep him. Not my type.'

'You do surprise me. So, what is your type? Certainly not Ian or you'd be married by now.' Milly stopped, a sudden gleam in her eye. 'I know, let's play Truth or Dare.'

'I don't really think—'

1

'No need to think, hon. I'll go first.'

'Oh, come on, Milly. Really! I haven't played in years.'

'And what about it? Now's the time to reacquaint yourself. Far better than I-spy or twiddling your thumbs checking out Bruce the barman,' Milly said, making a point of glancing in his direction. 'I have first dibs, by the way, as you're already taken.'

'You're incorrigible! Although he is quite cute, apart from the man bun, which I don't get on any level.'

'Hah. I never thought you'd be so fussy. I'll go first.'

'But I never agreed to …' Hannah glanced at her phone and the text that had pinged through.

A boring night in with a curry and my best boy. You enjoy, my love. See you soon xx

Milly settled her glass down on the table with a little bang, presumably to regain Hannah's attention.

'So, truth or dare?'

'Hold on a mo. I just need to reply to this,' she said, her fingers tapping away on the screen.

Hannah hated games of any sort apart from possibly Snakes and Ladders and, after the bottle of wine they'd managed with their meal, she was well on the way to being plastered. But with Milly staring at her with an eager expression pinned to her glossy lips, she felt she had little choice. She remembered back to the last time she'd played. A similar set-up but then there'd been more people around the table – four nurses intent on a good time. The dares had been increasingly obscene so …

'Truth then, if we must,' she said finally, dropping her phone back onto the table, her expression as resigned as her tone.

'We must! Don't worry. I'll be gentle. So, how many times has he tried to set a date for the wedding?'

Hannah laughed, settling back in her chair. 'To be truthful, I have no idea. Must be fifty by now.'

'Aren't you the lucky one … And when are you going to put him out of his misery?'

Never! Marrying Ian was never going to happen, despite accepting his ring in a moment of weakness. But that was something she wasn't prepared to tell Milly.

'That's two questions. My turn,' she said, suddenly remembering the rules of the game with a little sigh of relief. 'Truth or dare?'

'Oh, truth then.'

'Would you take Liam back if he asked?'

'Not on your nelly, even if hell froze over and the moon turned to cheese, and before you ask why, I'll tell you. He had his chance. One measly chance to stay faithful. If he did it once who's to say he wouldn't do it again.' She sat back, her glass aloft and her smile back. 'My go. Truth or dare?'

Hannah didn't know Milly all that well but she knew she didn't trust her when it came to pranks. At work she was always the one with the loudest laugh and the wildest of ideas. She probably had something in mind that would be mega embarrassing or completely gross.

'Truth then.'

'I don't think you trust me, Hannah,' Milly said with a chuckle. 'Okay. Truth it is. Mm, what will it be?' She propped her chin on her fingertip, pretending to think. 'Oh, I know. Someone asked me this a while ago. I found it really tricky but you'll probably do better. What's the one thing you could change about your life up to now if you could, and why?'

Hannah froze, the colour leaching from her cheeks. Her attention shifted from Milly to her glass, which she picked up and held between both hands like a lifeline.

To choose one thing over the many. Milly couldn't possibly realise that she'd given Hannah the hardest question of all. Hannah viewed her life like a house of cards but one where someone had removed the foundations, leaving chaos behind. She didn't like to dwell on the past. It was a very unhappy place but if she could come up with the catalyst that had changed the course of everything, it would have to be before meeting Ian. Even before Hunter's birth. Way before that.

'The plane crash that killed both my parents and my brother.'

Chapter 2

Gaby

Sunday 23 August, 12.30 p.m. Betws-y-Coed

'I have to admit to being pleasantly surprised. When you mentioned going away for a spa weekend instead of having a hen party, the only part of me that was happy was my liver. Although, I'm not so sure that DCI Sherlock is going to be that impressed with my fingernails,' Gaby said, inspecting her bright pink polish with a frown.

Newly appointed to the post of detective inspector, Gabriella Darin – Gaby to her friends – didn't have the money or inclination to take more than a passing interest in her appearance. Heading up the Major Incident Team over at St Asaph, she also didn't have enough hours in the day to manage her workload, which meant that her beauty regime consisted of five minutes to slap on a dollop of the face cream that lived on the bathroom shelf before grabbing her keys and bag and heading out the door. She'd never had a facial, and nail varnish was something that she bought with the best of intentions only to throw it away months later when the shiny liquid had morphed into a nebulous gloop in the bottom of the bottle. She'd been far more alarmed at the prospect of someone messing around with her feet than she was at the thought of a room full of criminals and had to remind herself at every juncture that she was only here because Amy had made her.

Amy Potter, small and slight with a mass of mousy-coloured hair, was family liaison officer, or FLO, back at the station. They'd been through much more than most friends and were closer than sisters because of it.

'He probably won't even notice and if he does, send him in my direction. Inviting the DCI to my wedding was a stroke of genius, don't you think? It's not as if he can give us a hard time for managing to squirrel the weekend off together when within days he's going to be quaffing my champagne.' Amy stared up at the overcast sky with a frown. 'I hope the weather stays nice for the wedding.'

'And if it's pouring from the heavens, it won't make a blind bit of difference to anyone's enjoyment, except perhaps your mother-in-law's and the photographer.'

Gaby strolled along the side of the river, her hands tucked into the pockets of her favourite blue gilet – a bright contrast to her black T-shirt and long black shorts – her handbag crossed over her shoulder. While she'd heard of Betws-y-Coed, it was the first time she'd actually visited. There was a quaintness about the place that meant she'd be visiting again, preferably in the company of a certain red-haired Irishman.

However, as with most things in her life, timing was everything, and with Amy's wedding on the horizon, she had no idea when she'd get the chance to sneak away for a couple of days of serious eating negated by the serious walking she planned.

She stifled a laugh at where her thoughts were taking her, her gaze drawn to a field of sheep grazing on the lush grass and to the little wooden gate beyond, which guarded a narrow path trailing off into the distance. The DCI owed her a bundle of time off in lieu, which she hadn't bothered to do anything about apart from diligently record it in the black diary that lived in reception. Now she had a mind to cash it in and book a mini break before the weather turned. It might be just the thing to shift her relationship with Rusty Mulholland, the resident pathologist, onto a more formal footing instead of the odd date whenever work and babysitters allowed.

'Did I tell you that my bouquet is to be a surprise? Tim asked me for ...'

Gaby nodded, adding a broad smile as she took in Amy's bright complexion and sparkling eyes. A very different Amy to the one she'd had to drag out of bed and forcibly push in the direction of the shower. It had taken a great deal of persuasion and numerous mugs of coffee to convince her friend that the hangover from hell would be far more manageable after something to eat. Gaby wouldn't have been averse to longer in bed either but the thought of a proper breakfast, instead of the bowl of porridge she normally opted for, had her dismissing sleep, at least for now. There was time enough for a mid-afternoon snooze later, under the large pear tree in the back garden of her tiny cottage.

'Has he given you any more hints as to where you're spending your honeymoon?'

'No. It's so annoying. The only clue he's allowed is that I won't need my driving licence as it doesn't have cars.'

'Ooh. Sounds exciting. No. It sounds like paradise.'

'That's all very well but I have no idea what to take.' Amy lifted her hands up to her hair and tightened her scrunchie. 'Makes for impossible packing.'

'Not really. He'd have told you if it was somewhere cold so one or two jumpers and a mac in case the rain hits but apart from that, beachwear should be fine.'

Amy grabbed her arm, pulling her to a halt, her face a picture of irritation. 'You know, don't you? The rat has told you and not me.'

7

'Well, he might have asked what my thoughts were but ...' Gaby backed off a step, pulling her hand out of Amy's grasp. 'It's no good trying to squeeze it out of me because I'm not even sure if he's gone with the idea or chosen something completely different.'

'But—'

'No buts, Amy.' She held up her hands, palms facing outwards. 'You'll have a lovely time wherever you are and whatever the weather. Now, no more questions. After all this walking, what do you say to a light lunch before we have to make tracks? The hotel is busy but they said they'd make room.'

'I knew I was right to book Paintings. Expensive but worth it.'

'You could say the same about us.' Gaby turned on her heel without waiting for an answer about lunch. 'I wonder if Marie and Diane have even surfaced yet?' she said, her thoughts turning to the other two women on the MIT who they'd left propping up the bar well past midnight.

'From the way they were putting the world to rights last night, I very much doubt it,' Amy said, resuming her usual good spirits. 'It was great to see Marie letting her hair down for once.'

'Yes. I can't help feeling that she's moving on with her life despite – and not because of – the actions of her ex-husband.'

The sound of Gaby's ringtone had her withdrawing her mobile from her pocket and glancing at the screen. She'd been hoping that it was Rusty checking up on her, but that wasn't what she got.

'Darin speaking.'

'I thought you were meant to be off?' Amy hissed.

'I'm never off,' she replied out of the corner of her mouth. 'Yes, sorry about that, Jax. It's not a great signal. What's up?'

Gaby closed her eyes to the beauty of the riverbank and her ears to the noise from the stream as she concentrated on Jax's words. With a discipline born out of experience, she switched back into the role of lead detective of the North Wales Major Incident Team with barely a glimmer of effort and, with the switch, any lingering trace of happiness deserted her along with the colour in her cheeks and any plans for the afternoon.

She finally finished the call but instead of returning her phone to her pocket, she turned to Amy, managing a smile of sorts. It wouldn't win any prizes but then Gaby had never felt less like smiling.

'Sorry about that—'

But if Gaby was a consummate professional then Amy Potter matched her step for step. Without so much as a change of expression, she increased her stride to a near run, the only thing stopping her from changing to a sprint the tree roots waiting to trip them both up.

'I'll phone Diane and Marie to let them know we're going back early and that I'll sort out the bill. Can you throw my stuff into my bag? Don't forget my make-up in the bathroom and my charger is still plugged into the wall.'

'Amy, you really don't have to—'

'Stop arguing. Are you in need of a FLO or not?'

'More than you know! Come on, I'll tell you all about it on the way back. Jax has rounded up Mal. We'll leave Diane and Marie to enjoy what's left of their hangovers in peace.'

Chapter 3

Gaby

Sunday 23 August, 1.15 p.m. Conwy

Gaby rarely had the time to visit the selection of small villages and towns that spanned across Wales in an interweaving ribbon. She worked long hours and, when she was at home, she had a list of DIY projects that she needed to carry out on her cottage. She'd heard of Conwy, the walled market town overlooked by an impressive medieval castle. She'd even had a person go missing from one of the marina properties, but that was about as far as it went.

Following the satnav in addition to Amy's frantic handwaving signals, she drove along Rose Hill Street and towards the perimeter of the town wall up ahead, Betws-y-Coed a world away. And yet Conwy was no less beautiful, just different.

'Once you're through the arch, take a sharp left. Mount Pleasant should be up ahead. Jax says he'll wait outside so that we don't miss it.'

'He's probably still cursing at having his sleep interrupted,'

Gaby replied, flipping on the indicator. 'As well as being on call, he's also working tonight. I had promised that he could take some of his time owing if it was quiet. Mal is perfectly capable of holding the fort for a few hours.'

Amy twisted in her seat, her mouth slightly open. 'I never thought I'd see the day when you'd have anything complimentary to say about Malachy Devine. I thought you couldn't stand the man?'

'You should know me better than that, and anyway I'm not in the game of pigeonholing colleagues as to whether I like them or not.' Gaby stiffened, altering her past with a metaphorical brush laden with regret. She'd learnt the hard way never to make snap judgements about people because invariably she'd been proved wrong. Her past was littered with her failings in that regard. While Malachy wasn't her favourite person, she was extra careful not to show her opinion one way or the other. She knew that a black officer could easily face bias during the performance of his day-to-day duties. She couldn't change the world but at least she could do her best to ensure that her small slice of the planet was managed in a fair and equitable manner.

'I have to give him credit where it's due. Over the last couple of cases he's proved that he more than deserves his place on the team.' She spotted Jax up ahead and started to slow her speed. 'You must remember that the postgrad, fast-track route Mal chose to become a detective means that he's missed out on all those invaluable and, to my mind, essential years pounding the beat.' She pulled up behind the CSI van and killed the engine. 'Come on, let's get this over and done with. With a bit of luck, we'll both be home in time for the six o'clock news.'

Gaby climbed out of the car and slammed the door shut, her mind ensconced in the task ahead. There were procedures to follow, strict guidelines that had been drilled into her from her early days on the force. She wouldn't even dream of entering the property until she'd divested herself of her gilet and climbed into the white paper bodysuit and accompanying blue overshoes. Latex-free gloves came next before she pulled the drawstring toggle on her hood, ensuring that all her hair was bundled underneath.

She quickly scrawled her name, date and the time on the clipboard handed to her by the uniformed officer guarding the door, then held it out to Amy. 'Right, Jax. Tell me what's happening.'

'The CSIs are on standby, waiting for you to give them the heads up, ma'am. I've also got Dr Mulholland on the way. He should be here shortly; he needs to sort out childcare first. Mal is with the victim's partner.' He paused, tilting his head towards Amy. 'He's going to be very pleased to see you. She's in b-b-bits,' he stuttered.

'Only to be expected. Okay, let's see the body then. There's no point in hanging around waiting for Rusty. He'll appear when he appears and it's not fair to ruin the CSIs' weekend. Which investigators have we got on duty?'

'Clive, but you'll be pleased to hear that he's called in Jason, ma'am. Jase is not happy about it, let me tell you. He had plans to go fishing.'

'Tough. Lead CSIs such as Jason, along with OICs, don't get the chance of a home life until they've cleared their desk for the day.'

'The same could be said for DCs,' Jax mumbled under his breath.

'What was that?'

'Nothing. This way, ma'am.' He held open the door, gesturing for her to go on ahead.

Gaby had heard what he'd said all too clearly but wasn't in the mood to tackle him on what was, after all, a minor transgression. Letting slip what he thought on occasion wasn't a bad thing unless it became a habit. For Gaby to manage the team she had to have an insight into what was going on inside their heads and the odd rebellious comment was far more useful than the hour-long catch-ups she had with each of them on a monthly basis.

The hall was minute with only room for a small table and little else. It led straight into the lounge, rectangular in shape with a small settee suite arranged around a fake fireplace, and a staircase that took up the whole of one wall. The room was also empty so they didn't linger. Instead Gaby followed Jax into the small kitchen, which was made to feel smaller by the two officers standing guard over the woman hunched over the table. Her head was buried in the security of her folded arms. Mal stood helplessly by her side.

Gaby had worked with Amy for long enough now to let her know her thoughts with only a flick of her head. But, in this instance, Amy didn't need any prompting to shrug off any visible trace of her banging headache and replace it with the veneer of composed officer on duty. Gaby watched a moment as she slid into the seat beside the woman, her tone calm and gentle, her body language open and expressive. Amy couldn't work miracles. She couldn't breathe life into cold lungs and quiet hearts. She couldn't revive the unrousable just as she couldn't rewrite the past. Her skills were deeper. Darker. Indefinable but no less important. Amy would stay holding the woman's metaphorical hand for as long as she felt it necessary. Tim and the wedding would be all but forgotten as she acted substitute mother, sibling and friend until help appeared from another source.

'Ma'am?'

'Coming.' Gaby turned away and followed Jax through a plain white door, almost invisible against the stark white of the kitchen walls and cabinets.

This was the part of the investigation that she both loved and hated in equal measure, adrenalin causing her blood vessels to fill and her pulse to quicken. The thought of the unknown lying up ahead. Both the start and the end of something. A life coming to an abrupt halt as the cogs of the police machine shifted into action. There was nothing she could do to prevent the loss of life but as to the rest? Only time and determination would tell.

The garage was the same as countless others she'd visited over the years. The bare brick walls surrounded by shelves with an assortment of boxes filled with the usual detritus that at some point would find its way into landfill. In many cases the need to house a car seemed an unnecessary luxury but not here.

The Toyota filled the space, leaving only a narrow path along either side and little else. Gaby wasn't a car aficionado by any means. If her vehicle had petrol in the tank and started when she pressed the ignition she was happy, but she'd be a fool not to recognise quality when she saw it. The orange sports model was obviously someone's pride and joy. Whose was yet to be clarified.

She strolled around to the front of the car to stare in through the windscreen at the man resting back against the driving seat. It almost looked as if he'd dropped off to sleep, all apart from the characteristic cherry-red mottling that caused her stomach to contract and her lips to purse. This wasn't the first time she'd come across the distinctive skin tone but that didn't make it any easier. Death was a nasty business but never more so than when it was self-inflicted. Accidental deaths from carbon monoxide poisoning were a rarity but sadly the same couldn't be said for suicides.

'Tell me again what happened,' she said, side stepping around a pile of vomit.

'Hannah Thomas returned home at around eleven o'clock, after a night spent at that new spa hotel in Ruthin, to find both her fiancé and son missing. She'd arranged to be back by eleven at the latest because the fiancé was due to play a match. As you can see, she found the fiancé but there's no trace of the boy. A lad of five. He's her son, but not her partner's.'

'You'd have thought the child would be in the car too, wouldn't you?' she said, bending down to peer in through the passenger window.

Jax shrugged. 'Unless the plan was to abduct him. I've set up a search and called in Marie and Diane to coordinate.'

They're going to love you for that. But all she said was, 'Okay, carry on. The CSIs are probably champing at the bit to get started. What else?'

'There's not a lot more to add. She opened the car to feel for a pulse while she waited for the emergency services to arrive. He was stone cold so death must have occurred quite a while ago.'

'When did she last see him?'

'About 5 p.m. yesterday.' Jax paused a moment, his stutter reappearing. 'T-t-the thing is, Thomas appears to be far more concerned about the whereabouts of her son than she is the death of her fiancé. Apparently, the boy suffers from diabetes but it seems more than that …'

'Okay, noted but let's hold back from theorising until we know more about what happened.' Gaby looked up, straight into the distinctive green eyes of Jason Moore standing in the doorway, no glimmer of a smile on his lips. 'Sorry about the fishing, Jase, I would promise to make it up to you but …' She shrugged her shoulders.

'Never mind. I've decided to give up on a personal life until you retire; that is, if they're ever able to drag you away after they've handed you your clock.'

'Ha, very funny, not.' She waved him ahead. 'Over to you and the team. I'll be in the kitchen if you need me.'

She headed for the door, only to pause at his uncustomary silence.

Jason, for all his faults and snarky sense of humour, was polite to the core of his rangy frame. He would never not reply despite being peeved at his lost weekend. It wasn't in his nature. She swivelled on her heel but not before she caught his sharp intake of breath.

'What is it?'

'You do know who this is, don't you? He's one of ours.'

Chapter 4

Gaby

Sunday 23 August, 1.55 p.m. Conwy

'One of ours? I don't get you?'

'Unless I'm very much mistaken it's that new copper. You know, the one who ended up crashing into the monument a couple of months ago?'

'You can't mean Ian Strong? But he's only a kid?' Gaby said, glancing back at the windscreen and the man beyond.

'What's that got to do with the price of fish? He's old enough.' Jason moved to the far side of the car to make room for the rest of the team.

Gaby lifted her hand to her hair only to drop it to her side, forgetting for a moment that she was covered in head-to-toe paper suiting. Instead she switched on her mobile and sent Owen Bates, her second in command, a quick text. He was the very last person she would choose to call in on a day off but a dead man was one thing; a dead copper, while equally horrific, opened up a completely different can of worms.

16

'Okay, do what you can. Remember there's a missing kid too so that has to be our priority. Anything, however small or insignificant, give me a buzz.'

Gaby walked into the kitchen only to step back at the sight of Rusty hurrying into the room, the hood from his over-suit dangling around his neck, his red hair in need of a good cut. Not that she felt she could tell him. Their relationship, for want of a better word, was too new to absorb the possible fallout from personal comments. Her mind swung back briefly to thoughts of that mini break in Betws-y-Coed that would probably now never happen.

'Sorry, babysitter problems.'

'Not an issue, Doctor,' she said, her voice pitched to professional. 'I know you like to be first on the scene but I've set Jason to work already. There's a missing child involved and, as you know …'

'Time is of the essence,' he ended, placing his medical bag between his legs so that he could fix his hood in place. 'That's fine by me. So, what do we know?'

'Not a lot.' She lowered her voice to barely a whisper, her head angled towards where Amy and Hannah were sitting. 'He was found by his partner a little after eleven. She'd been away for the night. I'll let Jason fill you in on the rest,' she continued. 'As soon as you have anything—'

'I know!'

Gaby ignored the tone, waving him towards the door with a brush of her hand. She had far too much on her mind to pull him up on his snarky response.

The kitchen had emptied leaving the two women sitting around the beech table, the soft sound of Hannah's voice the only thing to disturb the suddenly deathly quiet room.

'If only I hadn't gone away for the night.'

'There's no way you could have known …' Amy said, meeting Gaby's eyes over the top of the woman's downcast head.

'Ma'am, this is Miss Hannah Thomas – Ian Strong's partner and the missing boy's mother,' she said, handing her a scrap of paper with a name and address written in a shaky hand.

Hannah was dressed in jeans and a blue shirt dotted with tiny yellow flowers. Her eyes were puffy and, from what Gaby could see, red-rimmed and haunted.

Gaby dipped her head in acknowledgement before withdrawing backwards out of the room, unprepared to disturb the status quo quite yet. She'd need to talk to her, of course she would, but it could wait until at the very least the tears showed signs of abating. Amy knew the score. They'd been in similar positions many times. Hannah had found the body and phoned the police. A search was underway for her son. The rest could wait for a bit. Amy would provide tea and tissues until Hannah was in a fit state to answer questions – there were plenty of jobs Gaby could be getting on with in the meantime. There was the boy to find for a start but, with a team already organised and out searching, she also needed to contact the DCI.

She grimaced, starting to scroll through the list of contacts on her mobile. Her previous boss had warned her that DCI Henry Sherlock's weekends were sacrosanct. It had to be a dire emergency for Gaby to pluck up the courage to contact him.

'I'm sorry to have to interrupt your Sunday, sir.'

'This had better be good, Darin.'

'Yes. Well. I've just been called to a case in Conwy and it seems as if the victim is Ian Strong, one of the recent police intakes. In addition, there's a child missing. His partner's son.'

There was a long pause where presumably DCI Henry Sherlock was marshalling his thoughts.

'And what do you expect me to do about it?'

Gaby raised her eyebrows at that. There was more than one answer on her lips but there was no way she'd have the nerve to voice any of them.

'I thought it was best to alert you in case CS Murdock got to hear of it. There's obviously going to be a lot of media interest with this one, sir.'

A new pause fell into the conversation, this one far longer than the last.

'Right. I'll handle Murdock. Message me the salient points as soon as you have them,' he said, ending the call.

She squeezed the phone case, the imitation leather digging into her skin. For someone who had trouble with authority, playing the game was always more difficult when she never knew which set of rules to follow. Sherlock had been adamant that she kept him abreast of any serious concerns but obviously that didn't extend to interrupting his Sunday afternoon on the golf course.

Gaby cast her eye over the torn sheet of paper that Amy had given her and, after a quick word with Jason as to where she was going, headed back to her car. As much as Gaby hated having to call Sherlock on his day off, she dreaded her next task far more. Informing Ian Strong's parents of their son's death. As the lead in the investigation it was something she could easily palm off onto the boys in blue. It was also what most detectives in her position would have done. It would only take seconds to arrange and that would leave her to the whole host of jobs that she had lined up for the next few hours – top of the list being interviewing Hannah. But Gaby wasn't like other detectives. Despite soaring up the promotional ladder at a rate that landed criticism along with a great dollop of jealousy at her door, she'd never shirked a duty in her life.

She'd provide the Strongs with all the courtesy and kindness due to them, even if it was time she could ill afford. Gaby glanced at her watch as she set up the satnav. With a bit of luck, she'd be back in an hour or so for that interview.

Chapter 5

Gaby

Sunday 23 August, 3.55 p.m. St Asaph

Gaby was standing in reception ostensibly chatting with Clancy, the desk sergeant, when Amy escorted Hannah into the station, which gave her ample opportunity to study the young woman.

Hannah was in her mid-to-late twenties and of average height and build. Neither too tall nor too short, too fat nor too thin. Her shoulder-length, mid-brown hair was of the type most women of Gaby's acquaintance would have chosen to highlight. Interestingly, her face was also nondescript. Her skin was clear but hosted an insipid pair of blue eyes, and a nose and mouth a smidgeon too large for any accepted image of beauty. All in all, unremarkable.

Faces interested Gaby, which was probably in direct relation to a recent resurgence in her devotion to the science of criminal profiling. It was a rare criminal who could be typecast into the mould of deviant by the face they presented to the world. Most murderers and rapists looked normal. They were also primarily male, Gaby remembered. To a ratio of ten to one, if the recent

UK figures on suspect rates for male versus female perpetrators of murder were to be believed. Perhaps it was the very fact of Hannah's inconspicuousness that made her face more interesting to Gaby? If she passed her in the street, the woman would fade into the background. If she was standing in a line-up, the chance was that someone so unmemorable might just get away with murder …

The last two hours had taken their toll on Hannah's looks. Her shoulder-length hair was dragged back into a rubber band and, despite enjoying the luxury of an evening at one of Ruthin's top hotels, she looked pale, drawn, anxious and fatigued. Nothing could stop the feelings of sympathy that washed over Gaby but that in no way deterred her from the task ahead. She had one role and that was to get to the truth of what had happened on Saturday night. While she might be empathetic to Hannah having lost her partner, she couldn't rule out that Hannah was hiding the truth. Gaby's gut instinct told her that the emotions oozing from Hannah were genuine but it wouldn't be the first time that her gut had let her down. Her thoughts flickered to St David's and the biggest mistake of her career to date: the disappearance of Alys Grant.

Gaby held out her hand, her bland expression and firm grip showing no indication of where her mind was dragging her.

'I'm sorry for having to call you into the station but there are a few things we need to sort out. I'm sure you'll agree on the importance of finding out what happened, as quickly as possible.'

She directed her along the corridor into interview room four and waited for Amy and Hannah to take a seat before pressing the switch on the built-in microphone and reciting the usual introduction, which the station typists demanded in full.

'You're not under caution but if you'd like free legal advice that can be arranged?'

'No. I haven't done anything wrong. I just want this over so I can get back to looking for my son.'

'We'll arrange for that as soon as we've finished here. We shouldn't be too long. Firstly I'd like a recap of what happened on Saturday if I may?'

Hannah started to speak, her voice low and husky, her hands forming knots as she twisted her fingers. 'Ian was on earlies so he left at about half six so he could start his shift for seven, but you'll probably know that already. I got up after and tidied the kitchen, put the washing machine on, that sort of thing.' She looked up. 'Do you want me to tell you everything that I did or …?'

'You're doing just fine, Hannah – I can call you Hannah?' Gaby waited for the slight nod before continuing. 'Tell us as much or as little detail as you want. We'll interrupt if we have any questions.'

Hannah returned to her study of her fingers. 'I hung the washing out, which would have been about ten-ish. Then Hunter wanted to go for a walk down the hill.' She lifted her head. 'He loves the boats. I made some sandwiches from what was left over in the fridge and we wandered down past the castle to the quay. He's not meant to have too many sweet things but I did let him have an ice cream after his lunch. It's hard trying to be a good mum and manage his diabetes but I'm only pleased that I gave in for once.' She swallowed a couple of times, her gaze returning to her hands.

'Did you want to stop for a moment?' Amy asked, pushing a box of tissues in her direction.

Hannah sniffed, the sound loud in the suddenly quiet room. Then, instead of replying, she shook her head, plucking a tissue from the box and pressing it under her eyes.

'We didn't do much. It was too hot for that, just mooched around the boats and said hello to a couple of the fishermen to see what their catch was like. Fed the crusts of bread to the seagulls even though we probably shouldn't have. That sort of thing. Afterwards we made our way back up the hill. It would have been about half two, three o'clock – something like that. Ian had just arrived back.'

'Did you notice anything strange?'

'Not really. Ian was tired but then he found the job stressful. He went upstairs for a nap and, with Hunter ensconced in front of the television, I joined him. As you already know I had plans to go away for the night and I hadn't gotten around to getting ready. He was resting on the bed with his eyes closed so I took the opportunity to have a quick shower, get dressed and pack a few things. I'd decided to take my motorbike and there's not that much room under the seat.'

'And was it common practice for you to go away for the night?'

'Never. Milly, one of the girls at work, has just split up with her boyfriend but she'd already booked a night away and the hotel was being snooty about giving her a refund. She asked me whether I'd like to join her.'

'Okay. Let's shift things forward. Tell me about your overnight stay.'

'It was at Y Mwyar Duon in Ruthin. That big hotel on the riverbank,' she said, reaching for the glass of water that Amy had poured for her. 'Milly was waiting for me when I arrived. We went up to our room to get changed into the robes provided and spent a couple of hours relaxing in the spa, had a manicure, that sort of thing. After, we dressed for dinner and spent the rest of the evening in the bar ...' She paused, suddenly hesitant.

'And?'

'And ...' Hannah shook her head. 'We returned to the room and attacked the mini bar. After that ... next I knew we woke up.'

'Okay. So, you don't remember getting into bed or ...?'

'Not really. I woke up in my PJs, my face glued to the pillow, regretting every last mouthful of gin.'

'I think we've all been there,' Gaby said, making a note. 'And what is it you do?'

'I'm a nurse at Daffodils old people's home, only part-time because of Hunter. It's the first time I'd spent a night away from him because of his diabetes, which makes it all the more important that he's found quickly.'

'Okay.' The tip of Gaby's pencil pressed hard into the paper, making a deep hole, which she covered up with a squiggle. Looking for a missing child was always a priority but the desperation in Hannah's voice had just ramped up the importance of the search. 'Can you tell us a little bit more about his diabetes?'

'There's not a huge amount to say. Hunter is ...' She hesitated again, massaging the skin on her left wrist, which had the faint trace of an old scar breaking through. 'Hunter failed to thrive when he was born. It took the paediatricians quite a time to work out that he is a Type 1 diabetic. His pancreas fails to produce any insulin whatsoever. But apart from that he's a normal little boy. Full of mischief,' she said, her knuckles shining white through her work-reddened skin.

'He has a pump?' Amy said, her voice whisper-soft.

'Yes. A little device on his tummy that I'm not to remove unless it's being changed. And we never do. It's a godsend me being a nurse.' She paused again. 'Ian isn't ... wasn't good around anything medical. He hated being alone with Hunter. Oh, he was fine when I was there. Wonderful. The best substitute dad a parent could wish for considering he's only known Hunter for about a year. But a trip to the supermarket was about the sum total of the time I've spent away from my son since Ian came on the scene.' She glanced up before turning her attention back to her fingers. 'Not that I minded ever. It brought Hunter and me closer if anything. Last night was a bit of a test if I'm honest and the longest they'd ever been alone together. Ian kept harping on about marriage. I wanted to see if he even knew what parenting Hunter for more than an hour really meant.'

'Okay. Let's talk about this morning then. I know this is difficult but if you can take it from when you arrived back at the house.'

Hannah closed her eyes briefly, her voice low and soft. 'I dropped my bag in the hall and went looking for them both. The house was quiet – unusually so. There's always noise in our house, whether it's the TV or Hunter, so I knew immediately that

I was alone. I couldn't work out where Ian would have taken him. He knew I was coming home around that time. I'd even texted him to remind him. I called out a few times, lots going through my mind as to what might have happened.'

'What sort of things?' Gaby said, sitting back in her chair and watching the play of emotions on Hannah's face.

'Nothing that any parent doesn't think of on occasion. Hunter's diabetes. An intruder. Even Ian and Hunter playing a trick. I half expected them to jump out from the cupboard under the stairs shouting *boo*. It wouldn't have been the first time.'

'Okay. I know this is difficult, but we do need to go through what happened in the garage. If you need a short break I perfectly understand.'

'No. Let's get it over with,' Hannah said, after a second, her voice monotonous as she revisited the scene in the quiet of the room. 'I decided to get the car and search for them. The garage looked the same as ever. The usual boxes of Christmas decorations on the shelves. A few tools scattered about. Ian's pride and joy of a car. There was nothing different. Nothing to alert me that …' She took a breath, repeating her words. 'The garage looked the same. It even smelt the same or at least I think it did. No, that's not right.' She frowned. 'There was a smell like … like fumes. I thought it odd at the time then forgot all about it. When I glanced through the windscreen, Ian's head was lolling back against the headrest. I knew straightaway he was dead.'

Gaby opened her mouth only to close it at Hannah's next words. 'A dead person looks different, but it's not something that any nurse could ever explain. His eyes were open and staring. His skin had that particular carbon monoxide reddish-pink hue that we learn about during our training. I knew he was dead even before I felt for his pulse.'

'Okay, thank you. Let's talk about you and Ian. How would you say your relationship was?'

Hannah's head snapped back, her eyes suddenly alert where

before they'd been dull and flat, as if she'd only been going through the motions. 'What's that got to do with anything?'

'It's important to form a well-rounded picture of what happened, Hannah. I think you'll agree that it would be wrong of us not to conduct a *full* investigation, so please answer the question.'

'We muddled along like most couples. And like most couples there were good days and there were bad.'

'What about arguments?'

Hannah pressed her hand to her head, running her fingers across her forehead.

'We had our fair share. Ian wanted us to get married but I wasn't ready for that,' she said, her eyes wandering to the small solitaire diamond on her ring finger. 'We hadn't been together long, hardly any time at all.' She tilted her chin. 'Once bitten twice shy and all that.' She shook her head as if trying to shift a nasty image.

'So, if once bitten twice shy, what about Hunter's dad? Does he feature?' Gaby asked, again noting that almost automatic gesture of reaching for her wrist and massaging the skin as if it irritated her.

'Not since the night of conception.' She gave a laugh of sorts. 'Hunter's father was a mistake – a heady mix of sex and antibiotics – but it was a mistake that I never regretted even for a second.'

Gaby made another note on her pad for no other reason than to break the tension that was sucking all the air out of the room. She was struggling to maintain an open mind and if she wasn't careful, she'd miss what could be a vital clue. The most likely scenario was that it had been a tragic accident but there was still something about the set-up that she couldn't fathom – Hunter, and why he'd seemingly run away. Unless he'd found Ian and taken to his heels?

'What about your past?' Gaby said. 'Both yours and Ian's. Anyone out to get you? Any screwed-up work colleagues holding a grudge? Any reason that you can think of for this to happen?'

'No. No one. Don't you think I've been racking my brains for an answer? But there isn't one.'

'Okay. So, no colleagues but what about friends? Tell me a little about Ian and what he did outside of work.'

'We spent some time together as a family doing the usual sort of things but he was also obsessed with keeping fit, which took up most of his remaining spare time.'

'And his parents? Siblings?'

Gaby watched Hannah squeeze her eyes tight before snapping them open. 'There's only his dad. His mum died a few years ago now. He still talks … talked about her a lot. He was devastated, as was the whole family. There's a brother too, Dominic. He normally lives in Australia but he's here at the moment. I've no idea why,' she added, her voice faltering. 'I don't know him, not really – I've never met him.'

'And you, Hannah, what about your family?'

Hannah's jaw tightened. 'I don't have one, not now. That plane crash six years ago out of JFK airport? My parents and kid brother were on it. There's only some distant cousins that I haven't seen in years.'

'I'm sorry.'

Gaby dropped the pencil on top of her pad, the paper full of illegible notes, which would tide her over until the transcript could be typed up. There was still one thing she needed to ask but she felt a sudden reluctance to add to the burden of the broken woman sitting opposite.

Most people thought her hard and there was an element of truth in that observation. But Gaby wouldn't have reached the dizzy heights of DI without some grit in her bones and steel in her veins. There was never going to be a right time and she certainly wasn't in the business of either prolonging or repeating interviews.

'Hannah, I need to ask if you were in any way involved with the death of Ian and the disappearance of your son?'

Chapter 6

Gaby

'Well, that went well, not,' Gaby said, flinging her mobile and pad onto the middle of her desk. 'For all my faults I've always hated making grown women cry when they've already been through the wringer.'

'I take it you have no objection to upsetting the other half of the population?' Owen said, dropping into the chair opposite and crossing his legs. 'Poor Rusty. If I didn't think you'd met your match I'd almost feel sorry for him.'

Gaby glared across the expanse of wood but didn't have the heart to make a cutting retort. She already felt guilty at having dragged Owen away from his family duties. He was the most senior detective on the team after her, but he was also her friend and, with a young baby at home, ruining his weekend wasn't one of her priorities. The truth was she needed his expertise and his matter-of-fact common sense.

'Tell Uncle Owen all about it. Surely it can't be that bad?'

'I've just come from interviewing Hannah Thomas, who has to be viewed as a suspect in the death of her partner and the disappearance of her son. She went ballistic when I asked her. I've had to leave it to Amy to try and calm her down.'

'Ah! I'm not surprised. So, what are you doing for an encore in addition to slicing her heart with a serving of cold comfort on the side?'

'There are times I hate you almost as much as the job.' Gaby slumped back in her chair, slipping off her trainers under the privacy of the desk and wriggling her toes. 'I'll have you know I've arranged for Ian's dad to pick her up. He's well aware of the situation and, despite his own grief, was more than happy to offer when I told him that I'd have to get a witness statement from her.' She ran her hand over her forehead, brushing back a wisp of hair. 'We had a lovely hen weekend, wonderful, and now this. First Ian Strong. Then a missing kiddie. What next?'

'Poor old Ian. Clancy mentioned something about carbon monoxide poisoning when I walked in the door. While he might have been a prat, no one deserves that.'

Gaby didn't even manage to raise the glimmer of a smile at the speed with which the police grapevine had flipped into action. If Clancy didn't know the latest gossip then it hadn't happened yet.

'Right. Well as he hasn't been formally identified yet, let's keep that little gem to ourselves for now. Rusty is planning on performing the autopsy this evening after which we'll obviously know more. In the meantime, there's a five-year-old that's still missing. I've sent Mal on a door-to-door while Marie and Diane are coordinating the search. They've alerted the lifeboat and been in touch with Caernarfon to arrange a helicopter. At that age he can't have gotten far.'

Gaby eyed Owen over the lid of her laptop. His skin had that blotchy pallor of someone in need of a good night's sleep but, with a month-old baby, that wasn't coming anytime soon. She wasn't prepared to say any more on the subject of Hunter but

Owen was adept at reading her thoughts. Their most recent case, only wrapped up a few days ago, had also involved a missing child but there was a vast difference between a five-year-old and a ten-year-old.

'Is there anything we're missing? Because from where I'm sitting I can't see the sense in the boy running away. He'd have been too young to be involved with what happened to Ian for one … but what if Hunter found his body? For some reason I can't get that scenario out of my head.'

'That's all very well but surely someone would have spotted him and reported it?' Owen ran his hand over his beard. 'What about abduction? Kill Ian and then take the child or just take the child on the off chance. Either of those scenarios could work.'

Gaby ignored the second half of his comment because she knew only too well the usual outcome of random abductions. 'There's been no ransom request.'

'There's been no ransom request *yet*, Gabs,' he said, glancing down at his watch. 'There's still time.'

'I'll believe it when I see it. It's not as if a part-time nurse is going to be that great a catch,' she said, managing a brief laugh. 'I think we've covered everything unless you can think of anything we've missed?'

'Nothing apart from unpicking her alibi if you really do see her in the frame. The search is the main thing for now, isn't it? As soon as the boy turns up, we can all breathe a sigh of relief. Poor little chap. He must be scared witless.'

Gaby stood in front of the first of the new interactive white-boards, shifting from Hunter's photo to that of Ian. Ian was handsome with a mop of thick hair, cut into the regulation short back and sides that the force recommended. Blue eyes. A narrow chin with a deep cleft and a thick corded neck, which was testament to the amount of sport he did. What could have happened to warrant such an ending was the question that currently refused to be answered. Gaby blinked. She would far rather remember him as he looked in the photo than how he looked in that car, but only time and a successful resolution to the mystery of his death would dissolve that particular picture from her mind.

'That's a good point about her alibi. We also need to do a bit of digging about the couple. I'll get Jax to look into both Ian and Hannah's backgrounds when he gets here. The sooner we rule out any skeletons the better.'

'Are you expecting any?' Owen said, strolling over to his desk and picking up his phone, his eyes now on the screen as he swiped through his messages.

'Not really. Hannah lost her family in that tragic plane crash out of New York a few years back but I can't see how that would have anything to do with it. There's also her job at Daffodils Care Home but again that's unlikely to be relevant. I'll start by getting Jax to look into their finances. Any gambling debts. Any large payments. Loan sharks. That sort of thing. Right up his street.'

The sound of her phone ringing was a welcome interruption – until Gaby realised who was on the other end. Jason Moore.

Jason rarely rang. In fact, she could count on the fingers of one hand exactly how many times he'd used the telephone to share his thoughts. The tall, thin, senior CSI was quiet personified. He got on with his job and only contacted the team when he had some knowledge to impart. Something was up. She dreaded to think what.

'Hang on a sec, Owen. Don't go just yet,' she said, stopping him as he was about to pull open the door.

She picked up the receiver. 'Hi, Jason, what have you got for us?'

Chapter 7

Hannah

Sunday 23 August, 4.35 p.m. St Asaph

Instead of Ian's father coming to collect her he sent Dominic, Ian's brother, but Hannah was too churned up with worry about Hunter to know where she was, who she was with or what she was doing. She'd never met Ian's sibling so all she had to go on were the abrupt Zoom chats she'd been party to, along with the distinct feeling that he didn't like her. She had no idea why and at that moment she couldn't have cared less. Instead of a heart beating inside her chest, there was just a gaping dark cavern that no feeling or emotion could breach. The only thing that could fill it was Hunter returned to her side and, after losing her parents and her brother, there was no room left for hope. She dreaded the worst. Life had proven to her over and over again that she wasn't meant to be happy. There was no reason to think that this would be any different.

As a nurse Hannah had dealt with grief many a time throughout her career. She could almost say she'd become an expert, often stepping in as an intermediary until trained counsellors could be assigned. But no course or manual could ever prepare her for the gut-wrenching dread that filled her stomach with an unimaginable pain, or the mind-numbing anguish that refused to let a solitary tear fall. Ian was dead but it was all about Hunter. Only Hunter.

'You're very kind but there's no need to …'

'No. I *know* there's no need but my dad sent me so there we are.'

'You don't like me very much, do you?' she managed, buckling the seatbelt and resting back into the seat.

'I don't dislike you. Ambivalent would be more to the point. My brother always did have an interesting taste when it came to his girlfriends,' he added, his attention now trained on her ring. 'I never thought he'd be fool enough to marry one of them.'

'You're being offensive.'

'It takes one to know one. So, where is it to be?' he said, with an abrupt change of tone. 'I don't suppose they'll let you go back to the house quite yet.'

'No. But that doesn't mean I still can't search for Hunter. Just drop me off anywhere in Conwy and I'll do the rest.'

'Hmm.' He threw her a look. 'You should probably inform your landlord before they hear about it on the news.'

'And why would I need to do that, Dominic? I own the property,' she said, careful to keep her voice even.

His eyes widened. 'I didn't know that.'

'Why would you? It's not the sort of conversation I'd expect you to have had with your brother.'

Hannah turned in her seat to glance at his profile, something she'd been avoiding, simply because he was the spit of Ian. They weren't twins but by some trick of genetic fate they could have been. She didn't know what Dominic's problem was unless he thought she wasn't good enough for his brother. She probably wasn't! Ian certainly seemed to have more cash than her but they didn't talk about money much, apart from him contributing to the food bills. The house was hers but only because she'd decided to invest the money she'd got – following the death of her parents – into bricks and mortar on the advice of her parents' solicitor. She still didn't have two beans to rub together but at least it meant that she'd always be able to put a roof over Hunter's head …

The tears came in a sudden deluge, grief finally winning the silent war that was raging beneath her skin. Dominic's sharp intake of breath mingled with his foot on the brake as he pulled in to the side of the road. Anything else was lost under the gasps and snuffles as she struggled to coordinate taking in a lungful of air against what seemed like a river of tears.

Grief like this wasn't refined, certainly not in her case. It was noise and snot. Wails and crying moans. It couldn't be damped down with a quick pat or a sigh of annoyance just as it couldn't be contained by a sleeve or a flimsy tissue.

'Here.' He lifted her hand from where it was clamped to her face and thrust a tissue into her palm. That was all. There were no words. Words would have been superfluous. There was no other touch, which wouldn't have been welcome from someone who despised her. There was complete silence, awkward and uneasy.

Hannah didn't know how long she sat there. The tears eventually slowed to a trickle and, with a sharp blow of her nose, finally stopped – leaving a heavy silence. She felt raw, exposed, vulnerable; her inner self had been ripped apart. Dominic was the last person in the world she would have chosen to break down in front of. Another nail in the coffin of their non-existent relationship. There was only one thing she could think of to say.

'I'm sorry.'

'No need for that. You're obviously in no fit state to be by yourself. I'll drop the car off and come with you. Two pairs of eyes are better than one and all that—'

'No!' She hadn't meant to shout, her cheeks pinkening with embarrassment at the sound of her voice echoing in the narrow

34

confines of the car. 'Sorry, but I'll be better and quicker on my own. I know all the places that he might have—'

Hannah never got to finish the sentence. Instead she answered her ringing phone.

Chapter 8

Gaby

Sunday 23 August, 4.50 p.m. St Asaph

Gaby met them in reception, a shocked Owen hovering by her side. She felt she'd aged a century in the last ten minutes and could only guess at the thoughts flashing across Hannah's face.

Hannah knew. That was certain. People always did. Gaby didn't know whether it was by instinct, body language or some kind of sixth sense but Hannah knew what was coming. It was there in the defeated droop of her shoulders and the way her knees suddenly buckled.

It was only the prompt action of Dominic putting out an arm to support her that prevented her from collapsing into a heap at their feet.

Protocol dictated that Gaby should take her somewhere private but, with the reception quiet for once, protocol could go hang. Instead she led them both to the chairs lined up against the wall, her voice dipping a notch, her words heartfelt.

'I think you know what I'm going to say, Hannah,' she said, her teeth mangling the inside of her cheek until the sharp metallic taste of blood made her stop.

Hannah's head lifted, her attention shifting from where Dominic was holding both her hands in his, her skin losing what little colour it had.

'We've been searching for Hunter and—'

'Where is he? Where is my son?' she interrupted, her voice shrill, a little vein throbbing in her temple, her hands now free and fisted.

Gaby blinked. If she didn't know any better, she'd be worried she was about to get thumped. It wouldn't be the first time but rarely by a woman and certainly not one in the throes of grief. However, there was no going back once she'd started. No safe retreat behind Owen. She was in charge. This was her responsibility. Her problem.

With a measured tone, she continued to speak. 'Hunter was in your garden. He was well hidden so not easy to find. The team did what they could but it was too late. I'm so very sorry for your loss.'

There was no need to say any more. She'd said enough.

Later in the quiet of her cottage, Gaby would work the scene over and over in an attempt to discover what she could have done differently. Maybe next time she'd get it right. Maybe next time she wouldn't feel so inept as she watched Hannah collapse back into her chair, pale and silent.

She felt useless. No. She was useless.

Gaby watched on as Dominic took over. Somehow, he knew what to say and what to do to ease Hannah's haunting journey from hope to despair. Part of her wanted to know where he'd learnt the skill while the other part tried to file his methods for future use. It had taken one sentence for Hannah's world to come crashing down for the third time. The plane crash. Ian's death. And now Hunter's. Gaby had a workload to rival that of the most complex of investigations but her main priority lay in this small corner of Wales.

Chapter 9

Hannah

Sunday 23 August, 5.05 p.m. St Asaph

Hannah was led out to the car, barely aware of her surroundings or that Dominic was having to prop her up, his firm arm on her elbow the only thing preventing her from hitting the pavement.

'Come on. Let's get a coffee somewhere.'

She didn't notice the short journey, or when he pulled into the car park and unclicked her seatbelt. At some level she knew they'd left the station but that was all. She only truly became aware of where she was when he placed her hands around a hot mug and helped her take a sip. It took half an hour and two coffees for her to gain some control of her emotions. But the coffee was warm and laced with sugar. It couldn't lift her mood but it finally dragged her back to the present long enough for her to raise her head and take in her surroundings.

'You're very kind but there must be things you need to be doing,' she said, once her coffee cup was empty and back in its saucer. She was almost surprised at the words as she picked up her bag from where she'd placed it on the floor by her feet. It was the first time Dominic had shown any kindness towards her and, examining him from the security of her chair, she realised that it was something that didn't come easily. He'd probably been hurt in the past, not that she was particularly interested. He'd go back to Australia and she'd be left in Wales trying to pick up the fabric of her life from the memories of the old.

'Like what? I can think of nothing more important, Hannah,' he said, resting back in the wooden chair opposite, one leg crossed over the other, his eyes never leaving her face. 'What do you take me for? It's hard enough for me but to find out about Hunter too. It must be a million times worse for you than it is for me. I loved my brother but to lose a child …' He cleared his throat. 'I'm sorry. If I could get my hands on the person who's done this I'd wring their bloody neck. To kill …'

'So you think that they were both murdered then?'

'Don't you?'

'I don't know what to think.' She pressed her fingers over her eyes, trying to control her breathing.

'Sorry. It's neither the time nor the place for this. I'll drop you somewhere. You obviously can't go home. My dad will be happy to put you up for as long as—'

'No!' She softened her voice before continuing. 'Sorry, but I couldn't.'

'What about family then? I'll happily drop you off somewhere?'

She shook her head. 'There's no one. A hotel will be … No. Wait.' She searched in the pocket of her jeans and pulled out her phone. 'If you wouldn't mind dropping me off in Llandudno? I have a friend who will put me up for the night.'

'Okay. It might be an idea to inform that detective of your whereabouts in case there's any news.'

Chapter 10

Gaby

Sunday 23 August, 6 p.m. St Asaph Hospital

Instead of facing a quiet evening in her lounge, Gaby was staring down at the small body carefully arranged on Rusty's cold metal slab, her emotions shattering at the sight. There was no easy way. No well-trodden path. No guideline that would make it any better. There was a small boy decked out in dinosaur pyjamas, his skin already taking on the mottled hue that Gaby had long associated with death. There was a term for it but at that exact moment she couldn't for the life of her remember what it was.

After thirteen years in the force it would have been easy for Gaby to become blasé about crime. The truth was that most people were good. It was the small minority that kept her in the office long past her finishing time and persistently interrupted her sleep. The unexplained death of an adult was only a mystery to be solved. If she thought about it in any other terms, she'd never manage to keep an open mind – the central tenet of law enforcement. Policing, like most professions, was governed by strict guidelines. There were

40

long-established patterns that highlighted the way, torch bright. No matter how unique a criminal thought their crime, there was invariably always someone who'd gotten there first.

None of the above counted when the victim was a child.

There wasn't a mark on him that she could see, something she was thankful for if only to appease the family. What a thought. It could be worse. She'd seen worse. But this was bad enough.

'You all right, Gabriella?' She felt a brief squeeze on her shoulder but, instead of leaning in for a hug, she straightened her spine and pinned a false smile on her lips. She wasn't a good enough actress for it to reach her eyes.

'I'm fine.'

'Ah. The notorious *fine*, which means anything but. For the record, I'm *fine* too,' Rusty said, donning a heavy rubber apron and pair of wellington boots from the rack in the corner before heading over to the line of metal sinks that stretched across the back wall. 'I hope you don't mind me tackling this one first? The man appears to be straightforward but, of course, we won't know that until I open him up.'

'I'm fine wi—' She stopped abruptly, changing her words. 'Okay by me. You're the expert.'

He pulled on a pair of rubber gloves and turned to the pathology porter. 'Dean, we'll start by removing the pyjamas, if you wouldn't mind. And then you can bag and tag them. There's a CSI waiting to take them back to the lab for scrapings et cetera. You can also switch on the microphone.'

'Right you are, Doc.'

Gaby didn't respond; she couldn't. Instead, she concentrated on the mop of brown curls on the top of the boy's head and worked on her breathing. Anything to avoid looking at the scene unfolding in front of her. She was here because it was her duty. She could easily have passed that duty on to the likes of Owen but she wouldn't. Owen had a boy only a couple of years younger, which made the thought untenable.

She stood, her nails carving deep crescents into her palms, her eyes fixed, her ears trying to drone out the sound of Rusty's Irish lilt as he went through the motions.

'Here we have the body of a Caucasian male, approximately five years old. Brown hair, blue eyes. Height: ninety-six centimetres. Weight: thirteen kilograms. Both are significantly below the average for this age group but as he's a diabetic …' He droned on and on, only pausing a moment when the external examination was over, his hand depressing the microphone switch. 'No point in being a hero when there's no need, Gabriella. Pop the kettle on, there's a love. I'll be in as soon as I can.'

The kettle was cold, Gaby's mug long since empty, but still she sat, staring at nothing in the vague hope that her thoughts would get their act together. There were things that she should be doing but, after catching up with each of her team, she'd lost both the energy and impetus to do any of them. She certainly had no intention of reinterviewing Hannah in light of this new development. It was a task that could wait until the morning when they'd hopefully have more of an idea of what had happened.

Who'd kill a child? That was the question performing somersaults in her brain because she couldn't come up with one single explanation that made any sense. She could sort of get that some murders were bound to happen. She'd always remember one of her lecturers in the early days saying that they were all one step away from doing the unthinkable. The red mist that came out of nowhere. The car that cut off your path. The betraying friend or relative. The jealous lover. The greedy neighbour. She'd come across all of those in her time on the force. Each one came with a tick-box standard list of principles that had governed her actions and helped lead her to find the perpetrator, the crimes making an eerie sort of relatable sense.

Only serial killers and zealots fell outside of that cookie-cutter category, the stain of madness and obsession making a mockery of any rational reason for murder. But to find a killer, first they had to find the motive and that was where her thought processes floundered. What was the motive for killing a little boy?

'Why am I not surprised that you're sitting there doing nothing?'

The sound of Rusty's voice had her jerking to her feet. 'I wasn't doing nothing. I was thinking.'

He flopped into the chair behind his desk and, stretching, clasped his hands behind his head. 'About what?'

'The case, what else!'

'What indeed.'

'So, are you going to leave me on tenterhooks or let me know what you found?'

'An interesting puzzle, which leaves far more questions than it answers.'

She shook her head. She'd known from the outset how clever Dr Rusty Mulholland was, far cleverer than her, but, after the day she'd had, riddles were off the agenda.

'You have to be able to tell me more than that,' she said, retaking her seat. Her voice held a distinct edge. 'A little hint is all I need. I'm going to have to catch up with the mother at some point. Anything you can tell me that might help …' She dropped her gaze to the rigid set of his jaw and suddenly remembered how difficult it must be for him. Being a pathologist provided him little protection against the same emotions flooding her veins and, unlike her, he was a parent – a parent of a young boy. 'I'm sorry, I didn't mean—'

'I know you didn't.' He pushed his glasses up to his forehead and pressed his thumb and forefinger to the bridge of his nose, rubbing the dull red marks left by the pads. 'Despite everything it never gets any easier but me waxing on isn't going to help you.' He managed a small smile. 'It looks as if the boy might have been suffering from ketoacidosis, whether accidental or otherwise is yet to be proven.'

'What?' Gaby's eyes widened. 'Rusty, you lost me at keto whatever.'

'Sorry. Diabetic ketoacidosis, more commonly known as DKA. I haven't managed to pull his records yet but it's a pretty sure bet that he suffered from Type 1 diabetes.' He dropped his glasses back in place and reached for his notebook. 'I'm not sure how much you heard of my preliminary external examination but Hunter was wearing an insulin pump attached to his lower abdomen.' He started to sketch a torso and added a couple of probes and what looked like a small mobile phone. 'Diabetes is rare in such a young age group but not unheard of. It's likely that when he was born they discovered that his pancreas didn't produce sufficient insulin. Instead, they fitted him with an external device to administer a continuous dose of the stuff.' He looked up, his face more serious than she'd ever seen it. 'The skin around Hunter's umbilicus was stabbed with tiny needle pricks in what looks like a desperate attempt to get the pump working.'

'So, Ian … or someone, tried to reconnect the pump and failed, if the loose wire is anything to go by?'

'That's what it looks like.'

'And in desperation when he learnt that it was too late, he hid Hunter in the bottom of the garden and then topped himself, which does seem a little strange.'

'It may not be quite as clear cut as that, but I've sent off samples for blood glucose levels. We'll also look at the serum level of beta-hydroxybutyrate.'

'You're losing me again, Rusty.'

'It's difficult to put it simply but I'll try. Basically, insulin is needed to allow for the utilisation of glucose by the cells, thus removing it from the bloodstream. With no insulin, as in the case of Hunter's detached pump, the blood levels of glucose skyrocketed.' He lifted his head from where he'd been drawing molecules on his pad. 'You still with me?'

'Just about.'

'Good. So, the second part is where the DKA comes in. With all the glucose now stuck in the blood vessels the cells can't utilise it for energy. Instead they look to their mate, the liver, to convert fatty acid into the fuel that they urgently require. The by-product of this conversion is a chemical called ketones, which in large volumes is toxic to the body, hence the name keto-acid-osis.'

'And the beta …?'

He smiled across the expanse of desk. 'I'll turn you into a chemist yet, Gabriella! Beta-hydroxybutyrate, or BHB for short, is the name of the ketone that will prove whether or not DKA played a role in Hunter's death.'

'Played a role? I don't understand? I thought you meant that it led to it?'

'No. Not exactly. There are still some slides I need to check from his lung tissue for that. All I can say for now is that I suspect his diabetes was a trigger,' he said, smoothing his hand over his hair. 'I'm guessing you'd like me to work on Strong next and, if so, I have a favour to ask.'

Chapter 11

Gaby

Sunday 23 August, 7.30 p.m. St Asaph

The incident room contained all of the usual faithfuls sitting behind their desks and tapping away on their keyboards, apart from Owen who Gaby had left to catch up with the CSIs. Malachy Devine had divested himself of his jacket and tie and had rolled his shirtsleeves up to the elbows, revealing thick corded muscles and a fancy steel watch. Gaby's gaze shifted to the small diamond stud winking from his earlobe, before she moved on. Jax, the youngest member of the team, was behind his desk albeit with periodic yawns that he couldn't be bothered to mask with the palm of his hand.

Marie and Diane were looking very different from the last time she'd seen them, dressed up to the nines at Amy's hen do. With that thought, she glanced up to find Owen strolling down the corridor, Jason at his side.

Moving swiftly to the first of the three whiteboards, which spanned the wall on the left, she plucked up a black pen and recorded Ian and Hunter's details before turning back to the room.

'Right then, you don't need me to tell you how confusing the case is. I've just come back from Hunter's autopsy and it's even more complex than we first thought.' She spun the pen through her fingers, her eyes grazing each of them in turn. Jason was last.

'I know what you're going to say, so there's no point in trying to stonewall me. Anything at all from the CSIs would be useful at this juncture.'

'We found the body and yet you want more,' he said, spreading his hands in a form of supplication, his wrists facing upwards. 'I have some cracking arteries here if you'd like blood with it?'

'Come on, Jason. Enough with the funnies. I'm not in the mood.' She placed both hands on her hips and glared. 'We have a dead officer in addition to a dead child so any input from you would be most welcome, like for instance how you found the boy when the initial team had already combed the area?'

He relaxed back in the chair, his arms behind his head. 'We're nowhere near finished so all I'm able to provide is a brief outline of our findings up to now.'

'Fine.'

'For a start the garage didn't turn up anything extraordinary apart from the body, which I believe has been formally identified as Ian Strong.'

Gaby nodded her head in acquiescence.

'Poor git.' He compressed his mouth into a thin line. 'We only found three sets of prints in the car, all belonging to the three people living at the address. We also examined the petrol tank. It was empty.'

'So the engine ran until the tank drained.'

'That's how it appears.'

'And what about finding the boy?'

'You have Rachel, one of our newer team members to thank for that. I had to send her home after. Not an easy thing for anyone.' He swallowed hard, his attention on his long spindly fingers. 'I let her tackle the garden while we started on the house. I thought it would be good experience for her. I didn't really expect her to find anything after the initial sweep by the coppers.'

'Silly fools.'

'Don't be too hard on them. They probably didn't know what they were looking for. A pile of rumpled plastic looks exactly what it seems unless the child is small for their age. It seems as if Hunter was laid out on top of the compost heap and covered with grow bags.'

'Mmm and presumably the reason the back door was found open. What else?'

'The sheets in the main bedroom have seen some recent action.' He managed a smirk. 'I'm not sure how recent so we've taken them back for scrapings. Also it looks like there was a takeaway consumed, I'm guessing last night but the doc will confirm that with the autopsy report. We still need to backtrack through bank records to find out exactly when it was ordered and delivered. We also have Ian's mobile to look at. His girlfriend doesn't have the password. After that, we can get started on the timeline.'

'Good. Will you be continuing on after this or …?'

'Oh yes.' He bounded to his feet like a jack-in-the-box. 'Have to strike while the DNA is fresh and all that,' he said, turning to go.

'Hold on.' Gaby fetched her wallet from her bag, which she'd slung over the back of her chair, and withdrew four twenties. She wasn't usually so flush with cash but, with all the wedding festivities going on this week, she'd raided her decorating fund on the way to Paintings yesterday. 'It's not in any way a replacement for the weekend's fishing but fish and chips all round with my thanks.'

She didn't bother to acknowledge his grateful nod; instead, she carried on speaking.

'While the CSIs were doing their stuff, I caught up with the mother to break the bad news. After, I headed over to the pathology suite at the hospital. To cut a very long story short, you all know how Dr Mulholland tends to astound us with his superior knowledge—'

48

'I'm going to tell him you said that,' Owen interrupted, causing peals of laughter around the room, which were quickly suppressed.

'You do that and you'll be on nights quicker than you could ever imagine. As I was saying, before I was so rudely interrupted,' she said, darting Owen a severe look. 'We knew Hunter had diabetes from something Hannah said. The doc explained the condition to me and about how the pump on his tummy worked.' She placed her hand an inch or so below and to the left of her belly button. 'Apparently it's a common way of administering insulin these days. Early thoughts are that the boy's pump became detached. Strong couldn't revive him and, desperate with grief, decided to top himself.'

'That's all very well except for one thing,' Marie said. 'Why the hell didn't he call the emergency services? Being a copper, he'd surely know more than most the importance of getting help for the boy. It's drummed into them from day one in the force.'

'He did.'

They all turned to stare at Diane, who was doing a fine job of hiding behind the security of her computer screen. Diane had only decided to try for her detective exams at the end of the last case and, as the newest member of the team, was still finding her way. She was staying with the team until her twelve-week residential course started in the new year.

'Carry on, Diane, you're doing great. You were saying he made the call?'

'Yes, ma'am. Phone records are one of the easiest things to access, especially with Strong having the use of one of our mobiles.' She swept a strand of blonde hair away from her cheek, tucking the end of the long bob behind her ear. 'I'm not sure of the practice of using your work device for personal use but it's probably not a secret that we all do it.'

'We wouldn't work half as hard without that single perk,' Owen interrupted with a chuckle. 'They know all too well that they can contact us day or night and that's the reason they never give us a hard time over it.'

'Indeed.' Gaby agreed with everything he said but didn't have the time to get into an in-depth conversation over telephone usage. 'Carry on, Diane.'

'He dialled 999 at 3.59 a.m. but seems to have hung up before he was connected to a dispatcher.'

'But why would he do that?' Gaby headed back to the whiteboard and added the information, finishing with a huge exclamation mark.

'Perhaps he realised that it was too late?' Owen said.

'Why call in the first place?'

With no answers and only blank expressions Gaby decided to shift the conversation forward. 'Okay, we'll have to leave that for now. Mal, how did you get on with the door-to-door? Let's see if we can't pad out the information a little and, before you ask,' she added, noting their looks of dismay, 'I'm intending to wrap this up shortly. You all have homes to go to. Jax, I believe you've picked the short straw of being on call again tonight?'

'Yes ma'am.'

'Not to worry.' She smiled. 'Instead of using our Wi-Fi to stream whatever music your generation listen to, you can start doing backgrounds on both Strong and Thomas.'

'EDM.'

'Excuse me?'

'I listen to Electronic Dance Music,' he said, the blush reaching the tops of his ears.

She bit her lip, hiding a smile. 'I've heard it all now. What's wrong with normal dance music! In my day …' She pulled up short. 'Yes. Well, I'm sure you're interested in the kind of music I listen to,' she said, rolling her eyes. 'Right, back to Mal. What have you got for me?'

'Actually, far more than I'd hoped. Conwy has quite a community vibe about it. As a walled town, it's probably down to the limited expansion available. But, whatever the reason, it's good for us. The neighbours all know each other's business and were very happy to share.' He flipped through his notebook until he found the right page. 'In brief, Thomas has lived there for about six years with Hunter. Ian moved in about six months ago so he's a relatively new addition and not Hunter's father. Hannah tends to stick to herself. Either shy or stuck-up depending on which neighbour you speak to. Ian wasn't about much. A busy day job and a very busy social life meant they didn't see much of him, apart from him coming and going in a variety of either work wear or sports gear.'

He looked up, catching her eye. 'There wasn't much said about their relationship but, reading between the lines, the mother did most of the childcare but then as Ian wasn't the dad … There were reports of one or two shouting matches and slamming of doors but nothing that you'd think might lead to murder. They last saw her leaving at about ten past five yesterday on her motorbike. Ian had returned from work a couple of hours earlier. That's about it.'

'Very comprehensive, thank you. So their busy work and social lives meant that the boy rarely got to spend any quality time with both of them but that's less relevant than if Ian had been the father …' She uncapped the pen and, drawing a straight line, divided the top half of the third board into two. She annotated it with dates and times on one side and actions on the other. 'Hannah told us the time Ian arrived home and the time she left, now confirmed by the neighbours. We also have a good indication of the time Ian found the boy. What we need to do next is to look into the mother's alibi.'

'Surely you can't think that Hannah is involved in the deaths?' Marie said, pausing in the middle of unwrapping a chocolate bar.

'I don't think anything, Marie. I deal in facts, and statistically she's the most likely person to have helped Ian on his way, if indeed it does prove to be murder. We won't know more until after Rusty has worked his magic.'

51

Gaby strode over to the window and looked down at the car park, the pen hanging between her finger and thumb. 'The most likely scenario is that Ian panicked when he discovered Hunter dead but that's just one narrative. Another is that Hannah murdered Ian in a fit of madness when she found Hunter's body – then hid her son to throw us off the scent. Jax has already observed that she appears to be a lot more concerned about what happened to her son than her fiancé.'

Gaby stopped speaking to place the pen down on the nearest desk. 'And, as we all know, the prisons are full of people declaring their innocence. But we're not monsters,' she went on. 'Yes, we need to check Hannah's alibi with her friend, Milly Buttle, but that can wait until the morning especially as she's informed me that she's spending the night at Buttle's house.'

Chapter 12

Gaby

Sunday 23 August, 8.25 p.m. Old Colwyn

Gaby pulled up outside Rusty's three-bedroomed, red-brick house and shut off the engine. She wished it was as easy to shut off her mind but the image of Hunter on that slab simply wouldn't go away. She cared about what had happened to Ian – she wouldn't be a copper if she didn't – but it was always worse when it was a child.

She unclicked her belt and slid out of the car, a plastic bag dangling from her fingers. The next hour or so babysitting Conor, Rusty's eleven-year-old son, was what she should be thinking about. If previous occasions were anything to go by, she was in for a difficult time of it. The softly softly approach that Rusty had recommended meant that up until now Conor had completely ignored her, and his dad had let him. But there was nothing she could do about that if she didn't want to fall out with the testy pathologist. A relationship that involved two hot-headed individuals was bound to be challenging but she was reluctant to be the one to always give way. If he didn't know by now that she wasn't a doormat, she'd buy him a new one for Christmas and explain the difference.

The trace of her smile still lingered at the thought, only to be wiped when the bell was answered on the first ring. Rusty had mentioned the middle-aged neighbour who'd offered to help out on the odd occasion but, up to now, Gaby hadn't met her. At the sight of the skinny, black-haired beauty, she wondered why.

'About time too. Rusty said seven-thirty at the latest.'

'Yes, I'm sorry. I got here as soon as I could, Mrs Woods.'

'It's Miss. He's in his room playing one of them computer games.'

She spent a long moment eyeing Gaby up and down, from the top of her scruffy plait to her Nikes that she'd been wearing ever since she'd climbed out of the shower – was it only that morning? It felt as if a century had passed since she'd walked along the side of the riverbank chatting to Amy about her wedding.

Gaby took a step back and, being a no-nonsense sort of person, returned the compliment, noting the bad dye job and stretch leggings without revealing a smidgeon of her feelings for the woman. The idea that, as a single dad, Rusty probably didn't get much choice as to who to call on at the last minute, was as far as her brain was prepared to take her on that particular journey.

'Thank you. I won't keep you any longer then. You'll be keen to get off.'

She didn't care that she was a little on the left side of curt. If Rusty was fool enough to employ someone like Miss Wood to look after his son then he could sort out any fallout from Gaby's less than effusive words.

Once inside, she clicked the security chain in place and headed for the kitchen in search of crockery and cutlery. Rusty had asked if she'd mind preparing a simple snack for Conor, something like beans on toast, but instead she'd dropped off at the first fish and chip shop she'd spotted. She'd also made the executive decision to buy the same for Rusty, which she planned to keep warm in the oven. Not ideal considering the lateness of the hour but probably better than what he'd been planning – she'd spotted the pile of Heinz tins in the cupboard.

Gaby shouted up the stairs when she was done. Fish and chips had always been a rare treat in her house when she was growing up and she hoped that Conor would feel the same way.

He didn't.

'I'm not hungry.'

'Oh, okay. Not a problem. I missed lunch so …' Gaby sat down and proceeded to open up the chip bag and arrange the contents on the plate she'd set for him. 'In fact, fish and chips is my favourite of all,' she added, squirting tomato ketchup onto the side when she hated the stuff with a passion. 'There's nothing better than the smell of freshly cooked cod surrounded by thick crispy batter.' She chose the longest chip with care and dipped it into the sauce before popping it into her mouth, all the time aware of the death stare coming at her from the other corner of the room. 'It's all right, Conor. No need to stay and be polite. Off you hop back to your computer game.'

Gaby wasn't hungry, far from it, but she'd be blowed if she'd allow a kid to ruin what was a perfectly good tea. She worked through the plate, mouthful after mouthful, almost heaving as she squashed the last forkful down her throat. She didn't care about the wedding, less than a week away, where she'd hoped to be at least a half a stone lighter. At this rate she'd have to do what she'd always vowed she wouldn't – purchase a pair of body-shaping knickers.

At the sound of the key in the lock, Gaby shut off her phone, placing it on the arm of the sofa before standing to a full stretch and walking towards the door to free the security chain.

'No sign of Conor?' Rusty said, shoving his keys into his pocket and taking a step towards her.

'He's upstairs.'

'No, I'm not. I'm here. Hi, Dad.' Conor exploded into the room, forcing himself between them.

Rusty ruffled his hair. 'All right, son? Sorry I'm late.'

'She ate my tea.'

The bald, unadorned statement coming out of the lips of someone so young had Gaby restraining a smile although there was no humour in the quick look Rusty darted in her direction.

'I can't believe that.'

'It's quite true.' Gaby turned away to pluck up her phone, her fingers instinctively scrolling down to check if there were any new messages. 'Conor said he wasn't hungry so …' She shrugged her shoulders in lieu of meeting Rusty's gaze. 'There's bread in the bread bin and cheese in the fridge if he's changed his mind but I wasn't going to let fish and chips go to waste.'

'Dad?'

Instead of waiting for Rusty to decide who to side with, Gaby turned away, her fingers gripping on to her phone, pleased she'd decided to leave her car keys in the hall.

'It's late. Goodnight. I'll catch up with you in the morning.'

She'd reached the front door and had already started to pull at the latch when the sound of Rusty's bellow stopped her in her tracks. 'Gabriella, wait up a minute.'

She paused on the threshold, listening to the conversation playing out behind her, her hand resting on the latch.

'Bed for you but first, you need to thank Gabriella.'

'But, Dad?'

'No buts, Conor. Now, if you please.'

'But what about my tea?'

'What about it? You said you weren't hungry. If you don't say thank you to the babysitter, I'll curtail your electronic time.'

Gaby heard the muffled sound of footsteps and a quiet thank you closely followed by thumping up the stairs and a door slamming, as her own rage started to build.

Babysitter indeed! So that's what he thinks of me!

She had pulled the door open and was halfway towards her car by the time Rusty managed to catch up with her.

'Gabriella. Stop. Didn't you hear me telling you to wait up?'

She turned on her heels. 'And you think I'm going to follow orders from you just because you want it? I've had a shit day and an even shittier evening. All I want to do is crawl home because tomorrow is bound to be as bad if not worse.'

He lifted his hands only to let them drop. 'And me asking you to mind Conor hasn't helped any. I get that and I get that my son has been a beast but there's no need to take it out on me. Come on, what about I pour you a glass of wine and I can tell you about the results of Strong's autopsy.'

'You can tell me that here,' she said, fiddling with her keys. 'And anyway, I don't want to come inside and upset your son any more than I have already.'

'I think that it's probably done Conor the world of good having someone stand up to him for a change.' He ran his hand over his head. 'I know I've been far too soft since his mum left and that it won't help him in the long run …'

'Rusty, these things take time. But remember it's as difficult for me as it is for you.'

She started to unbend, the need to comfort him pushing aside any feelings of annoyance and disappointment. He looked aloof, alone and – it had to be said – lonely standing there, his hair all over the place. The conversation wasn't over, but it was perhaps better left for another day. Lack of experience made her feel awkward all of a sudden. She wasn't going to capitulate but someone had to shift the conversation into a direction they both felt comfortable with.

She took his arm and squeezed it gently. 'I won't have a wine but a cup of tea would be welcome while I watch you eat. You haven't eaten yet, have you?'

'I can get something later.'

'When there's cod and chips keeping warm in the oven?' she said, her brown eyes starting to twinkle. 'But don't tell Conor. He might never forgive me.'

He laughed, hugging her close before leading her back inside and towards the kitchen. 'I can't believe that you sat there and ploughed your way through his tea with him watching.'

'Yes, well, neither can I if I'm honest. But it was delicious. You sit there while I dish up. I hope they're going to be okay.' She frowned down at the plate she'd removed from the oven. 'They're always better fresh out of the fryer.'

'They'll be fine, perfect even.' He switched on the kettle and grabbed two pottery mugs from the cupboard above. 'So much nicer than having to make something from scratch.'

Within minutes they were sitting opposite each other, their knees almost but not quite touching under the table. Gaby sat back in the chair, cradling her mug between interlaced fingers while she watched Rusty tuck in. She only started to speak when he'd finished on the fish and was starting on the chips.

'So, did you find anything interesting?'

He balanced his knife and fork on the edge of his plate and, mirroring her, picked up his mug and cradled it between his palms. 'On the face of it there's no great mystery. Boy collapses because his blood sugar drops or, maybe even Strong went to check on him at some point and found him unconscious. We can only hypothesise at this stage. Strong was still wearing his pyjamas, with a pullover thrown on top, which again fits with the picture that's forming because—'

'In that sort of an emergency no one would bother to get dressed. Yes, I can see that.' Gaby took a sip from her drink. 'And that ties in with the phone call to the emergency services.'

'Phone call?'

'Sorry, I forgot you wouldn't know about that.' She shifted her head from where she'd been studying the small but homely kitchen with built-in oak cabinets and multicoloured tiles in an assortment of earthenware tones. 'One of the detectives traced back his phone records. A call was placed, but he hung up before it was connected.'

'Maybe he thought it would be quicker to drive, especially at that time of the morning when the roads would have been clear. The nearest ambulance station is probably the one in Llandudno Junction, the nearest hospital Llandudno General, so he was probably right.'

'That's all very well but why then change his mind, hide the boy's body and top himself?'

'Unless he hated the boy's mum?'

Gaby started, nearly tipping over her mug in the process. 'Now I wonder why you'd say that?'

'Well, look at it this way.' Rusty set his empty mug down and picked up his fork. 'She arrives home to find her fiancé dead and her son missing, only to learn hours later that her son is also dead. In the time between the first and second discovery she would have been going through hell. But there'd have been a degree of hope. Humans on the whole are an optimistic bunch. She'd have been hoping with every heartbeat for Hunter to be found safe and well, only to then have all those positive feelings bundled into a sack and thrown over that proverbial cliff. If you're ever in need of defining torture, it's right there.'

Gaby pulled a grimace at his words, her attention on the last of the chips, which he was spearing individually with the tines of his fork. Would someone be so cruel, or indeed cunning, as to plan Hunter's death in such a way? She had no answers, only more questions. 'There's only one problem with that scenario and that's why did he then decide to top himself? I get that guilt comes into it but if he hated her that much, surely he'd have wanted to stay around long enough to see her suffer?'

'Unless he thought it was partly his fault. Dislodging the pump through a bit of rough and tumble play is a possibility. You know as well as I do what big and little boys are like when their women are away,' he said, placing his fork down. 'But whatever caused the pump to dislodge is immaterial.'

She raised both eyebrows. 'How so?'

'Because his diabetes didn't kill him in the end, Gabriella.' He pushed his plate aside and propped his elbows on the table, his hands clasped in front of him. 'I haven't had a chance to collate all of the evidence yet for the final report but the lung slides I mentioned earlier prove that he was alive when he was placed on top of the compost heap, most likely unconscious but alive. The cause of death was suffocation from the plastic bags obstructing his airway.'

Chapter 13

Jax

Jax, at twenty-six, was used to late nights and early mornings so a second shift on call after working through the day wasn't as bad as it initially seemed. He'd even done a number of shifts where he'd stayed up all night and strolled into the station after a quick turnaround at home for a shower, shave and a change of clothing. Not to be recommended but it had always seemed a great idea at the time. Now he was in his element with a puzzle to solve and no one to interrupt.

He had a litre water bottle at his elbow and, with all of the other desks empty, the peace to listen to whatever he wanted on his phone. It also helped that Georgie, his girlfriend, was on nights too. The plan was to pick her up from the hospital when she finished her shift and go to Coast Café in Rhos-on-Sea for breakfast, but he pushed the thought aside in preparation for work.

Most nights at the station were boring. There were records left to update from the day shift and the usual routine check-ins with

61

the custodial and desk sergeants. All that changed if there was an active case but not until the boring stuff was out of the way first. Once he'd pulled out the night shift checklist and ensured he'd ticked off all the boxes, he flipped open the lid of his laptop and logged in to the system, his notebook open by his side.

Ian Strong was the sensible place to start. But Jax liked to do things his own way. He used to drive his parents to distraction by ignoring the meat on his plate until he'd devoured both the potatoes and vegetables and as for Christmas ... He was known to spread his gifts out across the day instead of opening them in one fell swoop, much to the annoyance of his siblings. But in this instance Ian wasn't going to be a challenge – far from it, for the simple reason that he would have already been investigated. As an entry-level officer, his life would have been turned inside out during his pre-employment screening, synchronising almost to the second with his application form arriving at the station. The force had to be careful with who they employed. An in-depth look at his finances and law-abiding status would have already taken place in addition to a full medical, including a psychological evaluation as to his emotional and mental health. For that reason, and that alone, Jax decided to start with Ian and leave his partner until last.

With security clearance through to access Ian's personal file, Jax turned up the sound on his headphones and was soon scrolling through Ian's original application form and medical reports. Having left school at sixteen with only two GCSEs, Ian had spent a couple of years in a career wilderness before settling down to an apprenticeship with a local plumber. At twenty-four he'd gone on to attain both his maths and English GCSE and started as a police community support officer, or PCSO. There were many routes to join up as an officer; this was only one of them. But it had still taken another three years for him to be accepted on to the force, a fact that had Jax reaching for his pencil and scribbling a note to find out the reason for the delay.

A brief dip into his social media presence was far from

illuminating. Ian, like most officers, had curtailed his usage on all the main forums since signing up and kept posts to a minimum. Prior to that he'd only posted occasional items and nothing with a hint as to his personal life.

His medical report came next but it was pretty standard stuff for a fit and healthy lad of twenty-seven. Jax hadn't known him well, but he'd seen him around often enough to recognise that he had the well-built physique of someone who took their sport seriously. Ian's health was textbook perfect with a blood pressure of 120/80 and 20:20 vision to boot. His psychological assessment was of far more interest, given his alleged suicide, but again he'd passed the written psychometric tests with flying colours.

Jax took a swig from his water bottle, his eyes still glued to the screen as he flicked through the standard assessment tick-box sheets to get to the summary at the bottom – a summary that left more questions than it gave answers.

In conclusion, Ian Strong achieved satisfactory scores on all his psychometric tests. Apart from admitting to a single incidence of cannabis use as a teenager, his drug and alcohol profile were clear. Finally, he demonstrated key behavioural characteristics and emotional traits that are usually found in successful applicants during both his one-to-one and group sessions. In light of these findings, I am happy to support his application as a police officer.

No one could have predicted the timeline of events that would lead to him being found in his garage but, if the psychologist was to be believed, Ian should have had the resources in his emotional toolbox to deal with them. Jax scrolled down to the name at the end of the report and added another note on his pad. It was far too late to give Dr de Jong a call. Reports were all very well, but a face-to-face meeting might be just the thing to iron out the questions popping up in his mind.

With a glance at his watch, Jax stood and walked over to the window. There was nothing to see apart from the car park lit by the tall security lights that surrounded the perimeter, nothing to distract him from the next part of his search. But still he lingered, hugging his arms around his navy hoodie. The office was warm but his busy day was starting to catch up with him, causing him to stretch his mouth in the largest of yawns before rubbing his hands over his face. What he needed was caffeine and perhaps one of the homemade muesli bars that Georgie had popped into his lunchbox earlier. He'd have been much happier with a couple of chocolate bars but the state of his finances and his girlfriend's recent conversion from vegetarian to vegan precluded that.

Turning away, he headed for the kettle and, choosing his favourite mug from the pile on the shelf above, spooned in a double helping of coffee granules. He couldn't really moan. While she was an absolute darling, he'd realised pretty quickly – in fact, on their first date – that roast dinners were a thing of the past unless he wanted to cook them himself, and a full plate of meat didn't hold the same appeal when she was sitting opposite munching away on a tofu burger. If that was the only thing he could find to moan about, then he counted himself a happy man.

The muesli bar didn't last two minutes but Jax barely noticed. He was having a much harder job in finding out about Hannah, something that was beginning to annoy him. The only good thing about it was that she hadn't turned up on any of his 'person of interest' searches on the Police National Database but as for the rest … Usually a name, date and place of birth were all that was needed to find out more about a person but not when you were called something as common as Hannah Thomas. As names went it was pretty innocuous but in 1995, the year of her birth, it was one of the most popular names in the land and not only Wales. There were hundreds of Hannah Thomases to plough through and not one that fitted the bill.

Police records in this instance wouldn't really help unless

there'd been a serious crime committed and, all he could find were parking offences and speeding fines – all immaterial until he'd pinned the right Hannah into the frame. The most surprising part in all of this was her invisibility on social media, which he'd mistakenly deemed a must in modern-day society; but, if she was there, she remained hidden from curious eyes such as his. None of the array of photos looked anything like her despite the number of women in her age bracket having an online presence. It was like looking for a single snowflake in a field of snow – pointless and impossible in equal measure.

Her social security contributions came next and confirmed that she was what she said she was: a qualified nurse. But that wasn't the reason his brow furrowed. Following her degree and, presumably tying in with the birth of her son, Hannah had started working at Daffodils, the same care home as his girlfriend.

Jax threw his pencil down in frustration and pushed away from his desk, rubbing the back of his neck as he continued to think through an alternative route in which to add to the information they'd already garnered. Police etiquette dictated that he couldn't ask Georgie about one of her colleagues. He could still remember, almost word for word, the Code of Ethics he'd signed up to – confidentiality being one of the underlying tenets. It meant they'd have to go down the formal path, via the nursing home manager. All that would take time and rule out the important little gossipy nuggets of information that his girlfriend would have at her fingertips. So bloody annoying.

Chapter 14

Gaby

Monday 24 August, 7.50 a.m. St Asaph

Gaby had a plan but, like most of her plans, it was bound to alter as the day rattled on to its ultimate conclusion. But by starting her Monday early, she hoped to spend some time later that evening adding the final touches to the paintwork in the lounge and reducing the size of her ironing pile.

She was sitting at her desk with a cup of tea in time to hear the eight o'clock news on the local radio, which, as to be expected, was full of the Conwy tragedy in all its graphic glory. She picked up her pencil and was busy scribbling notes on her A4 pad by the time the nasally challenged reporter had reached the weather. The forecast of wall-to-wall sunshine meant little to her apart from annoyance at the thought of her washing machine full of wet laundry but there was little she could do about that.

'Ma'am, I'm about to head off.'

Gaby lifted her head from where she was doodling a dinosaur

in the top right-hand corner of her pad. She hadn't heard the knock on her door but then again she'd all but forgotten that Jax had been lumbered with the night shift.

'Okay, thanks. Anything unusual overnight?'

'Like a graveyard, ma'am. I s-s-started on the backgrounds for both Ian and Hannah.'

'And?' Her tone was gentle at the sound of his stutter.

'And I-I-Ian appears pretty straightforward. No skeletons to be found in any of his cupboards.'

'Hardly surprising if they accepted him as a recruit. It's easier to get a job in the cabinet office than it is to be accepted onto the force these days.' She paused, noting his continued silence. 'So, I take it there are skeletons in Hannah's?'

'No, not even a teeny-weeny little bone shard. The thing is …' he didn't quite manage to meet her gaze '… I couldn't find out anything of any importance outside of her social security contributions and that only because it led me to her place of work.'

'You couldn't?' she repeated, jerking forward and nearly upsetting her tea, which she shifted to the other side of her laptop with deliberate care. 'What about a social media presence?'

'She doesn't have one or, at least not one that I can attribute to her. All I have is when she bought the house and her job history. That's it. Hannah Thomas must be one of the commonest names ever. I did a quick search after to check and both names made the top five rankings for her year of birth.'

Disappointment crept in under the waistband of her Zara trousers and hovered a moment before rising and finding its target – her stomach. She hadn't realised how much she'd been relying on a background dossier to help with the investigation until a spurt of acid from her belly full of fish and chips hit the back of her throat, nearly causing her to gag. Almost everyone could be tracked via a quick Google search if only to lead to their Facebook profile or LinkedIn page. Even a school photo of her on sports day holding a trophy would have been welcome.

Anything to get a feel for the woman outside of what they knew already, which wasn't much.

Gaby sighed with dissatisfaction. One of her former bosses was always banging on about the importance of preparation. Policework was ninety per cent groundwork and ten per cent inspiration mingled with a smidgeon of luck. She could almost hear the Cornish accent of her senior officer in Liverpool as he thumped out each point with the heel of his hand against the top of his desk.

She reached for her drink and took a long sip, swallowing hard, the image of Hannah Thomas breaking into her annoyance like a rain shower on a summer's day. A generic woman with a name that defied the investigative powers of one of the best up-and-comers in the business: Jax Williams. The man who'd managed to trace the whereabouts of the missing schoolgirl in their previous case by deciding to trawl through the street bins in Llandudno. If he couldn't find out anything useful about Hannah through dogged determination, there must be a very good reason why not.

'Don't worry about it, Jax. Either she's one of those rare animals that avoids an internet presence like the plague or we're not looking in the right places. Off you hop. You're back in tonight?'

'Yes, last one then two days off but—'

'No buts. Days off are far more important than days on.' She managed a brief smile, her thoughts already dragging her away from office banalities – the part of the job she hated the most. Gaby had a sharp mind and an even sharper wit but a kind heart. The only difficulty was she never knew which to use when dealing with staff and often felt that she got it wrong. Kindness could be seen as weakness. Intelligence as arrogance. Her knuckle-and-bone sense of humour on the borderline of being offensive. The truth was she wanted her team to get on with the job in hand with the minimum of input. They were all clever – they wouldn't have made it onto the MIT if they weren't. She was happy to lead them but as for holding their hands and mopping their brows …

well, they had partners and mothers for that. The 'Sleep well' she said next was forced from her lips, her hand already reaching for her mobile to check for messages.

She didn't see his ironic smile or the casual wave of his arm as he crossed the room. She also didn't hear the gentle click of the door shutting or the sound of his muffled footsteps echoing against the laminate flooring outside her office. Another text had pinged through – not a reply from Amy, who was a late riser. No, it was a message from Rusty to call him at her earliest convenience. Gaby didn't lose any time in picking up the phone, only to find that he was already on another call.

Chapter 15

Hannah

Monday 24 August, 8.55 a.m. Llandudno

Milly Buttle lived in a rented two-bedroomed house along Brookes Street, a narrow road situated near the railway station. The rooms were dark and poky and the furnishings had the distinctive smell that comes from years of nicotine use. It would have been the last place Hannah would have expected her to live but, as a healthcare assistant, it was probably all she could afford.

Hannah sat on the lumpy grey sofa in the lounge, ignoring the noises from the street outside seeping through the cracks in the rotten window frames, just as she ignored any effort on Milly's part to draw her out of her misery.

'Come on, Hannah. You really do need to eat something. It's been over twenty-four hours since we left the hotel.' Milly settled a tray on top of the coffee table, the smell of freshly buttered hot toast masking the underlying smell of stale smoke.

It took a lot to annoy Hannah. Most people thought her mild-mannered and it was easy to present that side of her personality to the world because it was the truth. Even when Hunter was at his most demanding, she always managed to take a deep breath and count to ten – sometimes fifteen.

A tray of tea and toast was an unusual trigger for her temper, but it came on the back of an hour of what could only be termed nagging, albeit with kindness at the centre. Her flare of anger was like being in the path of a tornado. There was nothing she could do to change the situation except say what she thought. There was no time to plan. No thought as to the damage that she might do to their friendship, or indeed their working relationship, by speaking her mind. All of the usual controls that prevented her from telling the truth were swept away on a tidal wave of grief.

'Really! And you think that eating something will make me feel better? That perhaps it will make the memories of my son and partner disappear?' Hannah's voice, initially soft, quickly rose to shrill. 'I don't want to fucking eat or drink. In fact, I shouldn't even be here. It's not going to help anything.' She picked up her phone and quickly stuffed it in the pocket of her jeans. 'I appreciate what you're trying to do but I can't stay.'

'But where will you go?'

Hannah hesitated, her hand still in her pocket as she shifted forward on the sofa and struggled to her feet. Milly had managed to hit the target dead centre, because of course she had nowhere to go. She reconsidered the question as it wasn't an answer that Milly was going to accept: it was there in the set of her jaw and the way her hands were entrenched on her hips. In truth, if their positions had been reversed, she wouldn't accept it either.

But Hannah's anger – although diminished – still lingered, not that Milly would be in a position to recognise it. She was a relatively new addition to the nursing home, only joining the team in the last couple of months or so. Yes, they'd hit it off straightaway but the length and breadth of their friendship wasn't such to allow for more than the most superficial of relationships. The truth was Hannah shouldn't have agreed to go with her to that hotel in Ruthin as a replacement for Milly's ex. If she hadn't agreed, what were the chances that both Hunter and Ian might still be alive? She had no right to blame her for what had happened. But that didn't stop her from doing exactly that.

'Look, I appreciate what you've done but it's not really any of your business where I go, is it?'

Milly's face flooded with colour only to melt away and be replaced by an awkward little laugh.

'No. Of course not. You have every reason to be angry with everyone right now but try and remember that I'm here if you need me. I'm worried about you.'

'Well, don't be. I'm not going to do anything stupid. I have far too much to do for that. Two funerals to arrange for a start.'

As soon as the front door closed behind her back, she leant against the black wood, heaving air into her lungs. Loath though she was to admit it, Milly had been right – she had nowhere else to go except home. With the death of both her parents and her brother, there was nowhere else. But she couldn't go back. Not yet.

Hannah wandered into Madoc Street, cutting around the corner of the auction rooms and into the heaving mass of Mostyn Street, Llandudno's main shopping area. Head lowered against the beating sun, she concentrated on the pavement, not bothering about where she was going or in what direction. It was as if her legs were in charge, leading the way, automatically following the well-trodden path along Church Walks to the North Parade and the pier.

It had been weeks since she'd visited the amusement arcade situated a few steps in from the start of the pier. The shove ha'penny game was a favourite of Hunter's and she'd used to take him on a Saturday morning as a special treat after she'd picked him up from his judo class in Craig-y-Don. But with the school holidays she couldn't remember when they'd last made the journey, something she now regretted with a fierce ache.

The pier was busy but then it would have to be blowing a

gale in from the Irish Sea to make a difference to the heaving stretch of Victorian architecture that followed the line of the Great Orme almost exactly. It was the go-to place for a daily stroll, the quaint little kiosks that bracketed the sides an ideal opportunity to escape the stifling heat.

But Hannah wasn't worried about the heat, just as she wasn't worried about the people milling about. She was barely aware of where she was or what she was doing, her fingers trailing the wrought-iron railings, her feet making little creaking noises each time she stepped onto another wooden slat. Her thoughts were consumed by images of Hunter as she tried to snag onto each memory and file it away for fear that she'd forget. His cheeky smile and slightly crooked teeth. The freckles that sprinkled his button nose. His serious eyes under heavy brows that almost seemed too old for his face. The way his hair refused to lie flat no matter how many times she brushed it. And with each successive thought, another little slice of her heart broke away and scattered into the wilderness, leaving a gush of blood and a stab of pain. She was mad with grief and yet in no fit state to do anything other than let the memories come, freefalling around her in a torrent.

There were no tears. Tears would have been easy – a release valve to spurt out her emotions, drop by solitary drop. She didn't want easy. She didn't deserve it. After all, wasn't she partly to blame for everything that was happening to her?

Hannah had reached the end of the pier, past the café, which was flooded with customers, and around the back to the steel railings and the fishing plinth that stretched out beyond. This was where she'd always ended up with her son, standing around exchanging token words with the fishermen. Hunter would watch wide-eyed as they hauled in an assortment of dogfish, mullet and, what they'd been reliably informed, were pollock. Hannah didn't know one fish from the other, apart from the cod they occasionally got from the fish and chip shop just inside Conwy Castle's walls, and neither did Hunter but he was enthralled all the same.

The sea had that distinctive greenish hue found far from shore. She stared down into its depths, her hands curled around the top rung of the railing as if her life depended on it and perhaps it did. Her mind emptied, her gaze pinned to the way the water lapped against the steel girders, the sound of tide against metal taking over from the noises behind her and the shrieks from the gulls overhead. There was nothing apart from the water. She felt small and insignificant. Worthless. She'd made a mess of her life and there was no going back to change it. No reprieve. No way to reverse what had happened.

Hannah melded with the water only a short distance from her feet, her mind following as her foot found purchase on the lower bar, her hands iron-tight …

Chapter 16

Jax

Jax had stopped off at the garage for the papers on his way to meet Georgie. It was only meant to be a pit stop but he couldn't resist searching through the flowers on display for a bunch that she might like. She was always telling him not to bother with grand gestures but that didn't stop her from giving him an extra big hug every time he made them. He ignored the large fancy displays that came at a large fancy price and instead chose a bunch of gladioli, their buds still tightly closed, their colour a secret until the glorious last. It meant that he was five minutes late in arriving at Coast Café but the blistering smile on her pale face made the delay worthwhile.

They didn't start to speak until they were halfway through their breakfast and on their second mug of tea.

'So, what kind of a night did you have?'

'Oh, the usual, you know. Busy.'

A usual night at the station was very different to the usual night working at the state-of-the-art St Tudno Annex Hospital. The new facility was situated between Llandudno and Colwyn Bay and a necessary addition to the NHS in their effort to reduce waiting times for routine procedures. With Georgie's surgical background she'd been lucky to be appointed deputy ward manager of the female orthopaedic ward. He'd tried to prise out of her what it was like but all she'd say was that he was best not knowing. The occasional bedpan story slipped out as did the odd moan about the other nurses but that was all he ever got from her. Confidentiality was key in both of their professions. He had to respect that she was rarely going to tell him anything of interest about her work and he certainly wasn't able to tell her anything about his.

He watched her take a bite from her vegan breakfast sandwich, her elbows ensconced on the table. She was small, with long brown hair that was normally restrained in a hairclip, but today she'd let it flow around her shoulders in a cloud. She wasn't pretty in the traditional sense. Her nose was long and thin, her mouth wide and full. But her twinkling brown eyes and ready smile made up for what others might view as minor imperfections.

Jax reached across the table and gave her hand a quick squeeze before returning to his full fry-up. He was happy to curtail his meat-eating at home but out of the house he was like a kid let loose in a sweetshop with a pocketful of change. Unstoppable.

'Anything in the papers?' she asked after a moment, picking up her mobile from where she'd placed it on the table. She started scrolling to her messages.

He placed his knife and fork together in the centre of the plate, chewing and swallowing his last mouthful of bacon before answering. He wanted to tell her about Hannah and the case but he couldn't. 'Just the usual drivel. I'm not sure why I read it.'

But instead of replying, she continued looking down at her messages with an unwavering stare.

'Georgie, you okay?'

She finally raised her head, the weight of the world in her eyes.

'Georgie,' he repeated, his voice whisper-soft, his hand curling around her arm. 'W-w-what is it?'

As a young man in his first serious relationship, Jax was desperate not to blow it. He'd even considered converting to veganism and he still might but that wasn't going to help him now. He didn't know what to do and he certainly didn't know what to say. Words for Jax were difficult. He'd had a stutter since he was seven and there were still good and bad days with regards to his speech. Some things made it better like being happy in his job and his relationship with Georgie. Stress made it almost impossible for him to get his words out. To see the woman he loved unable to speak had his stress levels rocketing off the scale.

She held up her phone and showed him the message, her hand starting to tremble. 'One of my friends has just texted me about a work colleague. Her little boy has just died.' She covered her mouth with her hand, pushing back from the table. 'I knew him. The loveliest little boy. I think I'm going to be sick.'

And with that she ran towards the toilets, her bag bundled under her arm, leaving Jax holding her phone.

Chapter 17

Gaby

Monday 24 August, 9.50 a.m. St Asaph

'Jax, what the hell are you doing here?' Gaby said, trying to work out what on earth would have made him drive all the way back to St Asaph instead of picking up the phone. 'I'm about to meet with Amy,' she said, the implication being to hurry up and get home to bed.

'I won't keep you, ma'am. I've just come from having b-b-breakfast with Georgie.'

He rubbed his hands across his face, unaware of the hollows and lines etched deep. He looked in need of a shower and bed, in that order, but something serious was obviously stopping him. Gaby bit back the words on her tongue and resisted the urge to glance at her watch. She hated being late with a passion. Amy would understand – of course she would – but that wasn't the point.

'You know my girlfriend works at an old people's home to top up her income? Her main job is deputy ward manager at the Annex but we're saving for a house.'

Gaby nodded, confused at where the conversation was leading but determined not to let it show.

'The t-t-thing is she knows Hannah Thomas. Would you believe it? I nearly said something earlier when I realised she worked at the same place. I'm not sure why I didn't except I knew I wouldn't be able to mention it to Georgie because of our policy on information sharing.'

Gaby had a lot to think about after she'd persuaded Jax to head home to the shower and bed that were waiting for him. She dropped into her chair and started doodling on the top of her pad, all thoughts of getting Amy a coffee pushed to one side. That Jax's girlfriend knew Hannah was the kind of lucky break they needed to shift the investigation forward. Okay, so there wasn't a great deal that they could do with the information but Gaby was sensible enough to know human nature was such that couples talked about work even when perhaps they shouldn't. She certainly knew that was the case between her and Rusty.

While Strong's death appeared to be self-inflicted, Gaby also knew that it wouldn't be the first time a murder had been disguised as a suicide. The criminal fraternity were adept at trying to deflect interest in their activities and what better way to stop an investigation in its tracks. If it hadn't been for the grow bags, she'd probably have agreed with them. But what father, even one with no legal claim to the role, would do such a thing? The more information they could get on Hannah's relationship, the better.

The knock on her door caused her to lift her head and pin a smile on her face, a smile that broadened when she saw Amy carrying two take-out cups and a bag from the bakery along St Asaph High Street.

'You little darling! How did you know that caffeine was just what I needed?'

'Because I know you.' Amy tilted her head in the direction of the croissants before adding, 'Was that Jax I saw heading off? I thought he was on nights?'

'He is but I'll come to that after we've caught up about Hannah.' Gaby prised the lid from her cup only to pull a face. 'Since when did you ever know me to drink green tea?'

Amy blushed scarlet, the colour clashing with the cerise pink of her long-sleeved T-shirt. 'That's mine!' She swapped cups. 'After the weekend I've decided that a detox wouldn't be a bad idea.'

Gaby raised her eyebrows in near disbelief at the words coming out of her friend's mouth. She'd never known her to be health-conscious. In fact, Amy Potter was the least health-conscious person she knew. It wasn't fair that someone so slim should spend most of their time stuffing their face with chocolate and crisps without putting on an ounce when Gaby only had to sniff at a cake to feel the waistband of her trousers tightening around her belly.

'So, what have you done with my friend and what do I have to do to get her back?' she said, making a point of bending sideways and looking under the desk.

Amy gave a half-hearted attempt at a laugh, which made Gaby suddenly sit up in her chair and take note. There was only one reason she could think of that would make Amy give up on caffeine, a reason she knew Amy had been hoping for ever since she'd met and fallen in love with Tim.

Gaby couldn't be happier, not that she gave any outward sign. Amy would tell her in her own time and not a second sooner. She managed to hold back the smile that was bursting to break out. Instead she lifted up her cup and took a quick sip while she marshalled her thoughts back onto a much more unsavoury path.

'What's your opinion about Hannah then, Amy?'

'I'm not sure, if I'm honest. Obviously she's devastated but I'd say more so for the loss of her child than her fiancé, if that makes sense?'

'Yes, that's the overall consensus although probably

understandable as she'd only been dating Ian a year,' Gaby said, the smell of warm buttery pastries shifting her priorities. 'Here. You look as if you need this.' She opened the bag and offered it to Amy before embarrassing herself by ramming one into her mouth whole. What was it with always feeling hungry the morning after a belly full of food?

'Thanks.' Amy sank her teeth into the flaky pastry, taking a moment to mop her mouth with the back of her hand. 'I didn't really fancy eating last night after everything.'

'I'm sure. Here, you might as well have the other one too in that case.'

'But—'

'No buts, Amy. I ended up stuffing my face with Conor's tea and—' She stopped her with a look. 'Before you ask, it's a very long story, which can wait until we have more time.'

She watched Amy devour the second one before returning to the topic at hand. 'I wonder why she and Hunter's father didn't stay together?'

'No idea. We didn't really get to talk about that. She cut me off at the pass when I tried to mention it.'

'Mmm … interesting. That fits with what Jax found out,' Gaby said, lifting up her cup and finishing the drink in one.

'Which was?'

'Absolutely nothing apart from the coincidence that Georgie knows her. They work at the same care home,' Gaby said, sweeping up the pastry flakes with the side of her hand and dropping them into the bin. 'With a name as common as Hannah Thomas we probably shouldn't be surprised. He couldn't even trace her on social media because he couldn't be sure whether it was the right person or not.'

'That's odd.'

'Very. Millions of people her age are on Facebook as well as Instagram. There's also a fair few that use Twitter although I don't get it myself.'

Amy laughed. 'That's because you're a complete neanderthal. I can't even get you to use WhatsApp.'

'And what of it?' Gaby snapped. 'I've seen far too many come unstuck by sharing their personal secrets to a world of strangers.' She glanced at her watch. 'Anyway, this isn't getting us anywhere. So, what did Hannah have to say before you left her?'

'Nothing of any note.' Amy lifted her hands, tightening her ponytail. 'But all that's immaterial because we're not really thinking that she had anything to do with the death of her partner and son – or are we? I thought the consensus was veering towards suicide? It takes a particular type of criminal to murder their child, and in most of the instances where it's happened, the perpetrator has been a man.'

'True enough, but there are exceptions to every rule and it's up to us to weed them out.'

Chapter 18

Marie

Monday 24 August, 10 a.m. Llandudno

There was nothing Marie liked better than getting embroiled in a puzzle, the more complex the better as far as she was concerned. It kept her mind off the other parts of her life that weren't so straightforward. Work was the best distraction of all, even if the case was as harrowing as this one.

Milly Buttle lived halfway down Brookes Street, a narrow lane situated behind Madoc Street and one new to Marie who was better acquainted with the North Shore and the shopping area behind.

The woman opening the door was of medium height with thick, dark hair held back from her face with a couple of funky hairclips. The handbag slung over her shoulder and car keys clutched in her hand told their own story.

'I was just heading out,' she said, starting to pull the door closed behind her.

'I'm looking for Miss Milly Buttle?' Marie opened her warrant card, noting with interest the look of concern that removed the smile from the woman's lips and the firmness from her grip as her keys fell to the ground.

'That's me. This must be to do with Hannah.' Milly reached down and picked up her keys before backing into the hall. 'Although I don't know how I can be of help. I don't know her all that well outside of work,' she said, leading her into a small lounge, which opened out into an even smaller kitchen.

Marie, after a moment's indecision, sank into the grey sofa and tucked her knees together. The smell of stale smoke caused her nose to twitch, which she tried to mask with a brief smile.

'To be honest, we're not sure either but you did spend part of the weekend together so that might be a good place to start. Why did you invite her if, as you say, you don't really know her outside of work?'

Milly laughed. 'Being new to the area, I don't know anyone well, not just Hannah. I came with my boyfriend for the summer season; he's a chef at one of the hotels along the seafront. We broke up pretty much within days of renting this.' Milly waved her hand around, her tone of voice saying more than her words. 'I'm stuck here for the foreseeable until I can afford to move on, and in the meantime, I intend to enjoy myself. Well, you can't blame me,' she said, her expression belligerent. 'He's living it up with one of the waitresses while I'm stuck in this hole trying not to lose the deposit.'

No. Marie couldn't blame her one little bit. If she had the money, youth and inclination, she'd do the exact same. But the five years or so that separated them ran deeper than the lines on Marie's face and the occasional grey strand that was starting to make its presence felt in her naturally blonde hair. Marie's days of drinking till dawn and working through the hangover from hell were long past but that didn't mean she didn't admire the woman in front of her for picking herself up and starting again.

'So, Hannah said in her statement that you booked a stay at Y Mwyar Duon as a surprise for your partner?'

'That's right. The hotel wouldn't give me a refund but were kind enough to change the booking to a twin room. And as I had no one else to ask …' She crossed one leg over the other, revealing a narrow gold chain circling her left ankle and the start of a tattoo, which Marie couldn't quite make out. 'We've worked together quite a bit recently and as we always have a good laugh, Hannah was the obvious choice.'

'Okay. And what about times? When and where did you meet up on Saturday and what time did you leave on the Sunday?'

'Let me see. It must have been about five or five-thirty at the hotel and she left around ten-thirty the next morning. Said something about having to relieve Ian as he had a game on.'

'And there's nothing untoward that happened? She didn't receive any odd phone calls or, for that matter, make any?'

'Not a thing. I think she messaged Ian at one point to check up on Hunter but that was quite early on in the evening. Later we'd had far too much to drink,' Milly said, her eyes widening. 'We both like gin.' She giggled. 'What's not to like about gin?'

'Indeed.' Nothing, apart from arriving home to find your son and partner dead. Nothing at all.

85

Chapter 19

Hannah

Monday 24 August, 10 a.m. Llandudno

Hannah removed her foot from the railing and straightened her shoulders in an effort to pull herself away from the drop in front of her. She didn't know how long she'd been poised on the brink. Time was as irrelevant as the cold, dark and lonely future stretched out in front of her.

It didn't take her long to hail a passing taxi. She slipped inside and, resting back against the hot sticky seat, expelled a long stream of air, all her energy draining away. It felt as if she'd just completed the most important race of her life. It would take her a long time to realise quite how important.

After a moment's indecision, she asked to be dropped off on Rose Hill Street. Hannah wasn't in the mood for a long walk up to her house but giving her home address would only cause a flood of questions from the already inquisitive cabby. She couldn't blame him that the deaths were all he had to talk about but listening to the theories he was spouting was the very last thing she needed right now. All she wanted was peace and quiet and time to think but it didn't look as if she was even going to be allowed that as she walked through the arch in the castle wall and started up the hill.

Mount Pleasant was a quiet residential street with little traffic outside of rush hour and the school run. Situated well away from the marina, it was rarely a place for tourists unless they were lost. But the large vans crowding the area had nothing to do with tourism. She hadn't reckoned on the media. In truth it hadn't even crossed her mind that her personal tragedy would pique their interest. The house was surrounded. The street was the busiest she'd ever seen it. The thought of trying to battle her way past the crowds was almost too much to bear.

As a qualified nurse, Hannah had learnt over time how to triage any given situation, how to decide what to do next. But this was different. She had no idea where to go except home, which now felt anything but. She couldn't go back to Milly's. She owed her an apology for a start, something she'd have to get around to but not yet. There was no one else. No friend in the wings waiting for an anxious call. No contacts on her mobile apart from work-related ones and friends of Ian's. No close cousins or indeed any family that she could rely on. She was on her own – something that hadn't worried her when she had Hunter and then Ian.

Turning away, she started retracing her steps, only to stop at the sound of her ringing mobile.

'It's Jon from next door. It's a bit of a madhouse outside. What about nipping around the back and going through the garden? I've already popped the kettle on.'

She looked up from her phone to find Jon waving at her from one of the upstairs rooms of his house. With a quick nod of her head, she cut the call and did an about-turn towards the narrow lane that backed onto the row of cottages. Hannah didn't know him well, not really. He was one of those men who seemed to get on better with other men than with women. She never knew what he used to chat to Ian about on bin night but it was far more than the usual moan about the weather. But he was being kind and that was something she needed right now.

The lane was cold, dank and smelt of cat pee, her nose wrinkling as the acrid aroma hit the back of her throat, almost causing her to gag. It was a place to store the bins and, as putting out the rubbish had been one of the jobs Ian had embraced, it was somewhere that she rarely visited.

Hurrying now, she darted a look over her shoulder to check that she hadn't been followed before clicking the latch on the gate and slipping into the small back garden, a mirror image of hers. She'd take the hospitality on offer because she had no choice. Her attention was focused on the four-foot fence that separated the two properties and the sturdy wrought-iron table below. With a bit of help and a hefty jump she'd be back in her own home in no time.

Hannah knocked on the back door, closing her mind to what she might find at home. The police had texted her to say they'd finished for the time being and that the car and all its contents had been removed. She couldn't think about the tiny shed and the compost heap beyond. It was enough that she knew what had been found. She didn't need proof or to see any of the tell-tale signs of what had happened only a few short paces away. Her imagination along with her thoughts were under strict instructions not to step in that direction – there was only so much she could take before her tender heart snapped along with her sanity.

Chapter 20

Gaby

Monday 24 August, 2 p.m. St Asaph

'Take a seat, Darin, and tell me how you're getting on with the Strong debacle? I had the chief superintendent on the blower most of yesterday in addition to the media hounding me. We need an early resolution closely followed by a statement to the press and it's up to you to engineer it.'

Detective Chief Inspector Henry Sherlock was a tall, dour man who wore his uniform with a pride that stemmed from his first career in the Army. He didn't stand to greet her, but then she would have probably rolled over in shock if he had. She settled in her chair, crossing her legs and adjusting the jacket of her trouser suit, before replying.

'Yes, sir.' She hesitated, taking a moment to choose her words. Sherlock was one of the toughest bosses she'd worked for and one of the sharpest. He was also adept at picking up on any failings on her part or threads of an investigation that hadn't been followed. 'Doctor Mulholland will have the reports from both autopsies later on this morning but I did have the opportunity to meet him yesterday for a quick catch-up. Hunter suffered from a medical condition called juvenile diabetes. He wore an insulin pump here.' She patted the lower part of her stomach. 'There are puncture marks on the boy's skin that appear to be attempts for the needle to be reinserted, which points to Strong finding Hunter, trying to reattach the pump, failing and committing suicide because of it.' She omitted to mention Rusty's thoughts on Hunter's cause of death – there was time enough for that when the report came through.

'I have Strong's original application here and psychometric testing.' DCI Sherlock dropped his reading glasses from where they lived on the top of his head, his hand lifting to tap the papers on his desk with a long bony finger. 'There's nothing to indicate that he was unstable or a suicide risk.'

'No. One of my officers came to the same conclusion.' She shook her head. 'And that's the reason we're continuing to look into both Strong's background and that of his partner, Hannah Thomas.'

He leant forward, his gaze trained on where she was mangling her fingers. 'I think you're not being entirely truthful, Darin. Or at least being economical with what you're telling me?'

Gaby swallowed but what little saliva she found did nothing to moisten her suddenly dry mouth. 'Dr Mulholland is still waiting for some pathology reports. There's the tox screen and the lung slides from Hunter for a start.'

'And?' he barked.

'And it looks as if the boy might have been alive when he was carried outside.'

'Which means that if Strong covered him in plastic, he killed him? Is that what you're saying?'

'I'm not saying anything until we get the report back,' she said, struggling to maintain eye contact.

'What about fingerprints?' he said, like a drowning man thrown a lifebelt.

'None on the plastic or on the child. We have to remember the in-depth, first-aid training Strong would have gone through, sir. He would have known the importance of maintaining an airway for a start.'

'Which is why he dialled 999, surely.'

'Then why didn't he stay on the line and request an ambulance? I'm sorry, sir.'

'Not as sorry as I am.'

Chapter 21

Jax

Monday 24 August, 6 p.m. Penrhyn Bay

'Wakey wakey, sleepyhead. It's time to get up.'

Georgie stretched, a large yawn emanating from her mouth, which she didn't bother to catch.

'What time is it?'

'Just six. I've made you cheesy pasta for breakfast.'

'Yum,' she said, her expression belying her words as she pushed her hair away from her face and swung her feet to the floor in search of her slippers.

'Yes, well I didn't think you'd want a second breakfast and you know my cooking isn't up to much.'

'You're always trying to put yourself down, Jax. There's absolutely nothing wrong with your cheesy pasta. I'm just pleased I didn't have to make it!'

'You always say the nicest things.' He bent down from his superior height and placed a quick kiss against her lips.

'That's because you deserve them.' She put the palm of her

hand against his chest and gently shoved him away. 'Now buzz off or I won't have time to do justice to my dinner.'

They didn't mention what had gone before although it was uppermost in Jax's thoughts. After his meeting with Gaby he'd tumbled into bed only to spend the rest of the day listening to the sound of Georgie tossing and turning beside him. The one good thing about it was that tonight was her last night. She'd be back on day duty but not until Sunday.

With the pasta dish in the sink soaking and mugs of coffee in front of them, they curled up on the sofa. Georgie's legs were tucked beneath her, her slightly damp hair loose around her shoulders.

'At least you're off tomorrow,' Jax said.

'Yes, although Tuesdays are usually the worst. We were due twelve admissions today and what are the odds that the day staff haven't been able to process them all?' She sighed. 'At least the night will fly past.'

'There is that.'

She entwined her fingers through his. 'I suppose you'll spend half the night tinkering on the case?'

'The case?' After what had happened at the café and their subsequent chat, where he'd told her that he was involved and little else, he was reluctant to be the one to broach the subject. 'A bit,' he said after a brief pause. 'I was trying to trace Hannah but she's not that easy to find.'

'No. Well, she wouldn't be. Been burnt in the past, although I don't know for sure – just a feeling I have. While she's a friend, we're not that close. Hannah isn't the type for close female friends. She was in the year above me at uni but we barely exchanged more than a couple of words before I met her again at Daffodils.' She squeezed his fingers lightly. 'I'm not going to be much help other than to say that she's somebody who keeps herself to herself. She never attends any of the work socials, of which there are many. You've been to a few so you know how full on they can be. Totally not her scene.'

'So, what about Ian Strong then? Did you know him?' he said, taking the opportunity to shift the conversation into a direction that interested him.

'Not really. We only met the once when my brother dragged me out for a drink a few months back. Mikey was between girlfriends at the time and I agreed, against my better judgement, to a pub crawl around Llandudno. I have to say I was quite surprised at her choice. Ian struck me as being a bit of a wide boy.'

'And how did you find her? Madly in love? Smitten?'

'Very wrapped up in Hunter if I'm honest. It was all about what he'd been up to whenever we were on the same break. I did offer to meet up for a coffee once or twice but she always used the boy as an excuse.'

'And Ian? Did she mention him?'

'Rarely. It was all about her son.'

Chapter 22

Gaby

Monday 24 August, 7.35 p.m. Rhos-on-Sea

Gaby knelt back on her heels, taking a moment to survey her finished lounge. It wasn't perfect but the Swedish sauna look of timbered panels on the lower half of the room was now a thing of the past. It had taken her six weeks to sand before painting the wood in a creamy buttermilk but the difference to the room was startling. Last weekend she'd stripped out the horrid, grey carpet to reveal the original floorboards, which were an unexpected surprise. She was now saving up for a large rug to tie in the colour scheme.

The other thing about decorating was that it gave her the opportunity to think. It was probably true to say that Gaby was obsessed with her job and with murder in particular. Crime had always interested her from an early age. No amount of badgering from her mother had made a jot of difference. She couldn't remember a time when she'd played with dolls and cuddly toys. With two older brothers she was far more likely to be found knee-deep in mud while they hurled footballs in her direction. But acting as goalie for her brothers wasn't something that bothered her as long as she was allowed to watch the true crime programmes on the television whenever she wanted. She was lucky enough to have parents who supported her despite wanting her to go into the family business. But a solid and dependable partner along with two-point-four kids and a job in the family restaurant had never been on Gaby's agenda.

After washing the paintbrushes, she wandered into the kitchen, flipped the switch of the kettle, and gathered together a mug and some cheese and crackers.

But the only problem with not bothering to cook a proper meal was the lack of washing up after. It was still only eight-fifteen and, with nothing of interest on the television, Gaby was at a loose end. She had no plans to contact Rusty, and Amy – with her parents having arrived from St David's earlier – would be on family duty. She could always open a bottle of wine and nurse a glass on her lap while she listened to music but Gaby was well aware of the dangers of drinking alone. The past thirty-six hours had been particularly trying, even for someone with her level of experience, and she was wise enough to know that she wouldn't stop at one glass.

Tomorrow was going to be full on with an eight-thirty meeting with DCI Sherlock already scheduled on her Outlook Messenger. What she needed was a good night's sleep but she also needed to be prepared, she thought with a sigh. There were things she could do from the safety of her lounge that would shave time off what was bound to be another very busy day.

With a mug of tea on the side, she booted up her laptop and started on her emails, which didn't take long to go through. There was an email from Rusty with an apology for not getting back to her and a confirmation that Hunter's slides confirmed what he'd been suspecting with regards to suffocation being the cause of death. She almost phoned him then, her hand curling around her mobile, her eyes suspiciously bright. But it wouldn't achieve anything. Rusty only dealt in hard facts backed up by rigorous evidence. She'd have to wait until he'd formulated the autopsy report or risk him telling her off for nagging. Instead she drafted a quick email inviting both him and Jason to a nine o'clock catch-up meeting and clicked send.

With her emails cleared, she turned to the next thing on her mental list of tasks. Finding out more about Hannah. Jax had been hampered by the popularity of her name and that's where Gaby's interest lay. She didn't like having to mop up after him but what if he'd been swayed by the scope of the task? It felt like a loose end, one she was determined to tie off.

Like most officers, Gaby didn't have a huge internet presence, but she did maintain a Facebook page, primarily so that she could keep in touch with what her brothers and nephews were up to. However, her current workload meant that she rarely got a chance to spend serious time doing anything apart from the job. The pages of unread posts reminded her of what a bad sister and aunty she was. Reams of photos and milestones in her little nephews' lives that she'd failed to celebrate. She banged off a few supportive replies and a promise to phone before turning her attention to her messages or, to be exact, the unread ones from her ex, Leigh Clark.

Leigh was both an emotional and career low point and one she didn't need reminding of as she quickly scanned his last couple of posts. He'd been instrumental in her being drummed out of Cardiff, an episode of her life that had taken her nearly a year to recover from. That he was always going to split up from his wife at some point was something she should have envisaged. After all, faithfulness had never been his strong point. But that he still thought he could make amends, in addition to a new life with her, was more than she could stomach.

Her hand touched the mouse, the cursor scrolling over his Hollywood looks and weak jawline before hovering over the unfriend button. It was something she should have done ages ago. Nothing good ever came from holding on to the dregs of the past. There was only one place for figurative dregs … She pressed the unfriend button.

Instead of celebrating with a laugh or a smile, she moved on with her search. She had Hannah's name, age and workplace, which should make it much easier to find her online. Using a search engine to help, she typed in relevant keywords to narrow it down. Her places of work. Her current location. It didn't take her long to come up with a news item about a Hannah Thomas in relation to the suicide of another young man. A suicide that had happened a few years ago.

Chapter 23

Georgie

Tuesday 25 August, 5.50 a.m. The Annex Hospital

Georgie Perrott sank into the deep leather chair and slipped off her black work shoes, a mug of hot chocolate cradled between her fingers and a pile of digestives in front of her. The first part of the shift had been as manic as she'd expected, the day staff too busy to do much with regards to getting the theatre cases prepped for surgery. In between taking observations, checking for piercings and recording dentures and crowns, she'd also had to care for the teenager who'd returned from theatre following a motorcycle accident, in addition to six others at various points in their recovery.

Of all the patients she was looking after, the fifteen-year-old concerned her the most. With multiple fractures and concussion, her distraught parents were guarding her bed in a tormented vigil. But now, with the glimmer of sunrise staining the sky a yellowish grey and signs that the girl was coming around from her ordeal, Georgie had managed to take her first break of the shift.

It wasn't unheard of for staff to go the whole night without pause but, with her blood sugar dropping and her eyelids starting to droop, Georgie knew that a few minutes now would give her the extra spurt of energy needed for the last two hours. This was often the busiest time of the night. They had the morning drug round to accommodate, closely followed by the rush to get those patients on the top of the list washed and gowned in preparation for their pre-meds.

She plucked her phone from her pocket and, with her mouth full of biscuit, started doing the one thing she'd promised herself earlier she wouldn't. There was something crawling through the back of her mind like an itch she had to scratch, despite knowing that it could possibly damage someone she both respected and admired.

The hospital grapevine was renowned for never missing a beat. It ran an information shuttle that only paused briefly to collect new juicy bits of gossip before proceeding on its way. There was always an element of truth in the stories it pumped out although how much of an element was questionable. Georgie had watched from afar as friends' and colleagues' reputations had been shredded by ill-conceived observations and speculation and, in a few sad cases, carried out with malicious intent. But by the same token if there was something she knew that could help the inquiry into Hunter's death, then wasn't she duty-bound to look into it?

The biscuits were long gone as was her drink, the sky now evolving in rapidly changing hues of orange and blue. One of her pet hates was tardiness, and unauthorised extended breaks at the expense of other members of the team made up for a big part of this. But she still lingered, ignoring her little blue fob watch pinned to the top of her scrub tunic top. She stared down at the grainy photo on the screen of her Samsung S9, her lifeline to the outside world and one she struggled to ration, much to the amusement of Jax who was nearly as bad. If it wasn't catching up with her friends on Facebook, it was searching her Instagram feed for recipe ideas. Cooking, despite Jax's glowing praise, wasn't her forte. But she wasn't doing either. Despite her dislike of gossip, and gossipmongers in particular, she was looking into something she had no right to. The tragic death of Stephen Lee, who'd died on Hannah Thomas's watch.

Chapter 24

Gaby

Tuesday 25 August, 9 a.m. St Asaph

The only good thing about the day as far as Gaby was concerned was the weather. After what seemed like weeks, the heatwave had finally broken, the skies now a paler blue and with a smattering of clouds to help dispel the oppressive heat. She liked nothing better than glorious sunshine. Hot, humid days spent pottering around her garden with a jug of iced tea on standby, but her workload precluded any such luxuries. Apart from a couple of tubs of pansies, which she was always forgetting to water, the garden was on its own when it came to maintenance. If it wasn't for the labours of next door's teenage daughter, who mowed her lawn every couple of weeks for a tenner, Gaby would be embarrassed to admit that it was her house. She certainly didn't have the time to treat it as a home: it was somewhere to lay her head and store her clothes, albeit a very expensive somewhere.

The incident room was busy, probably busier than she'd ever seen it despite their recent heavy workload. But there was nothing like the death of a fellow officer to hone the senses and focus the mind. It didn't matter that the word *suicide* had been bandied up and down the rank and file like a bad smell. Until it was proven or otherwise, the officers would work the case like they'd worked no other. She wondered whether they'd feel the same after she'd spoken to them – only time would tell.

'Right, everyone. Settle down. We have a lot to get through,' she said, sending a swift glance towards Jason who was sitting at the back and looking particularly disgruntled. There was no sign of Rusty.

Gaby rolled up the sleeves of her favourite Marks and Spencer shirt, her serviceable black watch the only jewellery on display. She didn't believe in wearing any of her finery at the station, despite having boxes of the stuff. Even out of work she kept adornments to a minimum, rightly or wrongly believing that her short stature was best suited to simple lines and unfussy accessories.

Picking up a green pen, she made for the line of whiteboards. She paused a moment to read over the timeline, her gaze resting briefly on the photos of Ian and Hunter on the top before turning to face the room, the pen rolling between her thumb and forefinger.

'First and foremost, there's already a huge media interest in the case by nature of both a police officer and a child being involved. Anyone who says anything to the press will face disciplinary proceedings, including immediate suspension and possible sacking. The DCI and super are being kept informed and will be the ones coordinating the release of statements and interviews. Is that clear?' She studied each of her team, knowing all too well the stress each and every one of them faced. While she trusted them all, up to a point, it wasn't only the media she was concerned about. It was the pressure exerted by well-meaning friends and family to divulge specifics of the case. She'd been put in the same situation many times. But there was only so much she could do to protect her staff.

'Now that's out of the way, we can get down to business and the reason for the warning. As you can see, I've invited Jason to attend … What have you got for us?'

Jason cleared his throat, his hands clenching a buff-coloured folder, which he opened out onto his lap. 'Hannah's house, over at Mount Pleasant, is squeaky clean of any evidence. We're still working on the car but there's nothing so far. Strong was wearing PJ bottoms and a T-shirt covered by a pullover, which was askew around the neck. We found some hair and cell traces from Hunter around the chest region, which would work with the theory that he found the boy unwell and carried him down to the car. But it could also be from ruffling his hair.'

He shuffled through the papers, reading through his notes before lifting his head. 'Now on to the boy. The grow bags were dragged across the ground from where they were stacked behind the shed, leaving trace marks on the paving slabs. But it's been a dry few days so there's no footprints to work with. The only thing not accounted for are some fibres from Strong's jumper and the boy's top – we'll know more when the results come back but they could be anything from gardening gloves to mittens. Apart from that there's nothing outstanding.'

'Except that Strong wasn't wearing either gardening gloves or mittens and …' she sent him a sharp look '… there were none found near to the body or lying about the house?'

'There's a drawerful in the hall, which we've taken away for comparison but I think it's unlikely we'll find a match.'

'Okay, thank you, Jason.' Gaby spent a moment updating the whiteboard before turning to Marie. 'The next thing we need to do is eliminate the mother from the investigation if we can. I don't have to remind you that she's currently our key suspect. Marie, you were going to check in with her friend?'

'Milly Buttle. Yes. There's nothing to say other than she confirmed Hannah's account almost word for word. They both arrived at about five or five-thirtyish, had a bellyful of gin and departed at ten-thirty the following day after a leisurely breakfast.' Marie hesitated, a frown brewing. 'I felt sorry for her if you must know. The house is no great shakes and being new to the area, she barely had time to settle in before she got dumped.'

'Okay.' Gaby made a note on the board under Milly's name before continuing. 'Next I'd like you to head over to Daffodils Care Home and follow up on the key points. In addition it will be an ideal opportunity to have a general nosy into what kind of a person Hannah is. Her sickness record. That sort of thing. We're lucky that Jax's girlfriend works there but we need to do most of the legwork for ourselves. Any questions?'

'No, ma'am,' Marie said, lifting her head from where she'd been frantically scribbling notes on her pad.

Gaby walked across the room to the one window that looked out over the car park below. It was a view as depressing as her thoughts. The only thing to brighten it was the sight of Rusty climbing out of his 4×4 and strolling towards the main entrance. She couldn't really believe that Hannah was involved in the death of her own child but she also couldn't leave her out of the inquiry. Who's to say that she hadn't returned early on some pretext or other, only to find Hunter dead? She could have decided there and then to help her fiancé on his merry way after suspecting that he'd had a hand in Hunter's demise.

'That brings me neatly onto the next point,' she said, leaning back against the cold radiator, her focus on Malachy Devine, who was stretched out in his chair, his brown loafers buffed to a bright sheen. 'For the most part, Hannah seems to like travelling under the radar, Mal. She doesn't have a social media presence that we can find, so I'd like you to drill down through the layers to find out why that's the case. The only thing of interest is a report on a case over in Bangor. The suicide of a young man called Stephen Lee. I've already checked the PNC but there's no record. See what you can do.' She took a second to locate Diane's neat blonde bob. 'I'm afraid it's another boring afternoon for you, Diane. You did too well with the CCTV on the last case for me to ignore your skills in that department.'

'Ma'am?'

'I can't see Ruthin, or Conwy for that matter, being overrun with cameras but see what you can come up with. It needs lateral thinking and that's right up your street.'

Gaby ignored the blush staining Diane's cheeks. Instead she turned her head to nod at Rusty who was racing down the corridor, smoothing down his hair with one hand and fiddling with the top button of his shirt with the other.

'Sorry, overslept,' was all he said, dropping into the chair beside Jason, the wood creaking under his weight.

'No problem. We've all done it.' Gaby strolled over to the cafetiere and, picking a mug at random, poured a coffee before handing it to him and returning to her position up front.

'We've just heard back from Jason about some suspicious fibres found on both Strong's jumper and the grow bags.'

Rusty nodded, the mug already empty and placed on the floor at his feet. 'I don't think anything would surprise me with the case,' he said after a moment, removing a sheet of paper from his pocket and unfolding it. 'I know you've been waiting for the autopsy results but I'm not going to apologise for the delay. I think you'll all agree that both deaths are unusual to say the least.' He pushed his glasses up his nose. 'I'm going to concentrate mainly on Strong as I'm confident that Hunter died from suffocation following being draped in plastic. His loss of consciousness from the DKA didn't help matters but that wasn't the primary cause of his death.'

There was a collective silence. No coughing or chair-shuffling. None of the tiny little noises that were usually found in a busy office. It was only momentary, but Gaby knew that everyone in the room was taking a second to work out the implications of his words: murder instead of death by natural causes.

'I've also managed to secure copies of Strong and Hunter's

medical notes. There's nothing unusual or noteworthy apart from the boy's diabetes, which we already knew about,' Rusty continued, the soft burr of his Irish accent more pronounced than she'd ever known it. 'Ian Strong was a well-nourished man with marked muscle definition, which tells me he looked after his body. There was nothing telling from the autopsy. No bruising on his skin. No evidence that he was forcibly placed behind the wheel of the car. No signs of needle marks. In fact nothing to suggest that he was under duress when he slid into the driving seat and died from carbon monoxide poisoning – something that has been confirmed by the high level of carboxyhaemoglobin in his blood.' He sat back in his chair, the paper loose on his lap. 'But I'm not telling you anything new. What I did find surprising was the high level of diamorphine floating around his system.'

Gaby nearly dropped the pen she was still holding along with her jaw.

'You're saying that Strong was a heroin addict?'

'A heroin addict?' Diane interrupted. 'But I thought you said morphine?'

'Diamorphine, Diane. It's the medical term for heroin and used widely for … for …?' She turned to Rusty to fill in the gaps.

'It's an opioid used for severe pain, primarily cancers but also some cardiac conditions – so following heart attacks and the like,' Rusty replied, refolding the piece of paper and stuffing it back in his pocket. 'And no, I'm not saying that he was an addict. The presence of opioids post-mortem isn't sufficient evidence for that label but the high concentration of 6-acetylmorphine found in his urine is indisputable.'

'I'm totally confused.' Gaby turned back to the whiteboard and added a note. 'Everyone's been saying about how health-conscious he was and yet he's full of the stuff. Large volumes?'

'A pretty impressive reading.'

'What about organ damage and track marks on his arms?' Gaby

threw out, impressed that she'd actually managed to come up with such an intelligent question. 'There should be signs, surely?'

'For long-term users, yes. In Strong's case no. I had a good look and there was none of the scarring or cirrhosis I usually expect to see in the dedicated addict.'

'So, if there's no signs of administration how the devil did he get it into his system?'

'If indeed he did administer it,' Owen said, standing to his feet and joining Gaby at the front. 'We all know that users can be inventive when it comes to hiding needle marks but the same goes for murderers too. There was that case a while ago where the pathologist eventually discovered a needle mark between the toes.'

'He'd have had to be pretty willing to have his feet injected,' Rusty said, his voice dry. 'Remember diamorphine crosses the blood–brain barrier within twenty seconds of administration, which means that within less than a minute he'd be riding a high. If you're thinking what I think you are, then how would someone have managed to manhandle him into the car without leaving a bruise?'

'Even so I'd like you to follow up on Owen's suggestion, Dr Mulholland.'

'By checking his feet?' Rusty raised his eyebrows.

'By checking his skin with a magnifying glass if need be for signs of a puncture wound. I know you've said that's something you've already done but I really would appreciate it.'

His expression shouted 'fed up'. His silence meant that she hadn't heard the last of it. 'Is there anything else?'

'No. I mean yes.' She stood still a moment, a deep frown in place. 'What about the car keys? You didn't mention them, Jase?'

'That's because we didn't find any.'

She turned back to Rusty. 'What about Ian's pyjama bottoms?'

'Nothing. Dean went through everything before sending it across to the CSIs.'

'I might not be known for my skills as a car mechanic but how do you explain Ian starting the car without his keys?'

The room fell silent for a second time.

'Okay, that's given us lots to think about. The keys. The heroin and whether it was self-administered or forcibly injected. We should probably bring Hannah back in for questioning but I think we'll wait a while until we gather a little more evidence.'

Gaby walked over to Rusty and placed a hand on his arm. But instead of speaking, she paused and turned back to face the room as if she'd just remembered something important.

'I'll just walk Dr Mulholland to his car. While I'm away, don't forget to sign Amy's card. It's tucked under my mouse mat. We can't let this get in the way of giving her a send-off she won't forget. Salt Inn, 6 p.m. tonight. Let's do everything we can not to let her down.'

Chapter 25

Georgie

Tuesday 25 August, 12.05 p.m. Chester

Georgie had never lied to Jax before. She'd never had occasion to. But going to Chester to look for an outfit for Amy's party was one thing. Arranging to meet with one of her friends and former colleagues, who now lived in Chester, was something entirely different. It wasn't wrong to meet up with a friend for an impromptu lunch, far from it. But what Jax didn't know was that the woman in question had been working on the same unit as Hannah when Stephen Lee had fallen to his death.

She spent the hour-long journey asleep, only jerking awake at the sound of the train screeching into the station. After a brief yawn and quick stretch, she clambered onto the platform. Apart from the fact she looked a little pale, no one would have suspected that she'd been up all night. Once out of the station, she picked up a taxi instead of walking the short distance to the Grosvenor Shopping Centre where she'd agreed to meet her friend, Tracy Robinson, for an early lunch before hitting the shops.

Chester was her go-to town when she fancied splurging on something special. It wasn't that Llandudno wasn't well off for shops because that was far from the case. It even boasted its own Primark in addition to the usual High Street faithfuls. But Chester, only a short train ride away, was the polar opposite to the quaint Victorian town. Its Elizabethan roots were embedded in the black, timber-framed buildings and an abundance of quintessentially English teashops.

Tracy was waiting with a coffee in front of her. She was a stunning redhead with long legs and a penchant for pink lipstick, which clashed with her hair but matched the tone of her bubble-gum T-shirt, heels and personality exactly. Georgie had known her so long that she almost couldn't pinpoint when they'd first met. She certainly couldn't remember how long they'd been friends, probably seven years or more when they were among the first cohort of nurses to start their Bachelor of Nursing degree at Bangor University. Tracy's squeal of delight and thick embrace, which nearly sent her cup flying – it certainly rattled in its saucer – drew a gamut of disapproving expressions from the four old ladies seated at the next table.

'It's been so long.'

'Far too long. What is it? A year?'

'More like eighteen months,' Georgie said, settling in the chair opposite and propping her elbows on the table, her conservative yellow sundress a perfect foil for her dark hair, her clear skin free from make-up. 'So, how's life? Adrian well?'

'As fit as a flea.' Tracy stretched out her left hand, the diamond cluster glittering in the sunlight spilling through the leaded windows. 'He's even talking about setting a date for the wedding.'

'Whoop. That's fantastic.' Georgie struggled to lower her voice at the sound of a distinct tut coming from the next table.

'Isn't it just. It will be you next, hon. So, come on, show me a pic then? I've heard so much about your man but—'

'Well. You know he's a detective, right?' Georgie scrolled

through the photos on her phone and, picking one, stretched the image between her fingers to fill the screen. 'There.'

'Ooh. Very handsome. A touch of the Ryan Reynolds around the eyes.'

'Do you think?' Georgie stared down at her phone, a broad smile turning her gamine face into a thing of beauty. 'Perhaps you're right. Lucky me!'

'Lucky you indeed, but as long as he's nice with it, it doesn't matter.' She caught Georgie's eye and descended into a fit of giggles. 'Although looks do help.'

'Yes but shush,' Georgie said, covering her mouth with her hand in an effort to suppress her laughter. 'You'll get us thrown out and I'm starving. I've barely eaten a thing since dinner and that was only a few biscuits at dawn.'

'Nights? They're the pits. It's nine to five for me all the way. A nice cushy number at a doctor's surgery administering jabs, redressing leg ulcers and other sundry easy-peasy chores.'

'You don't miss the hustle and bustle of the wards?'

'What, are you mad? Thirteen-hour shifts and the varicose veins to go with it. Not on your life.'

'But being at the beck and call of a GP all day.' Georgie shook her head. 'We'll have to agree to differ.' She picked up Tracy's empty cup and pushed away from the table. 'This is on me by the way. What are you having?'

'Just another coffee, please.'

'And a cake,' Georgie insisted. 'You know I hate eating on my own.'

Within minutes she was back carrying a tray piled with sandwiches, cakes and drinks.

'There's enough to feed a small army.'

'No, only one starving nurse and her skinny friend who insists she's always on a diet.'

'I'm not always on a diet.' Tracy pulled a grin. 'Only most of the time,' she said, picking up a pastry fork and sliding it into the slice of cheesecake Georgie had placed in front of her. 'But not today. So, what was this special thing that you couldn't discuss by email or even over the phone?'

'It's a little sensitive,' Georgie said, her voice a mere whisper, which had Tracy leaning forward in the chair, her fork back on the side of her plate.

'Intriguing.'

Georgie stared across at her friend, thinking of what to say and how to say it. Nursing was built on a foundation of patient confidentiality. However, Stephen Lee was dead. He'd been dead six years or more and it wasn't as if she was going to divulge the specifics of his care – she didn't know them and Tracy, who'd also been a student nurse at the time, wouldn't have been privy to the kind of confidential information found in a psychiatric unit.

'I wanted to ask about our second-year placements,' she said finally. 'Remember you and half the set were sent to the Beddows Unit for two weeks while me and the rest did our stint in Learning Disabilities?'

'Fancy you remembering that.' Tracy pushed her plate aside and, leaning back in her chair, cradled her cup between her fingers, eyeing her over the rim. 'I'm not sure I'll be of any help. You know what my memory is like for details.'

'Oh, you'll remember. I don't think I'll ever forget and I wasn't even there.' Georgie pushed her half-eaten sandwich away and, like Tracy, picked up her cup, the smell of double-shot espresso acting like super-strength smelling salts. 'The thing is,' she said, deciding to stick to the truth, 'I'm working with Hannah Thomas.'

Tracy placed her drink back on the table with far more care than the now empty unadorned white pottery deserved, her finger swiping at the smear of lipstick on the rim. 'Ah!'

'Ah is right.'

'You do know that we were sworn to secrecy, don't you? Matron dragged us all into her office and if there'd been a Bible handy we'd have had to place our hands on top. Serious stuff considering I wasn't even on shift. Hannah and Hardiman took the brunt.'

'Of course,' Georgie said, her voice trailing away. Hilary Hardiman, the senior staff nurse on duty the evening of the incident that had ended both her career and Stephen Lee's life. How could she have forgotten. The tremor that had run through the nursing fraternity had far-reaching consequences. It wasn't talked about, not publicly. It was as if some invisible hand had stretched out and gagged the nursing department in its entirety. But behind the doors of their flats, scattered across Bangor and beyond, the air was thick with supposition and gossip as to what could have happened, if only for them to learn from the experience. Georgie had never gone to the Beddows Unit as planned. It was closed for months and when it did finally reopen, a whole new band of management and nurses had replaced the old.

'You know I'd never ask if I didn't think it was important but, well, something's happened to Hannah, something horrible.' Georgie told her about Hunter and Ian, a gamut of expressions flashing across Tracy's face in a tsunami of escalating horror. 'So, if there's any possibility of a link …' she ended, spreading her hands, her meaning clear. She didn't want to press-gang her friend into divulging something that she'd sworn not to but, on the other hand, how could she not try and help Hannah?

'I don't know what to say. That poor girl. They tried to make her a scapegoat.'

'Exactly. If there's even a tiny little thing that you can think of?'

'There's nothing. Really. Nothing that wasn't dissected under the microscope of the media. Don't you remember it was the major news item for days? They probably knew more than we did by the end,' Tracy said, pulling a face. 'If I could help I promise I would. From what I saw, Hannah was the sweetest of girls.'

Georgie searched her face but there was no sign that she wasn't being anything but completely honest. She stood and, grabbing both cups, said, 'I need more caffeine.' But before she could take a step to join the end of the queue Tracy stalled her.

'What about checking out the library while you're here? As I said, the newspapers really had a field day.'

Chapter 26

Marie

Tuesday 25 August, 2.55 p.m. Llandudno

With more than fifteen years on the force, Marie Morgan was one of Gaby's most experienced officers, but being born and brought up in North Wales gave her an added advantage that Gaby's Liverpudlian roots could never match. Recently separated from her lawyer husband, Marie had thrown herself into work to the exclusion of all else – long hours at the station being the panacea she needed to survive the breakdown of her marriage. There was no thought as to the future or what next. At thirty-six, she'd watched any hope of becoming a parent disappear along with her cheating husband and she didn't have the energy to even think about starting again. Now she was living in Malachy's spare room on a peppercorn rent while she tried to build up a nest egg for the deposit on a flat.

Switching off the engine, she remembered all too clearly that she was one of the lucky ones. Ivo, her soon to be ex, hadn't died and she didn't have a child to lose, not yet anyway. Her fingers dropped fleetingly to her flat stomach. She had her health and if not quite the future she'd planned, then the makings of something to be proud of. Like Gaby, Marie was a staunch believer in the role instinct played in policing, not that she'd ever admit it. But Rusty's evidence about Hunter's death had only confirmed what she'd thought from the very beginning. Ian's actions as a distraught fiancé appeared off-key. Like most investigations it was now a case of sifting through the clues and piecing them together in a ribbon of explanation that made some sort of sense.

Daffodils Care Home was a long, low building squeezed in between the Sunnyside Hotel and a red-brick church along Llewelyn Avenue, a narrow road off the top of Upper Mostyn Street. The outside was painted a startling white, the immaculate lawned garden cared for by a loving hand. Marie took a moment to smell the pink rose bush that flanked the door, her nose wrinkling at the absence of scent. Her attention shifted to the fat bumblebee swooping between the flower heads. Gardening was her secret pleasure not that she got much chance now that the only outside space was Mal's roof terrace.

She'd barely pushed open the door to the reception area before she was accosted by a matronly figure, decked out in severe navy blue with a Peter Pan collar and a name badge with 'Gloria Dipton' picked out in gold lettering.

'Can I help you?'

In the early days of her career Marie would have been a snivelling wreck at the look of intimidation sent her way but that was before life had taught her a trick or two, not least the power derived from a warrant card.

'Good afternoon, I'm DC Morgan,' she said, flipping her card open and holding it up. 'If I could have a moment of your time?'

The office was small and obviously also functioned as a storeroom with filing cabinets beside the window and a floor-to-ceiling steel cupboard next to the door. There was no offer of tea and

Marie would have been left standing if she hadn't taken the initiative and plonked herself on the only other chair in the room.

'I really am very busy, Detective.'

'I won't take up much of your time, Mrs Dipton,' Marie said, her eyes hovering on the woman's gold wedding band before returning to the open notebook on her lap. 'I'm not sure if you've heard the news about Hannah Thomas?'

Gloria's expression softened briefly. 'Yes. A terrible business but surely nothing to do with her work here?'

Marie chose not to answer directly. 'What can you tell me about her?'

Gloria allowed her frown full rein. 'Hannah is a shy, quiet girl who is well liked by both the residents and staff.' She paused, her eyes sharp underneath her thick grey fringe. 'There's no reason for me to think otherwise, is there? Our residents must be protected at all costs …'

'There's nothing I can share about what is an active investigation. So, you had no worries about her work? No complaints from other members of the team?' Marie said, shifting the conversation away from the cliff edge it was facing.

Gloria spent a moment rearranging the top of her desk, moving the pen to one side and pushing the used coffee mug out of reach. 'No. Nothing. She joined us about five years ago, soon after the birth of her son – that poor lad,' she said, a little catch in her voice. 'She's one of those people one rarely notices, if that makes sense? In the old days, she'd have been termed a wallflower, always the one left sitting on the side when everyone else was out partying. She goes about her job quietly and efficiently and hasn't given me a second's concern until just now.'

Marie stared back, her expression not giving anything away.

Little Miss Wallflower, which was what Gaby had intimated. Someone no one took any notice of until something like this brought them into sharp focus.

Chapter 27

Georgie

Tuesday 25 August, 2.55 p.m. Chester

The Chester central library was housed in a refurbished former cinema. Georgie had time on her hands, so this posed the perfect opportunity to do a little snooping into Stephen Lee's death. She didn't spare a thought for her original plan, which had been to search the charity shops for something simple but stylish to wear to Amy's wedding. With money tight, a 'recycled' outfit seemed the best option – not that she'd told Jax. She still wasn't sure what he thought about most of her wardrobe coming from either eBay or jumble sales but, with her slight frame, she was usually lucky in finding something that few others were able to squeeze into.

Within half an hour of entering the imposing building, Georgie had garnered the help of one of the librarians and was sitting behind a screen scrolling through online versions of the North Wales newspapers. She didn't know what she was doing, not really, or even what she hoped to find. There was just this nagging doubt in my mind that wouldn't go away.

The death of a child was a tragedy, especially when the child was someone she'd met. Hannah had brought Hunter to the home on a few occasions at the behest of one of the residents and Georgie had thought him to be a delightful little boy, always clutching a dinosaur in his hand. But that wasn't why she'd decided to give up on her sleep. It was the clear impression she had in her mind of Ian Strong that evening in the bar with her brother. She didn't know him, not really, but that didn't change her opinion that suicide wouldn't have even appeared on his list of options. The situation didn't make sense to Georgie's confused brain, hence her interest in what was, after all, none of her business.

It didn't take her long to find what she was looking for, the story starting out as a one-liner buried on page four soon exploding into a shower-storm of front-page headlines. Her eyes scanned the screen, her little pink diary forgotten as she read through the columns.

17th July
A 29-year-old in-patient at the Beddows is reported to have fallen to his death yesterday evening.

18th July
An investigation is underway into the circumstances that led to the tragic death of a patient at the Beddows. Stephen Lee had been undergoing treatment for an undisclosed medical condition at the acute assessment unit. He is reported to have fallen off the roof, landing on the path below and sustaining fatal injuries at the scene. A third-year student nurse is currently assisting the police with their inquiries.

21st July
A 20-year-old student nurse, Hannah Thomas, was on duty on the evening in question. It is unclear as yet what led to Lee gaining access to the roof. The Beddows remains closed while an internal inquiry is carried out.

Georgie scrolled through a few pages until she came across the next reference, nearly three months after the initial article.

In a dramatic turn of events The Nursing and Midwifery Council, NMC, has issued a joint statement with the hospital trust, which in effect absolves student nurse, Hannah Thomas, of all responsibility for the death of Stephen Lee. Hilary Hardiman, the senior nurse on duty at the time of the incident, continues to assist the police with their inquiries.

What a shitshow! Georgie's hands were clenched into fists, all her thoughts going to Hannah and what she must have gone through. It made her blood boil that it had taken three months until common sense had finally won. As a student, Hannah would have only been carrying out the duties assigned to her by the senior nurse in charge of the unit, something the powers that be, in addition to the NMC, would have known from the outset.

She sat back in her chair, ignoring the way the hard wooden seat pressed into the backs of her thighs, as she tried to puzzle out what could have happened. It wasn't unheard of for someone with mental health problems to commit suicide, but not when they were being looked after in a secure unit where staff ratios were high. Georgie tapped her rounded fingernails lightly on the top of the table, trying to figure out what she should do next, which was to hand it over to Jax. But she wasn't going to quit yet. There was nothing to link what had happened to Hannah Thomas six years ago to what was happening to her now – in the unlikely event of her finding a link she'd happily pass the whole lot over to her boyfriend, and good riddance.

The next item on her hastily scrawled list was to chase up the findings from the inquest into Lee's death. However, a quick glance at her watch had her gathering together her belongings in a rush. She'd arranged for Jax to meet her off the four-thirty train and she hadn't even started looking for that dress.

Chapter 28

Hannah

Tuesday 25 August, 4.30 p.m. Conwy

Hannah was at a loose end. The only problem was she had nowhere to go and nowhere that she should be. Her doctor had signed her off work indefinitely, not that she blamed him. She was in no fit state to look after herself let alone the thirty-six residents who lived at the care home.

She'd wandered around Conwy for most of the day, spending time staring out at the marina, the minutes ticking into hours. It was only hunger and the search for food that finally drove her up the hill back into the town. She stopped off briefly at the SPAR but couldn't decide what to buy so left empty-handed, unaware of the awkward glances sent her way.

Conwy was a small community where everyone knew everyone else's business and, with the spotlight shining on their little town, it was hard not to know what had just happened – even harder to know how to respond. People weren't deliberately unkind but if crossing the road or diving into the nearest shop meant that they wouldn't have to face Hannah then that's what they did. Not that she noticed. She was oblivious to her surroundings, her footsteps automatically following the well-trodden path to home. She was almost at her front gate when she came to her senses, her eyes widening at the sight of the two newspaper reporters standing on her doorstep. But before they could intervene Jon bolted out of his front door and, grabbing her arm, propelled her inside.

'Sorry, love. I was in the back or I would have warned you.'

It was like waking up from a nightmare where only snippets remained. The time since Sunday lunchtime had passed in a dream-like sequence, everything afterwards dissolving into a cloud of dust.

Jon led her into the lounge and directed her to the sofa, tucked away on the furthest side of the room from the window. Hannah sat there, exactly where he'd left her, the ringing of the doorbell and the sound of a heated discussion barely registering in her tired mind. When he returned, he manoeuvred a mug of tea into her ice-cold hands and let time and the comfort derived from a hot drink work their magic.

'There, there. They've gone now. I told them I'd report them to the police for harassment. You should have seen them hightail it down the road as if the devil was at their heels.' She heard him rubbing his hands together, the sound finally dragging her back from goodness knows where but, wherever it was, she never wanted to return.

'This is very good of you,' she finally said, as social niceties reared their ugly head. She cleared her throat and, taking a sip of tea, tried again. 'Thank you for—'

But he interrupted her. 'No thanks necessary, my dear. No thanks at all. You'd do the exact same if it had been us in your position.'

Would she? Would she really? She didn't think so but thought better of airing her thoughts to a man who was one step up from a stranger. Jon was someone to talk to about the persistent problem of dog mess from the bulldog that lived in one of the houses opposite. That was it up until now.

'It must have been such a shock for you. And you had no idea that Ian was planning something like that?'

She continued sipping her tea, unsure of how to respond to Jon's gentle probing. She knew that the mild-mannered pensioner was nosy – it had been a topic of conversation between her and Ian when there was nothing else to talk about. The way he always seemed to pop up out of nowhere to waste what precious time they had together. They rarely saw Carmel, his wife. She probably had more sense, Hannah thought, a little spark of her usual good humour returning. The only time they saw her to speak to was when she had one of the grandchildren in tow, childminding for her daughter taking up most if not all of her spare time.

Hannah's mug was empty but Jon continued to witter on about this and that, despite her obvious reluctance to reply. She felt her eyes start to droop, the stress of the last two days, compounded by Saturday night's bellyful of gin, catching up with her. She only jerked awake at the feel of her mug starting to slip through her fingers.

'I'm sorry, Jon. Thank you for providing a bolthole but I really should be—'

'No, why not stay a while? Carmel will be back shortly. She'll give me a hard time if you leave without me inviting you to supper.'

'I can't impose …'

'I insist. She won't be long. She's just dropping Archie and Henrietta back to their mum. Come on. What about a slice of toast if I can't tempt you to stay for a meal? When was the last time you ate anything?'

She let him ramble on, knowing she didn't have either the energy or the inclination to put up much of a fight. He was right about the lack of food but it hadn't seemed important – it still wasn't. However, she needed to eat and, after her aborted visit to the supermarket, it was probably best if she took him up on his offer of toast. But she wouldn't stay much longer despite his entreaties.

The toast was still warm when the key rattled in the lock, the butter forming little golden pools on the surface of the barely browned bread.

'Carmel, my love, look who's here.'

Where Jon was tall and thin, with a full head of hair above faded blue eyes, his wife was a short, chatty dynamo with frizzy, grey-streaked hair and stylish, red-framed glasses. But instead of continuing the diatribe of questions, Carmel sat beside her and drew her into a deep hug, reminiscent of the ones her mother used to give her.

'I hope Jon has been looking after you, lovey?' she said, with a final pat on Hannah's back. 'He did right to deal with those reporters.' She shook her head. 'A scourge, the lot of them. Now eat your toast while it's still hot.' She lifted the plate off the coffee table and placed it in her lap. 'You'll stay for a bit of supper and the night. I'll make the spare room up for you.'

But Hannah was already prepared with a stream of excuses, which in part stemmed from the suddenly claustrophobic feel of the overcrowded room. Carmel had a love of chintz married with an overwhelming collection of china dolls. They littered every surface and must have been a bitch to dust but that wasn't the problem. It was their wide unblinking stares that creeped her out, just as they did every morning when she spotted them watching her on her return to the house. Hunter used to love them but then there was a wealth of difference between the imagination of a child and that of an adult. The fact that Carmel repositioned them every day, adding to the feel of their life-like appearance, had been nearly enough for her to want to put the house on the market and run for the hills.

No. She wouldn't stay. She lifted up the now-cold, soggy toast and, taking a deep bite, chewed and swallowed without tasting a morsel. 'Thank you for your kindness, both of you, but I'm expecting a call from the police.' She lifted up her phone as if to emphasise that fact and stood to her feet.

'But—'

'I can't thank you enough for your hospitality,' Hannah interrupted, finishing off Carmel's sentence with words of her own choosing. 'But I'm not going to disrupt your evening any longer.'

And with that, she made for the hall, pausing a second to peer out of the small window to the right of the door to check the way was clear. But Jon's earlier threat must have done the job or perhaps they'd decided to give up for the night because there was no one anywhere near her property.

Opening her front door brought no premonition of what she might find, only a deep sense of loneliness at what she'd lost. It might be selfish to think that way but she couldn't help it. Silent tears started to track down her cheeks, tears she didn't bother to mop up – there were plenty more to take their place. The truth was that Hunter and, to a lesser extent Ian, were the only family she had left apart from a couple of cousins she didn't hear from outside of an annual Christmas missive. Seeing them both, lying side by side on those cold steel trollies, had driven home once and for all that they were gone forever.

The first inkling that things weren't the way she'd left them was the sight of her overnight bag in the hall, the clothes and toiletries strewn across the floor. She swallowed, trying to moisten her suddenly dry mouth. There had to be a rational explanation but the truth was she'd left the bag zipped up and clogging the hall on Sunday morning – there'd been no reason or inclination to move it.

She headed into the lounge and almost wished she hadn't, her thoughts of moments ago disappearing at the sight that greeted her.

The room had been vandalised: the mirror over the fireplace now glistening in shards on the rug below, the crisscross knife marks on the sofa allowing the stuffing to poke out, the photo frames from the mantelpiece stamped into the rug, the pictures removed and torn into strips.

Hannah had heard of burglars desecrating houses. Drug-fuelled delinquents spreading excrement over the walls like some new age art movement … but this, this was different. This was personal.

She dropped to her knees and started to gather together the scraps of paper, ignorant of the broken glass scattered like leaves on a windy day, a steady river of tears hampering the exercise. The last photo of her parents and her brother, taken only hours before they'd boarded their fated flight and sent via WhatsApp to her along with a cheery 'wish you were here' message. A picture of Hunter on his first birthday, his arms and legs still layered with baby fat. The photo of Ian and Hunter, taken on a rare trip to McDonald's. All priceless or, at least, priceless to her.

She had thought that life couldn't get any worse. She was wrong.

Chapter 29

Gaby

Tuesday 25 August, 6.35 p.m. Conwy

'Do you think she could have done it?' Owen said, standing in the doorway, his gloved hands hidden behind his back.

'Possibly but it's far from likely, is it? Have you seen the state of her? It looks like the site of a massacre with all that blood streaked on her face and hands. Have a heart, Owen. She's beside herself with grief.'

Gaby grabbed his arm and pulled him away from the lounge and back into the hall, leaving the crime scene officers to work their magic. 'I don't know what to do with her. She's refusing to get her wounds checked. What if there's glass embedded?'

Owen shrugged. 'What if there is? You can't force her unless she's sectioned under the mental health act.'

'True enough.'

Gaby wasn't sure that mad with grief would pass the stringent tests that doctors put their patients through to achieve such a certificate. It certainly seemed to be having a detrimental effect on Hannah's behaviour if the state of her ripped jeans and visible wounds were anything to go by.

'So, what are we thinking then, Owen? A robbery or …?'

'I'd go with "or" myself,' he said, with a lack of his customary twinkling smile. 'It takes a special type of bastard to trash the home of the recently bereaved, particularly when the dead includes a small child.'

'Exactly my thoughts. It doesn't look as if theft was the motive, so the only gain is emotional anguish for the mother. It's a good job she called us when she did.'

They stared across at each other, their expressions layered with feelings that neither of them could translate into words. Gaby wasn't a parent but she'd seen first-hand the bond forged almost as soon as sperm infiltrated egg. It had happened to her brothers and she suspected that it was happening to Amy. Owen, a father of two, shared her distress. As he'd already said, it took a particular type of person to have performed such an act and Gaby, for all her years as a PC in Liverpool before taking her detective and inspector exams, had never come across anything like it. To rip up photos was one thing; despite the horror, they could be replaced easily enough. But to strip Hunter's bedroom in its entirety of every scrap from the bears on his bed to the clothes in his chest of drawers was the worst kind of crime.

There were no toys. No posters or books. They'd even taken the bedlinen and curtains. Apart from the furniture the room might be a hotel room for all the personality it displayed. All that was left to Hannah now were the photos on her phone and her memories. Nothing to touch, feel, smell, experience – all destroyed by the worst kind of evil imaginable.

'It looks as if we're back to the drawing board on this one but in the meantime, it doesn't need the two of us here. You pop off and send my apologies to Amy. Tell her I'll join the party as soon as I can.'

'But you need to be there …'

'I also need to be here until we get Hannah sorted with some-where to stay for the night.' She placed her hand on his arm and turned him to face the door. 'Buzz off. I'll be along shortly.'

'Ma'am, can I have a quick word?'

Gaby noticed the young PC guarding the door, a clipboard and pencil held to his chest.

'What is it, Craig?'

'There's a man outside. I've tried to get him to leave but he won't go. He says he's known to the family.'

Gaby let out a long drawn-out sigh. That was all she needed. It was always the same when a crime was committed. It brought out the worst in people, the nosy need-to-know gene pushing away any thoughts of common sense and basic human kindness.

Her gaze landed on the tall, dark-haired man filling the gateway. 'Strong's brother. Okay. You stay here. I'll be back in a minute.' She pulled back the hood on her over-suit before striding out of the door.

'Hello, Mr Strong. Can I ask what you're doing here?'

'What I'm doing here?' He took a step back. 'Surely it should be me asking that? After all it's my brother who's dead.'

'Okay.' Gaby relented, her attention on his hands, which were clenched into fists, the broad knuckles gleaming white through the skin, the muscles of his forearms bunching along with the cords in his neck – all indications that he was quickly losing the war with his raging emotions. 'Come this way but make sure to keep your hands in your pockets; the CSIs are far from finished.'

'That's very American-sounding and, yes, we do have the show in Australia.'

'A recent change from Scene of Crime Officers. I'm not sure what the advantage is except that the general public now know what we're talking about,' she said, unable to dim the sarcasm lacing her words.

She followed him, only to pause beside the door. 'Before you go any further, I need to warn you that there's been a burglary and Miss Thomas has been injured.'

'She was attacked?' he said, his colour fading underneath his tan.

'No, not exactly but she is hurt. I really need to get her to see a doctor but she's having none of it.'

'Well, that's easily sorted,' he said. 'I'm one. A gynaecologist, or at least I will be when I've completed my exams, but the basics are the same.'

'Oh. Right!'

She led him past the lounge, throwing an apologetic look at the CSI on her hands and knees picking up glass and placing it in an evidence bag, her gloved hands stained red.

'That's a lot of blood.'

'When Hannah arrived home she came into the lounge and …'

'I get the picture. So, can I see her? It sounds as if those wounds need medical attention as soon as.'

Gaby couldn't see any mileage in keeping him in the hall when clearly he could do some good in the next room. But she suddenly stopped outside the kitchen door where Hannah was sitting with her head in her hands.

'She obviously can't stay here. It's still a crime scene …'

'You don't have to continue, Detective. My father will put her up gladly for as long as she needs.'

Chapter 30

Gaby

Tuesday 25 August, 7.35 p.m. The Salt Inn, St Asaph

'I never thought you'd get here.' Rusty walked towards her and planted a quick kiss on Gaby's mouth before holding her away from him and studying her blue dress and matching shoes. 'You look amazing. The way Owen was speaking, he expected you to turn up in your suit.'

'Ye of little faith, Rusty. Us girls have ways and means of slipping into our glad rags that you men couldn't even begin to envisage.'

'What, you mean you popped a change of clothes in your car before leaving for work this morning?' Rusty winked.

'Something like that,' she said, unprepared to confirm exactly that. Picking a stray hair off his tweed jacket, she thought what a handsome man he was. With his auburn hair freshly cut since she'd seen him earlier, he looked good enough to eat, which was a salutary reminder that she'd missed breakfast, worked through lunch and, as a result, could quite happily eat a horse if it presented itself. 'Where's the couple of the hour?'

'Smooching on the dance floor. The sooner that man makes an honest woman of her the better.'

Gaby followed his gaze, a smile budding at the sight of Amy wrapped around Tim.

'I see what you mean.'

'So, do you fancy a dance or something to eat first?'

'You know me so well, Rusty,' she said, scanning the room for signs of food.

'No, not yet, but I'm getting there.' He nodded in the direction of the table set up to the left of the bar. 'Come on, I skipped lunch. You get the plates while I get the drinks. A wine or …?'

'No, it's going to be a tough enough day tomorrow as it is without adding a hangover into the equation. Something soft that looks alcoholic – I don't want to be called a party pooper.'

'I don't think anyone would dare. You do know that this means you're doing the driving? I have no compunction in asking as I've managed to swing the night off both parental and work duties,' he said, his blue eyes twinkling behind his black-rimmed frames. 'What about a gin and tonic, ice and a slice, without the gin?'

'It will, at least, look perfect if not taste it!'

Gaby was standing at the table trying to decide between chicken wings and spareribs when she felt an arm encircling her waist.

'At last. Owen did say that you'd be late,' Amy said, giving her a little squeeze before removing her arm. 'So, what's going on?'

'I'm sure you don't want to hear about the case and I certainly don't want to tell you about it.' Gaby managed a laugh. 'You're officially off duty until after the honeymoon – not that I should have to remind you. Tim would have my guts for garters if I started talking shop at your party.'

'I know but …'

'But nothing, Amy. This time the case is going to have to get solved without your input. Just forget about it,' Gaby said, adding a spoonful of coleslaw and potato salad onto the side of each plate. 'Do you think Rusty would prefer mustard or tomato ketchup?'

'Rusty would prefer both, thank you very much,' he replied, chortling somewhere in the vicinity of her left shoulder. 'Sorry, Amy, I didn't get you anything. What are you having?'

'Oh, I'm good, thanks,' she said airily, wafting a hand in the general direction of Tim, who was chatting to Jax and Georgie on the other side of the room. 'I've had far too much as it is.' She focused on the plates. 'Well, I'd better leave you to it while it's still hot. Come and join us when you're finished.' And with that, she hurried off.

'That was a bit odd, don't you think, Amy refusing a drink? I've never known her to before.'

Gaby lifted a finger to her lips. 'Shush and use your brain, would you. Either she's suddenly discovered that she's allergic to alcohol, has decided to be the designated driver at her own party or …'

'Ah. Right. Got you.' His lips twitched along with his left eyelid. 'This chicken is good,' he carried on, neatly changing the subject.

'Yes, as are the ribs. So, what have you done with Conor then?' she said, wiping her mouth with a napkin and finding room on the bar to deposit her half-empty plate. Her appetite had suddenly deserted her as her mind caught up with the fact that Rusty was childless for the night.

'He's been invited on a sleepover around at one of his friend's. I don't have to pick him up until tomorrow evening.'

Gaby didn't know what to say to that. The air between them was suddenly thick with tension and unspoken questions, which she certainly wasn't going to put a voice to. Their friendship, as she liked to term it, was meandering along pretty nicely. With work as it was, she hadn't given much thought to where they were heading. She was still scared, as well as battle-scarred, after the disaster of her time with Leigh Clark. Going out with a man who had a challenging eleven-year-old in tow wasn't what she'd hoped for but the gleam in Rusty's eye told her he had no such concerns. She damped down a sigh at the way he was downing his pint of Guinness. He couldn't possibly drive so there was no way out of the dilemma. She was only glad she'd decided on a whim to wear her fancy underwear for a change. If the crew she'd been working with could have seen what she'd been hiding under her suit they'd have probably collapsed. She giggled, her colour rushing up into a deep blush at the thought.

'Something funny?'

'No. Far from it. Tragic, more like. Oh look, there's Jax and Georgie,' she said, her turn to change the subject.

Georgie was wearing a long, figure-hugging red dress with fitted sleeves and diamante detailing in a size that Gaby wouldn't get her left leg into, let alone her right – not that she was bothered. After years of yo-yo dieting she was finally coming to terms with her shape. Her friendship with Amy had helped, as had, funnily enough, her job. There were far more important things to think about than size. She was fit and healthy, if not quite happy – but happier than she'd ever been, she mused, her gaze flickering down to where Rusty had taken her palm in a firm grasp, his thumb absentmindedly smoothing over the back of her hand.

She cleared her suddenly dry throat. 'If I was a betting woman, I'd say that they'll be next to walk down the aisle.'

'But they've hardly been dating two minutes?'

'That's all it takes, less than that. Totally smitten. Young love!'

'Ha, you're not so old yourself.'

'Old enough!'

'Well, there is such a thing as the value of experience,' he said, pulling her around to face him.

'Stop it and ask me to dance.' She mock-slapped his arm away, embarrassed by his overt display of affection.

He stepped back and offered her a small bow. 'Your wish is my command,' he said, again offering her his arm along with another deep chuckle. 'You do know that the whole department is aware we're seeing each other?'

'That's as may be but I'm the one who has to direct operations tomorrow and I won't have them sniggering behind my back.'

'Now you're being silly or stupid, maybe both,' he said, with a return of his old arrogance.

She glared at him, trying to pull her hand out of his suddenly firm grasp. 'I've changed my mind about the dance.'

'No, you haven't,' he said, drawing her onto the floor, the pull of his jaw giving away the fact that she'd annoyed him. 'I'm not making a fool of you in front of your team. I wouldn't dare, but it is time you learnt to let your hair down.' He looked at her hair and where she'd tweaked her plait into a messy bun, loose tendrils circling her cheeks. 'You're a great boss but also a woman, a woman who's becoming increasingly important to me.' He wrapped her close, her head only reaching his shoulders. 'What do you think Sherlock is up to right now with his wife over at the golf club?'

Gaby snorted, her bad humour dissolving with his words, and a little glow exploding inside. 'Have you met his wife?'

'No, I haven't yet had that pleasure.'

'No. Well, you're certainly in for a treat. I don't think he'd let her set foot in the golf club. She'd be running it within five minutes of joining.'

After two dances, Gaby made her excuses and headed for the ladies', not that she needed it. Instead she sat on the chair inside the door and removed her heels, cursing that she'd decided to wear them. Years on the beat had reinforced the benefits of wearing low-heeled loafers for work and, when she wasn't at work, she was either in trainers or slippers.

'So, this is where you're hiding.'

Amy meandered into the room and, checking that the cubicles weren't occupied, poured her glass of clear liquid down the sink before leaning against the wall and avoiding Gaby's gaze.

'I'm pregnant.'

'Oh, Amy, you lummox. As if I didn't guess.' Gaby jumped to her feet and padded across the room in bare feet, drawing her into a deep hug. 'I'm delighted for you.'

'We weren't planning it or anything.'

'These things happen, my love,' she said, gesturing for her to sit on the only seat. 'How far are you gone?'

'Nearly four months. I didn't even guess until Sunday. I'd been fine up to then, no signs of anything and with my periods always being erratic.' She looked up, her face deathly pale. 'When I told Tim that I'd been sick he made me take a test.'

'That's wonderful. So exciting. A new job, home, man and baby in little over eighteen months. That's some going.'

'But what about all the alcohol? I don't normally drink as much as I did on Saturday.'

'Which you vomited most of back up. Your clever body's way of keeping your baby safe.'

'Gaby, I'm scared. You will help me, won't you?'

Gaby frowned at the comment, which was so unlike her strong, independent friend. It must be her hormones running rampant, or the fact that her relationship with both her mother and future mother-in-law was sketchy at best. Whatever the reason, Gaby was determined to have a quiet word with Tim at the earliest opportunity. But for now she was happy to reassure Amy that she'd do everything she could.

'As if you'll be able to stop me. With two nephews and now Conor, I'm a mine of useless, child-related information – not that it's done me a jot of good,' she said, compressing her lips.

'How's it going with Conor?'

'It's not.'

'Well, if you will eat his tea …' Amy laughed, with a return of her usual good humour. 'Here.' She opened the back of her phone case and removed a couple of plasters. 'I had a suspicion you might be needing these. You should know better by now.'

They walked back into the bar, arm in arm.

'Ma'am, I'd like a word if it's convenient,' Jax said, his hand on Georgie's shoulder. Owen was at his side, sipping from a glass of lager.

'For God's sake, I'm not the flaming queen. Gaby will suffice when I'm off duty, Jax.'

'And when would that be?' Owen said.

'When would what be?'

'You being off duty?'

'Oh, go boil your head and get me a low-alcohol beer while you're at it. I've suddenly lost my taste for … gin,' she said, sending Rusty a quick smile across the room.

She directed them to a quiet table in the corner. 'Is this all right or do we need to go back to the office?'

'No. Here is fine. It's not really me who needs to speak to you. Go on, Georgie, she won't bite.'

Gaby hid a frown at his terminology, instead managing the sweetest of smiles. She didn't know his girlfriend well, hardly at all, but the young woman obviously had something on her mind.

'It's all right, Georgie, and do call me Gaby.'

'It's about Hannah. Hannah Thomas,' she said, her voice a mere whisper in the noisy room. 'I work with her on occasion.'

'Yes, Jax did say.'

'She's a nice person. Lovely. Kind.' Georgie was staring down at the table, her eyes riveted on the bubbles floating up her glass of fizz. 'She wouldn't hurt a fly but …' She lifted her head, catching Gaby's gaze. 'I think you should know about Stephen Lee.'

Gaby perked up at the name, a name she recognised. She had no idea what Georgie was about to say but she'd guessed at it being some grapevine gossip of little importance. This was obviously far from the case.

'I don't know if you know anything about nursing but it's a three-year degree course interspersed with time spent on a variety of wards and departments. During the second and third year we get to choose what we term "spoke placements" – two weeks in an area of our choice. One of the options was the Beddows.'

'The Beddows?'

'An acute mental health assessment unit.'

'Oh right. Do you mind if I make notes?' Gaby asked, pulling her diary from her bag and turning to the clear pages at the back.

'Not at all. Anyway, Hannah was in the year above me so the story is only from what I've heard bandied about but …' She glanced at Jax briefly. 'I was in Chester earlier so I took the opportunity to do a little digging while I was there.'

Of course you did, but Gaby kept her mouth shut, unwilling to disrupt Georgie's train of thought.

'Anyway, to cut a long story short, Stephen Lee was a patient on the unit,' she said, fiddling with the folds of her dress. 'He died under Hannah's watch. There was a huge kerfuffle at the time. The nursing body was involved. There was rumour that she'd be let go but, as a student nurse, they couldn't lay any responsibility at her door. The qualified nurse on duty wasn't so lucky.'

Gaby nodded a thank you to Owen, who'd placed a tall glass of lager in front of her, before returning her attention back to Georgie. It also gave her valuable thinking time. 'And you think this could be in some way connected to the death of her partner and son?'

Georgie shrugged. 'Maybe. Maybe not. Hannah fell pregnant shortly after and only got to sit her finals after Hunter was born. I hadn't seen her in ages until I started picking up some shifts at the nursing home and I certainly wasn't friendly enough with her to start discussing her past.'

'Ma'am, er G-G-Gaby, that is,' Jax said, blushing right up to his hairline. 'When she told me, I had a quick look at the report from the original inquest.'

'I would have expected nothing less, Jax.' She glanced over her shoulder but the party was still in full swing, the dance floor and bar area packed. Rusty was deep in conversation with Mal and Marie, a full pint in his hand. He caught her eye and, raising his glass, saluted her briefly, before resuming his tête-à-tête. No one was taking any notice of what was going on at the table in the corner – just as well. 'A brief summary, if you please?'

'The inquest was at Ruthin County Hall,' Jax said from memory, his speech, for once, clear and even. 'The coroner – I can't remember her name off the top of my head – said that the post-mortem examination revealed Lee died from extensive external injuries following a fall off the hospital roof. He'd been admitted to the unit a week before with severe depression, thought in part to be related to his dependency on Class-A drugs. The final conclusion was suicide.'

'Which shouldn't have happened, bearing in mind that he was at the Beddows for his depression. Interesting.' Gaby lifted her drink and took a sip, her nose wrinkling at the bitter taste. Setting down the glass, she pushed it aside and leant back against her chair. 'It's certainly something we'll check into. Thank you for bringing it to our notice, Georgie.'

'Hannah won't be in trouble, will she?'

'After all this time? I can't see it myself. But we do need to find out whether the accident in any way influenced what happened at the weekend. It's unlikely after so long but not impossible.' She picked up her diary and stared down at the couple of scribbled notes she'd made. 'There's only one other thing. The name of the nurse on duty, if you can remember it, that is?'

'Hilary Hardiman.'

'Okay, thank you.' Gaby watched as Jax led Georgie back onto the dance floor, her red dress swirling around her ankles as if she didn't have a care in the world. Gaby, on the other hand, now had another name to add to the growing list of people needing to be investigated.

Chapter 31

Hannah

Tuesday 25 August, 10 p.m. Llanrhos

'Ouch.'

'Sorry. Only one more to go,' Dominic said, pouring a little more iodine onto a square of gauze and patting the cut on her knee. 'Are you ready?'

'As ready as I'll ever be.' She gritted her teeth, her fingers fisting into the side of the mattress as he attacked her again with his father's tweezers. Hannah would never have put herself down as a coward but then she'd never had her knees peppered with shards of glass before. Her jeans, her favourite pair ever, were now only fit for the bin. But instead of trying to pull them down over her wounds, she'd watched as he'd slit the seams and fashioned them into shorts, albeit the raggediest pair of shorts she'd ever seen.

'I'd be far happier if you'd allowed me to take you to the emergency department. A couple of these are deep enough for gluing. They're bound to scar.'

'If you think that I'm bothered by a scar or two you're sorely mistaken,' she said, studying the top of his head as he rummaged through his dad's first-aid box in search of plasters.

'No. I know. You're a roughie-toughie miss who's fine managing on her own.' He sat back on his heels, glaring out from below winged eyebrows that most women would kill for. But not her.

Hannah didn't know what it was about him but the more she got to know Ian's brother the less alike she found them. In appearance they were like carbon copies but looks were only skin-deep. Underneath, Dominic was harder, something that was reflected in the firmness of his chin and the narrowing of his gaze every time she caught him scrutinising her. Part of her wished that she'd taken Jon and Carmel up on their renewed offer to spend the night, but the state of her legs had stopped her. She would have stayed with Milly if the home hadn't called Milly in to work the late shift and getting the keys would be too much of a faff in her current fragile state. Now all she wanted was for Ian's brother to leave her to her own devices with maybe a cup of tea and a biscuit as she realised there was probably an easy remedy for the gnawing pain in her stomach.

'There. You're all done.' He stood and, walking over to the door, leant back against the jamb, his arms crossed in front of him. 'I'll find you something to wear and—'

'There's no need. Honestly. I'll be fine.'

'I know you'll be fine but it will upset my father if we don't offer you the rudiments of a comfortable stay like a towel and a toothbrush – or did you remember to bring your own?'

All she could manage was a little shake of her head. She'd been hurried out of the house so quickly that she'd barely had a chance to grab her bag and phone.

'Your phone. Does it need charging?'

She darted him a look at his 'bang on the nail' question. 'I'm not sure.' She fumbled in her jacket pocket a moment. 'Out of charge. I'm sorry.' She felt her eyes start to fill.

'No need to apologise. You weren't to know you were going

to be burgled. It's the same make as mine so no problem,' he said, picking up the phone and checking the charging point. 'There's a bathroom next door. My dad has left you a towel and some other bits and pieces. You sort yourself out and I'll be back shortly.' With that he left, closing the door behind him with a resounding click.

The shower was hot, the towels thick and fluffy. The water stained a rose red as it drained through the plughole, her eyes on the smear it left on the white ceramic tray. She knew there'd been blood, but not quite how much. She didn't care. Nothing was as important as it might have been three days ago.

Redressed in her T-shirt, she attacked the shower with cream cleanser before heading back into the spare room – if Ian's dad was to be believed, her room for however long she needed it. She'd seem him when he'd opened the front door, his dogs by his side. But after only a few words he'd made himself scarce, leaving the hosting duties to his surly son.

She hopped into bed, feeling like a child sent to their room without their supper. No food. No drink. No phone …

The knock was sharp and decisive with barely a pause for her softly spoken 'come in', before he entered, a tray in one arm and a charger and pair of pyjama bottoms under the other.

'Oh, you shouldn't have gone to all that trouble,' she said, her eyes on the mug of tea and plate of what looked like cheese and ham sandwiches.

He didn't reply. Instead he sent her another glare while he set the tray and the pyjamas on the edge of the bed before stooping to plug in her phone.

'You'll be back on Facebook in no time.' His derogatory tone told her his thoughts on social media.

'Actually, I'm not on Facebook.'

'You do surprise me,' he said, with a noticeable twang at the end of the sentence.

'I take it you don't approve?'

'It's not up to me to approve or otherwise. It's your life to waste as you see fit.'

It was easy to see that he could hardly bear to be in the same room as her, despite his pseudo-solicitous behaviour. After all it would reflect badly on him if he was rude to his dead brother's partner, wouldn't it? Hannah had no idea why he disliked her and, the way she was feeling, she couldn't give a damn either way. She wanted to tell him to leave, but she didn't think he'd take kindly to being ordered around in his own home.

She picked up her mug and, after taking a deep sip, placed it on the bedside table, struggling to ignore the sandwiches despite her growing hunger pangs. She'd eat but only after he left.

'Well, thank you again for everything. You must have somewhere you'd rather be than babysitting me,' she said, the nearest she'd go to addressing his most odd behaviour.

Her mobile pinged through a message closely followed by another, a welcome diversion from the suddenly, tension-filled room. She reached for the device, her eyes drawn to the illuminated message lighting up the phone – her way of reinforcing that it was time for him to leave.

'Goodnight then. I'll see you in the morning.'

She wasn't listening. She'd stopped listening as soon as her eyes had connected with the words displayed on the screen. A little cry left her lips even as the phone tumbled from her hand onto the bed before rolling to the floor.

He was back by her side, his expression changing to one of concern in an instant.

'What is it? What's happened?'

Chapter 32

Gaby

Tuesday 25 August, 10 p.m. Rhos-on-Sea

'I hope they won't mind that we disappeared off early,' Gaby said, slipping the key in the lock.

'I don't think anyone would have noticed and, as we have a full day of work ahead of us, it's only common sense.' He took the door from her hand, pushed it open and gestured for her to go before him.

'Right.'

Gaby slipped off her shoes, walked over to the lounge window and set about drawing the curtains. Switching on the table lamp, she tried to analyse how she was feeling. Nervous, certainly. A little scared too but also excited. It was nearly two years since she'd been alone with a man outside of the office, apart from the plumber – a happily married fifty-year-old who would be horrified where her mind was dragging her. He had no interest in her as a person – only in the state of her pipes. She stifled a laugh.

'I don't know about you but I feel like a cuppa,' she said over her shoulder. 'Want to join me?'

'Perfect.' He settled on the sofa and, picking up the TV remote, started flicking through the channels. 'Anything you want to watch?'

'I'll leave it to you.'

She was back within minutes, a bowl of Mini Cheddars in one hand and two mugs in the other.

'Here you go.' She handed him his drink and placed hers on the coffee table before sinking into the squashy sofa, leaving a good few inches between them, her attention on the blank screen.

'I thought you wanted to watch TV?'

'Nothing on worth watching.'

'Music then,' she said, starting to get up, only to be detained by a hand on her arm.

'No music. No TV. No more excuses. I'm happy to phone for a taxi if you'd prefer? I take it there's still no bed in the spare room?'

'Not yet. It's being delivered on Thursday. For Amy,' she added, wanting to make it clear what she meant. 'She's staying here the night before the wedding.'

Gaby frowned, trying to work out why she was so anxious all of a sudden. She liked him and he liked her. She allowed him to draw her close. The time for words was over.

'Hello. Darin speaking.' Gaby slipped her feet out of bed and, reaching for her dressing gown, pulled it around her shoulders, aware of the soft snore coming from the other side of the duvet.

'Ma'am, it's Clancy from the station.'

'As if it would be anything but work at this time of night,' she whispered, glancing at the luminous dial on her watch, which told her it was heading for midnight.

The floorboards were cold underfoot as she made her way across the room, but she didn't waste any time trying to remember where she'd left her slippers. Instead she closed the door behind her and made her way to the lounge and the comfort of the sofa.

'Sorry for disturbing you but we've received a call from Mr Strong over at Llanrhos. Miss Thomas has received a death threat.'

'Dear God. In person?'

'No. A message via her phone.'

Gaby couldn't say that she was surprised, not really. The nature of her profession meant that she was rarely surprised at anything. She didn't believe what she was told until it was backed up by facts but, with the time as it was and most of the team off until the morning, there was very little she could do except secure Hannah's safety.

'Okay, see if you can arrange for a car to park outside her current address. Not much can happen to her until morning and I'll visit her myself before heading into work. Is there anything else?' She looked up to find Rusty framing the door and signalling that he'd make her a drink.

'No. Sorry for disturbing your night, ma'am.'

'That's what I'm paid for. Hope you have a quiet shift.'

She ended the call and followed Rusty into the kitchen, almost laughing at the sight of him warming milk in a pan, his bare legs on show beneath his shirt tails.

'Everything all right?'

'Not really. There's been a death threat made to Strong's partner.' She plucked a couple of mugs off the shelf and started spooning hot chocolate powder into the bottom of one. 'Chocolate or only milk?'

'Chocolate will be fine. Not what she needs after the last few days I would have thought.'

'Exactly.' She poured hot milk into the mugs and handed him his along with a spoon. Instead of making her way into the lounge she leant against the work surface, reluctant to make eye contact but forcing herself to do just that. She'd never been any good at après-sex pillow talk but, unlike her time with Leigh, at least they had something to talk about outside of their shifting relationship.

'She's had more than most thrown at her. It's a wonder she's still standing.'

'Unless she set up the message as a diversion,' Rusty said, squaring his glasses onto his face.

She laughed. 'You're more suspicious than me and that's saying something.' Ignoring her drink, she folded her arms across her chest. 'So, why do you think that it would be necessary for her to do something quite so horrendous on the back of the death of her son and fiancé?'

'To put you off the scent would be my likely guess,' he said, copying her in crossing his arms, his back resting against the closed door. 'She is the chief suspect and, as she's also not stupid, she'll know that.'

'But why?'

He shook his head. 'That's your department, not mine.' He picked up his drink and, pulling open the door, continued to hold her gaze. 'It's well past my bedtime. Coming?'

She walked past him and up the stairs, trying and failing to put the idea of Hannah's guilt out of her mind. It was only when Rusty reached for her hand that the thought slipped away. There'd be time enough to think about conspiracy theories in the morning.

Chapter 33

Gaby

Wednesday 26 August, 7.30 a.m. Rhos-on-Sea

Gaby raced out of the house, the pressure from Rusty's lingering kiss almost forgotten in her rush to get to work. He'd made her sit down at the kitchen table and force down a piece of toast she didn't want but felt obliged to finish, her mind wholly centred on the day ahead. She'd barely reversed into the road, her gaze alternating between her mirrors and the view up ahead of the Welsh coastline when her phone started ringing.

She pulled into the side of the road, much to the annoyance of the milk van driver behind her. He wouldn't have gesticulated in quite such a fashion if he'd realised he was dealing with the very long arm of the law. But then again, if he had, he might have had something to say about the finger she flipped him out of her open window as he overtook her on a squeal of rubber.

'Darin speaking.'

'It's Jax. I'm g-g-going to be late in today.'

'That's fine.' She forced her voice to soften at the sound of his stutter. 'You know you don't have to phone me this early. At nine would have been fine.'

'You don't understand, ma'am,' he said, the sound of air being dragged through his lungs audible across the waves. 'It's G-G-Georgie. She's been called into the nursing home. They found a discrepancy with the controlled drug register and she was the last one to check it.'

Gaby was tempted there and then to return home and hide under the duvet, with or without Rusty. She knew from experience that her day could only get worse. But she wouldn't. Her first responsibility was to her team, a strange view perhaps for a serving copper but one she'd hold right up until retirement. Without her colleagues she wouldn't solve even a fraction of the cases that came her way.

'Jax, don't worry about us. You go and do what you have to do to support Georgie but keep me updated. You know as well as me that if drugs are missing then we'll end up being involved one way or the other.'

It only took her seven minutes to drive the distance from Rhos-on-Sea to Llanrhos, the short journey marred by her thoughts of what Jax and Georgie must be going through. She didn't have to be a copper to know the seriousness of drug theft. By the time she'd pulled up outside the smart semi-detached bungalow with an overindulgence in the garden gnome department, she'd come up with a variety of reasons for the missing drugs from mathematical to falling down the back of the drug cupboard – none of which included theft by Georgie.

After a quick word with the uniformed officer sitting outside – who had a look of controlled boredom on his face – she walked up the short, paved path, searching for a non-existent bell to push.

The door was opened on the second knock by Dominic Strong, something she hadn't been expecting. If she had, she'd have made more of an effort with her expression, which must have held a haunting reminder of the trick the brothers' genetic code was

150

continuing to play on her mind. They weren't twins, far from it. But they looked like twins, which was all that mattered.

'Good morning. I believe Miss Thomas is here?'

'You'd better come in.'

He closed the door behind him but remained in the hall, staring down at her from his superior height, but he needn't have bothered. Many people over the years had tried and failed to intimidate her with their lofty stature but at five foot and half an inch, she was well used to being talked down to. Gaby wasn't worried about things she couldn't change. What did concern her, however, was why an intelligent man like Dominic Strong would deem such behaviour necessary, closely followed by the observation that she was glad he wasn't her gynaecologist.

'I'd like a word first. As far as I know she's still sleeping.'

'I'm surprised she managed.'

'That would be down to the sedative I sneaked into her cuppa and, before you lecture me, she was dead on her feet. In my professional capacity I deemed it the right course of action.'

I'm sure you did! But instead of commenting, she secured her bag on her shoulder and waited, following the best tip she'd learnt as a probationer. The power of silence.

'I wanted to take the opportunity to ask how you're getting on with the investigation before my father returns – he's out with the dogs. It's far too stressful for him. He's not a well man.'

'I'm sorry. At this stage there's really not a lot that I can tell you.'

'Or won't.'

'Excuse me?'

'You heard.' He turned on his heel and, pushing the first door on the left open, stormed into the room.

Gaby followed, the only thing she could do under the circumstances. She barely glanced at the untidy lounge, books and papers layering most of the surfaces, a distinct smell of dog detracting from the clutter to the exclusion of everything else. He was standing in front of a red-brick fireplace, his hands clasped behind

151

his back. She didn't take the seat he'd indicated with a tilt of his head. She'd played too many games in and out of the office to be tricked into a subservient position, despite the persistent ache in her calves, a remnant from last night's dancing.

'Mr Strong, your brother's death is top priority at the station. As he was a serving police officer, it's incredibly important to us that we turn every stone. The nature of the job means that we make enemies. If there's any reason to suspect that it wasn't self-inflicted, believe me, we will discover it.'

'He was murdered. End of!'

Her eyes widened at his emphatic reply. 'How can you be so sure?'

'Just because I live on the other side of the world doesn't mean we weren't close. I chose to study medicine in Australia because it was the only place that made me an offer and I felt like a change of scene. Ian and I were in touch most weeks, sometimes most days, via WhatsApp if you must know. He'd never been happier. Hannah was the love of his life and when he was accepted onto the force he felt on top of the world.' He sighed, collapsing onto the nearest chair and staring at the floor, his hands dangling between his denim-clad knees. 'There is no way he'd have committed suicide under any circumstances.'

Gaby sat on the sofa opposite, almost as worn out by his speech as he appeared to be. The truth was his words were only confirming her opinion, first formed when she'd seen Ian hunched over the steering wheel; an opinion compounded by his psychological evaluation. The idea of him taking his own life didn't ring true. Maybe at a push if it had been his own child, but Hunter had been around four when they'd met. The paternal bonds might have been growing and expanding but they were still very different to if Ian had been his dad. Her thoughts derailed, some sixth sense telling her they were no longer alone.

Hannah was standing in the doorway, her hair on end and uncombed, her top crumpled and stained, her feet bare. But it wasn't her clothes that Gaby was interested in. Despite the seda-tive, she looked as if she hadn't slept a wink. The shadows grazing her cheeks and pressing under her eyes were dark enough to give her a hollowed-out appearance, as if someone had scooped out the goodness, leaving only the dregs behind. She would never be termed good-looking, but now she looked positively plain. Gaby dropped her gaze to Hannah's hands, her attention trained on the mobile gripped between her fingers.

'Hey. How are you doing?' Dominic strolled to her side and, with one hand lightly on her arm, walked her over to the sofa and waited until she was settled.

'Slept like a proverbial log, which is funny considering I didn't expect to,' she said, her expression glacial and her meaning clear.

He had the grace to look embarrassed. 'Er I thought you needed to after the shock you had.'

'Which one?' Hannah glanced down at her phone before putting it on the arm of the sofa with all the care of an unex-ploded bomb.

Dominic didn't answer. Instead he headed to the door. 'I'll just go and put the kettle on while you have a word with the detective.' And with that he was gone.

'I don't mean to be rude to him, but he rubs me up the wrong way, not to mention that he's the spitting image of …' Hannah stopped, unable to continue.

'I completely understand,' Gaby said, nodding in agreement. 'It must be incredibly difficult for you. Apologies for the early visit but I've been told about the text you received?'

Hannah lifted her phone, unlocked it and scrolled to the correct message. 'Here.' She handed it across. But instead of remaining in her seat, she walked over to the window and peered through the fancy nets across at the old school beyond.

Gaby took a photo on her phone, trying not to think about what the words must have meant to the woman even now hiding her face from view.

They died because of you, which makes you next.

Instead of saying what she wanted, which was to try and offer some comfort, Gaby stuck to the task at hand, missing Amy with each passing second. Amy was the expert in these situations while Gaby was tongue-tied by her own insecurities about her ability to make Hannah feel better, and a dread of making her feel worse.

'If it's all right with you, I'd like to take your phone back with me? It's amazing what the team can do with tracking these things.'

'Fine. There's no one left to call me now anyway.'

The sound of footsteps in the hall reminded Gaby of the phrase 'saved by the bell', simply because she didn't have any sort of an answer to such a statement and again wished that Amy was by her side. One of the first things she'd do when she got back to the station would be to check the arrival date for Amy's locum, which had been set back due to sickness.

'Here you go. I thought tea and toast would be in order as you've yet to eat,' Dominic said, staring across at Hannah. 'There's sugar and spoons.'

Gaby hid a laugh at the sight of the milk carton and sugar bag plonked on the tray but the tea was strong, hot and very welcome.

Hannah ignored the mug and plate he handed her, instead setting them down on the mantelpiece before returning to her viewing position beside the window, her thoughts obviously miles away.

The silence grew and Gaby was reluctant to break it because there was nothing to say, no information or support that she could give. Instead she nearly burnt her throat in her rush to finish her tea. She placed the mug on the coffee table and pushed herself to her feet, feeling the strain in the back of her calves as she again cursed last night's foray into heel-wearing.

'If there's nothing else, I'd better shoot off, a busy day and all that.'

'I'd appreciate a lift back home, that is if I'm allowed?' Hannah said. 'I need to pick up my bike.'

'Sure thing. It only means a slight detour.'

'But what about your breakfast?' Dominic said with a frown. 'You should eat. I'm happy to take you anywhere you need to go after that.'

'No. I've relied on your hospitality as it is and …' Hannah caught his eye briefly, her skin tone rivalling that of the panna cotta Gaby's mother used to make for special celebrations. 'If I eat anything I'm going to throw up.' With that she made for the door and waited, one hand grabbing the frame for support.

Dominic looked at Gaby but all she could do was shrug her shoulders. She understood that he was trying to help but he had a funny way of going about it. He needed to gain Hannah's trust – drugging her, even if it might have been done with the best of intentions, wasn't the way.

Out in the car Gaby twisted in her seat, her hands on the steering wheel.

'Are you positive about going back home? I'm not sure it's a good idea. I can put a PC watching the house but …'

'There are things I need to do and it's not as if I can afford taxis. It's too much to expect people to drive me everywhere.'

Gaby didn't ask her what she had to do. It wasn't any of her business and she probably wouldn't tell her anyway. Instead she plucked a card from her wallet and dropped it onto the dashboard in front of her. 'All my numbers are on there. Call me whatever the time and no matter how stupid you think it is. I'll get your phone back to you as soon as …' She paused, her foot hovering over the clutch, her hand wrapped around the gearstick. 'I take it you'll be sleeping at home tonight?'

'There's nowhere else to go. I'm not imposing on Milly again and Dominic is too … No.'

Chapter 34

Hannah

Wednesday 26 August, 8.25 a.m. Conwy

'Thank you for the lift.'

Hannah slammed the car door shut and walked towards the house. There was no sign of the reporters but with a police car filling the driveway that was hardly surprising. If she wasn't feeling quite so anxious, she'd have offered the poor man sitting outside her house a drink but she'd had enough of the police to last a lifetime. There was also no sign of Jon or Carmel. Either they were out or the police presence had driven them back behind their green velour curtains. Whatever the reason, she was thankful for being spared their kind but claustrophobic presence.

Pushing open the hall door was a lesson in bravery but she had a plan all worked out. There was no need to go into the lounge or upstairs, where she already knew what she'd find.

She blinked in an effort to stop that thought before it grew and grew into the unwieldy monster it threatened. Even a glimmer pulsed like a stab to the heart, ripping and tearing up her flesh in an explosion of grief. It was bad enough losing her son but to lose everything else … She bit down on her lip hard, pushing the thought back where it belonged and sliding the deadbolt in place for good measure. She had a plan, which she must stick to. A plan with hope at its centre. No deviation. No question.

Hannah was tidy, obsessively so, when it came to the main rooms of the house but her ironing pile was legion. The utility room next to the kitchen was a mess but a mess of her own making. The tiny room contained her washing machine, tumble dryer and two B&Q storage boxes full to overflowing, piled on top of each other like a modern-day leaning Tower of Pisa. And this was where she headed in search of two things: clean clothes for herself and the hope that the robber hadn't checked this most unimportant of rooms for items belonging to Hunter.

Why pick on Hunter? The thought raised its ugly head again, only to be battened back into place by the sight of his favourite T-shirt poking out the side of the dirty washing basket. She felt like shrieking at the sight but she didn't; instead she lifted it free and held it to her nose in an attempt to fill her mind and her senses with the essence of her son. A hint of his shower gel. The smidgeon of chocolate syrup from the ice cream he'd dribbled down the front and the reason he'd changed it as soon as they'd returned from their walk on Saturday. He hadn't bothered to go to his room – like mother like son – instead he'd raided the washing pile and thank God for that.

She gripped it to her chest, trying to memorise the smell as if somehow it would fill the emptiness that had racked through her since his death. She missed Ian too, of course she did. After a relationship that had spanned nearly a year she was bound to. But she'd never loved him. Certainly not as much as she'd loved Hunter – nothing like. Part of her felt that her capacity to love had been skewered by the death of her family and the fallout from what had happened shortly after. The term 'damaged goods' popped out of nowhere only to join all the other negative thoughts bounding around her mind. None of this was her fault. All she wished now was for someone else to believe that.

Dropping to the floor, the T-shirt on her lap, she tore through the baskets. There were soon three piles. One of Hunter's clothes, one of Ian's and one of hers. Hannah wasn't rich, far from it. The money her parents had left had gone into the house, the little left soon frittered away when she'd had to take time off work after having Hunter. Like her, Hunter didn't have masses of clothes. What he did have was in the dirty washing pile, the ironing basket, the washing machine or tumble dryer. She shouldn't be feeling triumphant, far from it, but she couldn't help herself.

Hannah wandered back into the kitchen wearing a clean pair of jeans and a short-sleeved top with butterflies printed onto the indigo fabric, chosen because it had been one of Hunter's favourites. There were things that she needed to do like get a locksmith around. She wouldn't be able to sleep until all the locks had been changed, simply because one of the first things the police had told her was that there'd been no signs of a break-in. Dominic had volunteered to find a locksmith, but she'd turned him down.

She frowned, recalling Dominic's overbearing presence through all of this. She got that he was a doctor and as such used to taking the lead. It was something that seemed to be in the blood of every medic she'd ever worked with. But what she couldn't understand was his need to interfere in her personal life too. She was nothing to him – as his brother's now former partner, less than nothing. So why the interest? It couldn't all be down to compassion – she'd hazard a guess he didn't have a compassionate bone under that thick sheet of muscle and impervious smile. Perhaps he used too much of it in his professional life to have any room left in his personal one.

The sound of the landline pulled her up short. Hannah didn't know how long she'd been standing with Hunter's T-shirt clutched in her hands but the stiffness in her fingers indicated longer than she feared. She also didn't know who could be calling. It was most likely the police with news or Milly checking up on her. Just as long as it wasn't Dominic …

Chapter 35

Jax

Wednesday 26 August, 10 a.m. Daffodils Care Home, Llandudno

It wasn't the first time that Jax had visited Daffodils. That had been when they were investigating the disappearance of the care home's resident hairdresser in a case that had challenged both their minds and resources and ended in the arrest of Wales's third serial killer.

Situated halfway along a narrow road off Upper Mostyn Street, the long, low building was dressed in white and surrounded by splendid gardens that would do any owner proud. But Jax didn't notice the gardens and he certainly wasn't interested in the state of the paintwork. He'd been waiting outside in his car for what felt like hours but in reality was only thirty minutes. Georgie hadn't wanted him to come in with her and rightly so. He certainly wouldn't have wanted her there if their roles had been reversed.

He stepped out of the car, slamming the door behind him in a clear indication that his normally placid demeanour was anything but. The car was his pride and joy, the sportscar something he'd started saving for as soon as he'd gotten his first Saturday job stacking shelves at Asda. The Figaro wasn't as flashy as Malachy's Jaguar F-Type but it was old and reliable, like a dear friend he never wanted to part with. The paintwork might be scratched in places and the boot never enough for the supermarket shop but that wasn't a reason to retire the old lady off to pastures new. With the soft top down and with the wind in his hair he felt like king of the road, which was priceless by any measurement scale.

The home was just as he remembered. A dark place with heavy antique furniture and an underlying smell of polish and air freshener. The entrance hall was small and narrow, the forty-watt bulbs not man enough to reach the dark corners and high cornices. But Jax was as interested in the interior as he was in the outside appearance of the building, his feet automatically heading for the stairs and the sound of loud voices drifting through the mahogany banisters.

'Jax, what are you doing here? I thought you were waiting in the car?'

'I was, all of half an hour ago,' he said, standing to his full six-two, his fingers looped around the belt of his trousers.

Jax hovered in the entrance, taking in the scene in one glance, again ignoring the decor and fittings in favour of the four other people in the room, including the woman wearing a severe dark navy uniform and a scowl to match. His attention lingered on the name badge pinned next to her fob watch before moving on. It was rare for Georgie to have a bad word to say about anyone but, when she did, Gloria Dipton's name usually featured; he'd only met her the once, but that was once too many. The other inhabitants consisted of a portly man, dressed in tatty jeans and a checked shirt, standing beside a tall woman in beige separates. Georgie was standing in the middle, surrounded, a large A3 ledger between her fingers.

'Can I help you? This is a private discussion.'

Jax suppressed a sigh. He knew he wouldn't be welcome by anyone and that included his girlfriend.

'It's more that perhaps I can help you,' he said finally, trying to expel his breath in equal measures. To stutter now would be the worst possible time.

'Really!' Gloria exploded, a snide smile adding to the scowl and revealing lipstick-stained teeth. 'This is private business and I'd like you to leave. Your *girlfriend* is surely old enough to speak for herself.'

'You think that three people questioning one is right under any circumstance except a job interview?' His voice was calm and collected, unlike his thoughts, which were skittering around his head in a mad rush to get over the finishing line. He reached into his inside pocket, withdrew his warrant card and flipped it open, in the sure knowledge that by doing so he was in for a hell of a row later. But it couldn't be helped. No. He couldn't and wouldn't help it. Walking out and leaving Georgie, even with an argument on the horizon, wasn't going to happen in this room.

'If you have something that you'd like to discuss with me, like missing drugs for instance,' he said, eyeing the ledger, 'then I'm happy to help. The presumption of innocence, as set out b-b-by Article Eleven of the UN's Universal Declaration of Human Rights, still stands unless you know something that I don't?' He studied their suddenly alert expressions. The involvement of the police was obviously an unwelcome addition to their Wednesday morning foray into staff brow-beating.

But before any of them had a chance to reply, the sound of running feet on the stairs had them all turning to stare past Jax at the sight of Hannah hurrying towards them, her ponytail sweeping around her shoulders.

'I came as soon as I could, Gloria. What's this about missing drugs?'

Chapter 36

Gaby

The incident room was sweltering, the forecast of long-awaited rain showers yet to materialise. The distinct smell of sweat and spices were testament that at least one of her officers had partaken in a late-night curry after the party had wrapped up and who could blame them. Certainly not Gaby with the remains of her breakfast causing her to squash down the latest in a series of acid-wrenching burps.

'Right everyone. Settle down. Jax has something on but, as we have a huge amount to untangle, we won't wait for him,' she said, waving an arm in the direction of the first of the whiteboards, which was already overcrowded with information. She draped her black jacket on the back of her chair and tucked in her white shirt from where it had shifted out of her waistband, before checking her phone for the umpteenth time. 'I've been in touch with Jason. He's just catching up with the rest of his team and then he'll be down for an update but first, a little recap.'

Gaby headed for the third whiteboard, picked a black pen from the tray underneath and started writing Ian and Hunter's names in the centre. After, she drew squiggly lines radiating outwards in the form of a wonky-looking spider diagram – art had never been a strong point.

'I'm not going to bore you with Strong and Hunter's demise. We know the main points already and Jason will fill us in on the rest. It's what happened next that we need to get our heads around and link to what we know already. With last night's burglary it looks like someone has it in for Hannah. They even followed it up with a late-night text, sent to her mobile while she was staying over at Ian's father's house.' Gaby plucked up her phone from where she'd placed it on her desk and scrolled to the right page. '"They died because of you, which makes you next". Not the nicest of things to send on the death of the only family you have,' she said, lifting her head and scanning the room in search of ideas.

Malachy was sitting behind his desk and, unusually for him, silent. To an outsider it would seem he wore a look of intense boredom, but Gaby had come to realise it actually meant anything but.

Owen's thinking pose included leaning against the nearest wall and touching his beard. His hooded expression could be easily taken to mean inattention but that was far from the case. Owen was one of those rare individuals with an eidetic, or photographic memory, something that was the envy of everyone he came into contact with apart from his wife. Marie's expressive face was now showing distaste as she continued jotting down something on her notepad. Diane was too new to the team for Gaby to form a judgement. She was currently tapping away on her keyboard with an enviable speed that put Gaby's own two-digit version to shame.

But Mal was different. Her gaze again rested on his face. He never gave anything away. He'd make a great poker player, she thought suddenly, not that she knew or cared anything about the rudiments of gambling. But the skills of her team were immaterial at present if none of them had any ideas worth sharing.

With a sigh, she added both the burglary and the phone message to the board before recapping the pen and tapping it against the edge of the desk, with no thought to the inner workings of the interactive device. 'Initially it looked like Ian found the boy dead and took his life because of it, fearful of Hannah's reaction, no doubt. But all the nonsense that follows brings up a new set of questions that we've yet to answer.'

'Ian's motive is a little sketchy for that scenario, don't you think?' Owen moved away from the wall and, flexing his shoulders, pulled out the nearest chair, his feet stretched out in front of him. 'For a start his psychological profile doesn't fit that behaviour.'

'I agree wholeheartedly but, remember, that same profile didn't find any of the addictive behaviours we'd expect with diamorphine floating around in his system.'

'No, I give you that and we know from experience that psychometric testing isn't perfect.'

'There's another thing,' Gaby said, remembering back to what Rusty had said. 'The way the deaths were executed led to the maximum distress and emotional damage to the mother. Finding her partner. Thinking that Hunter was still alive only for him to be found later. The removal of all his belongings – what's that all about anyway? – closely followed by a late-night text when she'd be at her most vulnerable.'

'If indeed it wasn't her all along. It does all seem a little too flawless for my taste,' Owen said, cracking his knuckles, a recent and most irritating habit that she'd yet to speak to him about. 'I know it's not what any of you want to believe, a woman murdering her child and then her partner, but history tells us it's not only men who can turn on their offspring. Remember that woman whose kids were found in the freezer?'

There was a pause, no one knowing quite what to say.

Gaby swivelled the pen between her fingers, reluctant to follow his train of thought but well aware he was only speaking sense. 'So, what would you suggest Hannah's motive would have been?'

'If we're talking about crazies, they don't need one, do they?' Marie said, toying with her watch.

'Good point but that doesn't take into account the timeline.' Gaby tilted her head in the direction of the second board. 'By her own account, she wasn't even meant to be at Y Mwyar Duon. It was all a last-minute thing arranged by that friend of hers.'

'Milly Buttle, ma'am,' Marie interrupted.

'Yes, thank you, Marie.' Gaby removed the lid from the pen and, making space on the lower half of the board, started scrawling down an action list. 'Next up we need someone to head over to Ruthin and meet with the barman at the hotel. If we are going down the road of Hannah as possible murderer, and I for one can't see it, then we had better be sure we have an ironclad case. The media will be over it like a dog chasing a rabbit down a burrow – all claws and yapping teeth. I can see the headlines now if we cock this up. But …' She rotated her shoulders to ease the sudden tension in her neck. 'We might as well give it a look and see what pops up. You never know, we might get lucky.'

Gaby stared at the board in the same way a grand master would plan their next move but, in this case, instead of chess pieces she was positioning the team to make the best use of their individual skills. Malachy was solid and reliable but, it must be said, without Jax's dogged determination or Marie and Diane's flair for thinking out of the box. His skill lay in getting people to open up even when they were determined to stay silent, which made him the perfect choice to carry out the interviews over in Ruthin, she mused, adding his name beside the hotel. Marie could stay in the office and act as liaison while continuing to look into Strong's background. She'd also ask her to check out Dominic Strong while she was at it, her mind twisting back to the interview she'd lined up with Hannah.

Gaby really missed Amy, even though she'd only been gone a day, not least because she would have been the ideal choice to sit in on that interview. In her absence she chose Owen, her second in command. He wasn't good at managing the emotional stuff. That would be left to her and she was the first to admit that she wasn't good at it either, but it couldn't be helped. She needed Marie glued to her laptop and it wouldn't be fair on Diane. That left one item remaining. Stephen Lee. She lifted her hand and, rubbing her brow, opened her mouth to speak only to snap it shut at the sight of Jason and Jax wandering down the corridor.

Jason looked his usual serious self. He was the only grown-up she had ever met who seemed to have a persistent problem with keeping his shirt tails tucked inside his trousers. Her gaze dropped to his brown cords before shifting to examine the man she was more concerned about.

Gaby had a soft spot for Jax Williams, not that he'd ever be able to tell by her manner. She strove to treat each member of the team the same, while trying to make use of their particular skill set. But the tall, gangly twenty-six-year-old with boy-band blond looks and lopsided grin was easy to like. There was no evidence of the grin today. Instead there was a frown.

Shifting her hip onto the edge of the nearest desk, she turned back to Jason. 'What have you got for us then?'

'Another puzzle I'm afraid.'

She leant forward, her hands pressing down on the top of the desk. 'Well, you know how we all like a puzzle, Jase.'

'Not this one you won't.'

He crossed one leg over the other, his brown loafers clearly chosen for comfort over design but, with the long hours he put in, she couldn't really blame him.

'Every item belonging to the child has been stripped from the house. The lounge. His bedroom. Even down to the plastic cups and plates that he used to eat his meals off and his bath toys. They even removed the drawings scattered around the kitchen and the posters from his bedroom walls,' he said, his voice deliberately controlled. 'The only items they missed were in the small utility room off the kitchen and that might have been because they were disturbed. It wouldn't have been a quick job to search so thoroughly. Sadly they'd also gone to the trouble to wear gloves and possibly even a hat and long-sleeved clothing. We haven't found any trace DNA, apart from in the hall and the lounge, which is to be expected,' he qualified. 'As we know, visitors tend to have access to those two areas.'

'Anything else?'

He opened the palm of his hand, revealing a small plastic specimen bag. 'Only these. They were in the master bedroom, hidden under a pile of socks.'

Gaby should have been expecting it. After all, she'd read Strong's autopsy report. But the sight of the ten glass ampules was a shock. However, before she could question him further Jax rose to his feet and crossed the room.

'Do you mind?'

Instead of waiting for a reply, he lifted the bag from Jason and, raising it up, slowly swivelled the plastic so that he could read the small lettering on the side of each ampule.

'Diamorphine, five milligrams, expiry date June 2022, as if I didn't know that already,' he said, his words as colourless as his sudden pallor.

Gaby bit her lip, knowing where this was going. There was nothing she could do to help except let him continue even though he was barely able to get the words out in a steady stream of understanding.

'I-I-I-I've just come back from the old people's home that Georgie and Hannah Thomas work at. They've both been called in over a discrepancy in the controlled drug register. A box of twenty ampules of diamorphine, five milligrams, expiry date June 2022, has gone missing.' He lifted his head from where he'd been staring down at the sample bag, which was now back

168

in Jason's lap, his eyes shifting between the sea of faces in front of him, clearly unable to focus on anyone in particular. 'There's no explanation that makes any sense. The drugs are counted on a twice-weekly basis by two qualified nurses. They have to sign the controlled drug book to that effect. The last time they were checked was by Georgie and Hannah on Friday.' He took a deep swallow, his Adam's apple shifting in his neck, his hands now loose by his sides.

'But what about the keys?' Owen said. 'There must be another explanation.'

'Only one set that's kept at the home, which is in the possession of the nurse in charge at any one time.' Jax ran his hand through his hair, causing it to stick up in clumps.

'That means any one of them could have taken them?' Jason said.

'No, I'm afraid not. They were the only trained staff on since the check, apart from the matron and deputy matron, who have both worked there since the home opened twenty years ago. Hannah and Georgie are clearly in the frame. They either took them or allowed someone else access to the keys.'

'Like whom?'

Jax crunched his shoulders. 'Who knows. Georgie says the only person she'd ever let near the drug cupboard would be another trained nurse, a pharmacist or a doctor.'

Gaby didn't know what to say and, by the deathly silence encompassing the room, neither did anyone else. No one wanted to believe that Hannah was anything but a victim in all of this, but the evidence was starting to stack up against her. Missing drugs found in her house and a partner riddled with the stuff. But while they had enough to question her about the theft, the rest was circumstantial when sitting alongside her bulletproof alibi – an alibi Gaby needed to break. The only issue now was whether Strong had injected the diamorphine voluntarily. She'd have to check back with Rusty because an isolated needlestick jab was akin to looking for a needle in a proverbial field full of hay bales.

There was still the question of Stephen Lee's death. But the likelihood of a suicide six years ago being relevant was fading into the background of the picture that was starting to build.

Chapter 37

Gaby

Wednesday 26 August, 3 p.m. St Asaph

'Thank you again for coming back into the station, although you didn't need to go to the trouble and expense of hiring a solicitor for an informal chat like this,' Gaby said, nodding briefly at the man sitting opposite Hannah.

Andy Parrish was a good, solid solicitor with a penchant for paisley ties and flash cufflinks. His presence was a surprise but probably a wise move on Hannah's part. All Gaby needed to know now was whether she'd hired him to help prove her innocence or because she knew she was guilty. Only time would tell.

'Really? I was under the impression that I was on the top of your list of suspects?'

'We do understand what a traumatic time it's been for you,' Gaby continued smoothly, ignoring her question. 'Today we need to confirm a few things from our earlier discussion.'

'Such as?' Hannah fumbled in the pocket of her denim jacket, removing a tissue, which she must have placed there in preparation for the interview.

'If we can take it back to how Milly ended up inviting you to the hotel instead of her boyfriend?' Gaby asked, her notepad open in front of her.

'Milly's a nice enough person. Quite sweet but her boyfriend walked all over her. The stories she used to tell when she first started. We all felt sorry for her but there was little that we could do until she recognised what a prat she was going out with. It turns out that he found someone else and basically dumped her on the spot, leaving her with a night booked at Y Mwyar Duon and no one to go with.'

'And what about the arrangements? How did you get to Ruthin?'

'I took my bike.' Hannah rubbed her hands over her face, her fingers pressing gently on the fragile skin under her eyes. 'It's not that Milly didn't offer me a lift because she did. It's just it was a nice day and I felt like giving it a run.' She lifted her head. 'When I arrived Milly was in reception signing in. We went to our room, got into the robes provided and went downstairs to the health suite for a swim and jacuzzi. After, we had a drink at the bar before heading into the restaurant.'

'And you left the restaurant at about what time?'

'We moved into the bar after our meal and left about twelve. Maybe one. I couldn't really say. Like most parents of young children I was making use of the opportunity of being let off the leash.'

'I believe you said you don't remember much after that?' Gaby said, flipping back through her notebook.

'No but that's to be expected surely? The hangover was proof enough of how much alcohol we consumed.'

'Okay, what about the next day then?'

'We got up late. Breakfast serves until ten and we made it at a quarter to, not that either of us were in the mood for food. My

172

head was banging so I took two headache pills, washing them down with a glass of orange juice and a bit of toast. That's it. We left about half ten.'

'Right, let's move on to when you arrived back home.'

'We've gone through all this before.'

'I know that but if you could humour us,' Gaby said, tapping the stapled sheaf of notes peeking out from under her notebook. 'You might have remembered something new and now is as good an opportunity as any to tell us.'

Hannah shook her head, her ponytail moving along with her neck. 'There's nothing really. I parked outside. Walked through the house from top to bottom, shouting as I went. I finally decided on the garage as a last resort ...'

'Why?'

'Why? Because I thought I'd take Ian's car and check a little further afield.' She shook her head a second time. 'I don't know why. I can't really remember.'

'Okay. Thank you.' Gaby glanced down at her notes again even though she knew what question to ask next. She'd primed Owen to concentrate on Hannah's body language when she asked it. 'We still need to discuss the problem over at the care home and the fact that our team found what look to be corresponding vials of diamorphine during their search of your property. But first I'd like to ask you about Stephen Lee.'

Chapter 38

Malachy

Malachy Devine had never been to Ruthin. The youngest son of Nicholas Devine, QC, he'd spent his youth in a small, select mews in a lane tucked behind Harrods before being shipped off to board at Harrow, closely followed by a law degree at Durham University. But, unlike his father, law wasn't his passion and, despite the nagging and posturing about the financial rewards such a career would bring, he decided at the tender age of twenty-six to add a degree in criminology to his list of qualifications.

Wales was a whim, only that. A chance to move away from the increasingly cloying atmosphere at home created by a mother who had too much time on her hands and little with which to fill it. He wanted independence – the opportunity to live his life as he saw fit without expecting to fill the very large shoes of both his father and older sister, who was quite merrily following in the family firm. The fact that his mother made it her new mission to pop across the country every few weeks to check up on him in addition to stocking up the fridge and sorting through his washing was an irritant that he was yet to solve but he was working on it.

He spent his time either at work or in his loft apartment listening to his extensive collection of smooth jazz while he worked his way through an exciting array of crime fiction on his Kindle from the likes of Peter James, BA Paris and SE Lynes. When he wasn't doing either of those things, he was messing about in his home gym, keeping his muscles toned and his fitness level at peak performance. An overweight child and lazy teen, he'd turned his body from soft and flabby to ripped and hard over the course of his early twenties and after all that effort, he wasn't about to let it slip.

Ruthin, for all its picture-postcard quaintness and Welsh charm, wasn't his thing at all. He wasn't a party animal, far from it, but desultory river walks followed by a little shopping and a meal in one of the many hotels wasn't his bag. He had no idea why Darin had picked him for the jaunt.

He pulled into a parking space at the side of the river and sauntered across the road to Y Mwyar Duon opposite. The receptionist was blonde and attractive, a bright smile painted on in a pillar-box shade of red lipstick. Putting his shoulders back, he returned the smile with one of his own, his eyebrows lifting at the sight of her slight blush.

Malachy knew he was good-looking. It would have been impossible for him not to notice that women took a double take in his presence, but he wasn't interested, far from it. Body image was something that had concerned him when he was overweight and insecure but not now because of the time he spent slaving away on the rowing machine and cross-trainer. And as for the rest – he simply wasn't interested, which was part of the reason for his mother being on his back all the time: his lack of a girlfriend, or a boyfriend for that matter. She wouldn't have cared either way, which was all part of the problem because neither did he. At a push he'd have described his sexuality as confused. He'd never had either a girlfriend or a boyfriend and, if current patterns continued, he wasn't likely to change that status quo anytime soon and, to his mind, why should he? He was perfectly happy with his own company. In fact, he relished it. The only person he deemed a suitable living companion was Marie, which was the biggest surprise of all.

He presented his warrant card, which caused the woman's blush to fade, a look of anxiety pushing it aside. It didn't take long to find himself in the manager's office, the hotel register on the screen in front of him, and a glass of ice-cold water in his hand; it was far too hot for coffee.

Y Mwyar Duon was part of a global hotel chain and thank goodness for that, he mused, taking out his notepad and jotting down the times that Milly Buttle and Hannah Thomas had checked in and out of the accommodation. Everything was item-ised even down to what they'd eaten for their evening meal, the mini massage in the health suite, and the two bottles of gin and tins of tonic removed from the mini bar.

He drained his drink in one, the shards of ice tinkling in the bottom. That wasn't what he had come for – not really. After all that sort of information was only a phone call away. No. He was here to speak to the staff to see if a sliver of clarification could be added to the sketchy picture of their evening. He was also here to inspect their guestroom, not that he expected it to tell him anything. Any traces would have been cleaned away after their departure but again the chambermaid might be able to add something.

The room was situated at the side of the hotel, the wrought-iron balcony affording delightful views of the paved courtyard below with trees on the right and a distant view of the riverbank on the left. Everything was in impeccable condition, from the freshly painted balustrade to the top-of-the-range fire escape, which blended in with the Tudor-style façade perfectly.

The bedroom was beautifully presented in shades of mocha

and gold, the cream carpet thick and decadent. The twin beds were dressed in coordinating linen with the distinctive blackberry logo. It was exactly the kind of place his parents enjoyed staying at, and there and then he made a mental note to enquire as to the pricing. He had been in the dark as to what to buy them for a wedding anniversary present – a weekend at the hotel would be perfect especially if he could time it for when he was away. Jason kept nagging him about a fishing trip. Perhaps now was the time to give in.

The bar was busier than he'd been expecting on a hot day in the height of summer but there was no accounting for taste and he could quite see the advantage of sinking into one of the squishy sofas with a book and a beer for the afternoon. Instead he ordered a glass of bitter lemon and, flipping his badge open, asked the barman to join him when there was a lull in service.

'So, what have they done, then?' the barman said, staring down at the photos that Malachy had placed in front of him. His name badge said Bruce, the eager expression at war with the bodybuilding physique and designer man bun. But it only took one glance at the innocent faces of some of the more extreme serial killers to know that judging a book by its cover was a major mistake in law enforcement. There were exceptions of course but, in Mal's experience, people's outward appearance rarely matched their inner one.

'I'm sorry, sir. That's confidential business.'

'You can't object to me asking,' Bruce said with a sly wink, looking more than a little ridiculous in his black suit and bow tie with the sun shining through the windows. 'We were very busy last weekend but funnily enough I do remember them. Intent on a party, if you know what I mean? There was another group of women but far more sedate,' he said, lowering his left eye in another sleazy wink.

'So they were both drinking then?'

'Absolutely. G and Ts all the way. I ended up having to escort them to the lift. This one' – he tapped his finger against the edge of Milly Buttle's photo – 'could barely stand. It was enough to put me off drink for a lifetime.'

The doorman was older, shorter and far less helpful.

'Nah. Dickie would have been on duty, he works the weekends. He's saving for a house so the bit of extra he gets on the night shift makes a huge difference. Me, I like my sleep.'

Mal folded his arms across his chest, popping his elbow against the reception desk. 'But you know his routine?'

'Too right. The job is a piece of piss at night to be honest. This is Ruthin and not Rhyl,' he added, his third chin starting to wobble. 'After the last guest returns, which is usually about eleven, half eleven at the latest, we lock the front door and do a tour. You know the sort of thing. Checking the outside doors are all shut and locked. Checking the bar and the toilets to see that no one has sneaked in for the night. After that, we sit behind the reception desk, manning the phones. But it's not all play. There are a few jobs left for us and we occasionally get asked for room service or to call out the doctor if one of the guests becomes ill.'

'And you log all these jobs, do you?'

'They make us, each and every bleedin' one,' he said, his cockney accent allowing him free range with the English alphabet. 'Hey, Lily, show us the night book, would you, darlin'?'

He flicked through the pages of the green ledger to find the right page, his short stumpy fingers pointing at the couple of entries. 'Mmm, busier than normal.'

Malachy eyed the record with interest and, pulling out his phone, took a quick snap of the relevant page.

Chapter 39

Diane

Wednesday 26 August, 3 p.m. St Asaph

Diane Smith loved her new job on the MIT. She also loved her little flat and her two grown-up children. She hated her ex but then again, she was sensible enough to realise that she couldn't have everything. Born and brought up in North Wales, she had a stable of female friends who had helped her through a messy divorce where her husband had taken gleeful delight in forcing her to sell the family home and divide the spoils because the children had left home. But she could honestly say she felt as if she was having the last laugh with a career as a detective on the horizon – not bad for a middle-aged blonde who'd been thrown on the scrapheap. She'd upgraded her greying locks for a smart blonde bob and was in the process of upgrading her wardrobe. As soon as she could afford it, she also intended to upgrade her car from compact four-door to low-slung and racy. But that was for the future. Now she had a job to do.

Pushing her empty mug to one side, she rebooted her laptop

and quickly logged on to the police network, thankful for once that she'd finished checking out the CCTV footage, not that there had been many cameras to check in and around Ruthin and Conwy.

There were a few ways to track somebody down and, with the explosion of social media, it was now very difficult for someone to live under the internet radar. But Stephen Lee was different again. For a start the fact that he was dead made it easier, if not for him, then for her. Within minutes, she had his death certificate in front of her in addition to the coroner's report from the inquest into his death – all of which was salutary reading considering that he was only twenty-seven when he'd died. The fall had resulted in fractures to his thoracic and lumbar spine in addition to fractures to both ankles and legs. However, the cause of death was put down to a subarachnoid haemorrhage when his head had smashed against the concrete pavement following the drop. The inquest had included pictures of the scene and it was clear to see the distance from the top of the fire escape to the tarmac path below.

She jotted down a couple of notes on her pad, a small knot appearing between her finely arched eyebrows, which owed nothing to her make-up bag and everything to the expertise of a local tattoo artist. The truth was Diane couldn't see the sense in investigating a suicide that had happened six years ago and one that Hannah Thomas was proven not to be responsible for. But instead of moaning she decided to get on with the job. She printed off the relevant sheets and spread them across the desk, her frown back. The one thing that was missing was a photograph of the young man. She found it within seconds of launching Google.

Newspaper reports and the like were of little use to detectives. The information only added a flavour of the truth and no clue as to what might have been embellished for the greedy eyes of headline-seeking members of the public. That didn't stop her from printing off the relevant articles, her attention drawn to the serious-looking man with the weight of the world pressed deeply into the grooves and shadows of his sallow complexion. As a member of the police Diane was interested in what internal stresses had resulted in his outward appearance but, as a mother, her heart ached for what his parents must have suffered following his death. Her mind switched briefly to Hannah and what she must be going through before she captured the thought and forced it back into place. Sentiment was all very well but it wouldn't help her prepare for Darin's next team meeting.

With a little shake of her head, she returned to her screen and typed in the name Hilary Hardiman, the person ultimately blamed for Stephen Lee's suicide. The Beddows, by nature of the type of care it provided, had been a locked unit. All entry and exit points were keypad-controlled. All windows barred. All staff trained in special breakaway and de-escalation techniques – all apart from the student nurses on placement whose sole purpose was in the capacity of observer.

The professional body that governed nursing and midwifery, the NMC, was a mystery to Diane but their website was easy enough to navigate and she soon found her way to the fitness to practise section and the result of the hearing.

Legal lingo was the one thing about the job she hated the most, for no other reason than she found it incredibly difficult to interpret what the lawyers meant with their wordy phrases and complex sentence structures. But she struggled on through the lengthy document, her eyes squinting as the lines and paragraphs ran into each other in an explosion of jargon. She got that Hardiman had been struck off the register and as such would never practise as a registered nurse again. The key phrase, referring to 'her lack of insight into her own clinical failings and ultimate refusal to take ownership of her actions', was damning enough, but when combined with her persistent assertion throughout the proceedings that Hannah Thomas, a nurse in training, was to blame, completely abhorrent.

Diane pursed her lips at the stupidity of the woman, as she

scanned through the sketchy notes she'd managed to make. It always surprised her when people refused to apologise for something that was clearly their fault. Far better to get it out of the way and move on.

She pulled back the sleeve of her blouse to check the time, the pale blue Liberty print shirt a welcome addition to her wardrobe. She still had a good hour left before the meeting and there were a few loose ends she wanted to tidy up, like the current whereabouts of Hardiman. If she had the time she might manage to squeeze in a quick meal at a local café as she'd worked through lunch. It would save her having to think about cooking later.

Chapter 40

Gaby

Wednesday 26 August, 3.25 p.m. St Asaph

Back in the incident room, Owen pulled up a chair and placed his hands behind his head, his fingers splayed.

'Andy Parrish is acting above his remit don't you think, stopping the interview almost mid-sentence like that? We had no reason to warn either him or her about the direction the conversation was going to take.'

'With all due respect, Owen, I think it would have been far better if Amy was getting married next week instead of this one. This needs her careful people-handling skills, something that you have to admit we both lack. It's a huge shame that her replacement won't be here until next week. We'll have to muddle through until then,' Gaby said, tightening the clip on her plait. 'Did you see Hannah's expression when we mentioned Lee's name? I thought she was going to faint. It was only Andy's swift intervention that prevented it.'

'And instead she'll have a good half-hour in which to prepare.'

'Come on. Give the woman a break. She's just lost her family, been burgled and now tied up in some way with those missing drugs from Daffodils. It's hardly likely that something that happened six years ago is going to be in any way related to what happened at the weekend.' But it was easy to see by his intransigent expression that Owen wasn't having any of it.

'You might as well call me an unsympathetic bastard, Gaby. Who's to say that she wasn't involved in all of this? It would have been quite easy for her to fudge her alcohol intake and pop on her motorbike as soon as the friend was asleep. What better excuse than to burgle your own house, making it look like the worst thing possible to happen to a bereaved mother?'

'Owen, you *are* an unsympathetic bastard! So, how come she didn't remove the diamorphine ampules then? The one thing that implicates her over everything else?' She glanced at her watch and, turning her head, spotted Malachy, Marie and Jax walking down the corridor, their hands full of coffee and a plate of what looked like the station's famed jam doughnuts. 'Great. There's enough time for a quick catch-up before we have to rejoin Hannah and Andy.' She tilted her head. 'Hurry up, you lot. I do hope you have some doughnuts to spare.' She paused, remembering the dress she had to squeeze into in less than four days' time before adding, with far less enthusiasm: 'Owen is in need of refreshment.'

Gaby stood and, picking up the cafetiere from the shelf nearest her desk, eyed the murky black liquid with the exact same expression she would if she'd just stepped in dog poo. But as it was hot and calorie-free, it was all that she was allowing herself, the memory of Conor's fish and chips long outstaying its welcome. Gaby was far from glamorous but still vain enough to want to look her best at Amy's forthcoming wedding – not least because of a certain Irish pathologist who'd agreed to accompany her.

'Right then, we don't have much time left,' she said, glancing down at her watch. 'Lucky for us her solicitor asked for a short recess when we brought up the name of Stephen Lee. So, what have you got?' she said, her gaze landing on Mal.

'Staff at Y Mwyar Duon were very helpful, ma'am. They didn't even ask me for a search warrant so I got to see their room, which was a superior twin with views over the car park and a small balcony overlooking the river,' he continued, after swallowing a mouthful of doughnut. 'Obviously it's been cleaned since then so there was no point in delving too much. The bill included numerous alcoholic bar beverages in addition to gin from the minibar in their room. I spoke to the bartender who confirmed the opinion that they were there with the sole purpose of having a very merry time.'

'So, all in all you haven't found out very much apart from to confirm her story?'

'That's about right. I did manage to check with the doorman and the out-of-hours register.'

Gaby perked up. 'And?'

'And nothing. Reception received a call at 3 a.m. from their room for some paracetamol,' he said, pulling out his phone and swiping across the screen.

'Therefore confirming their alcohol consumption or a ruse to reinforce that they were both still in their room around the time of Strong's demise,' Owen said with a smirk.

'Unlikely though after what they put away,' Marie interrupted, taking a swig from her water bottle.

Gaby nodded. 'Anything else, Mal, before we move on?'

He frowned, his attention still on the screen. 'Not in relation to their room. No.'

'If you're going to keep me in suspense, the very least you could do is stop eating and speak quicker.'

'Sorry, ma'am.' He shut off his phone and slid it back into his pocket, the half-finished doughnut back on his desk. 'Reception had a call about a suspected prowler an hour later. A pair of honeymooners thought they heard someone outside their room but when the porter went to investigate there was nothing to be found.'

'Mmm. Interesting but without CCTV irrelevant. What about you, Marie. Found any nuggets of delight on the Strong brothers?'

'More like a few coins' worth. I started with Ian. There's not much to say outside of what we know already. Liked the gym and his rugby. Nothing else. I'm still waiting for clearance to access his bank account. The brother is far more interesting,' Marie said, swiping to the notebook app on her phone. 'Moved to Australia at eighteen when he was accepted to read medicine in Brisbane. He's currently working at a women's and children's hospital while he completes something called a specialist obstetrician and gynae-cology training programme. When he's not at work he lives in a riverside property located on prestigious Hamilton Hill with views over Brisbane River.'

'Very nice. Why didn't I think of gynaecology as a profession?' Gaby said, with a lip curl.

'Because staring down criminals instead of staring at women's nether regions is far more your style,' Owen said, struggling not to laugh.

Gaby sent him a withering look before turning back to Marie. 'Ignore him. What else?'

'When I said prestigious I really meant it, ma'am. I did a quick property search and he bought the place two years ago for five million Australian dollars.'

Gaby whistled through her teeth. 'Which translates to?'

'About two and a half million, give or take.'

'Which is way more than a twenty-eight-year-old doctor could be expected to earn. Okay, we could always ask him when we're interviewing him later but I'm betting he'll object to the question.' Gaby started nibbling her thumbnail before popping her hand in her pocket, the temptation to pick at the varnish almost too much to bear. 'If you can nudge Ian's bank for his records, and we'll take it from there. Oh, you might as well look at the dad's finances too while you're at it.'

Gaby shifted her attention to Jax who'd spent the course of

the conversation chewing his bottom lip. It was obvious he was worried about something, less obvious as to whether he was going to share his concerns with the team. But before she could question him, Diane burst through the door, throwing her mobile, bag and notepad on her desk.

'Sorry I'm late. I got caught up with Hilary Hardiman.'

Gaby leant back in her chair, her gaze unwavering. 'So you went to see Hilary Hardiman and …?'

'No.'

'No? I don't understand?'

'Going to see Hilary Hardiman would be impossible, ma'am. She died over six months ago. Cancer. Which means that there's no way she could have been involved in the current situation.'

'Okay,' Gaby said, trying to work out how exactly her death tied in with the case and failing miserably. 'Anything else?'

'I also managed to track down Stephen Lee's family, not that there's much to say. He left home when he was sixteen. Reading between the lines, he was kicked out. I spoke to the mother on the phone. She was more interested in missing the afternoon soap on the telly than she was in discussing her son. I'd say we should invite them in to give a statement but my gut feeling is that it will be a waste of time.'

'Which also means that there's little point in asking Hannah about Lee except for her near-faint earlier.' Gaby placed a small cross beside the name Hilary Hardiman on the board before shifting her head towards Jax. 'What about the message sent to Hannah's mobile? Anything?'

'I'm afraid not. Jason traced it via the service provider. A burner phone bought from Asda and only used the once. It's probably in landfill by now.'

'And the mobile data? Surely he should have been able to pin a location?'

'Afraid not. We're talking about anywhere within a ten-mile radius based on the cell mast signals.'

The room was silent for a moment before breaking out into conversation, most of it negative and despondent.

'Shut up, the lot of you, and let me think,' Gaby said, banging the heel of her hand against the nearest desk.

The case was getting away from her. There were too many angles to follow, all of them leading to a dead end. If no one had a reason to harm Hannah Thomas then why had her home been burgled and who had sent her that text message? Gaby picked up her phone and, swiping the screen, found a new message from Rusty. A message that changed everything.

Chapter 41

Gaby

Wednesday 26 August, 3.45 p.m. St Asaph

Gaby had never seen Andy Parrish flustered but there was always a first time for everything, she thought, regretting with a passion that she hadn't been allowed to leave the microphone running on their private conversation. Like many detectives before her, she strongly believed that the protection afforded to clients and lawyers in the disclosure of what could be important evidence made her job far more difficult than it should have been.

There was nothing she could do other than take note of Andy's look of annoyance, which was reflected in his uncharacteristically messy hair. If she didn't know any better, she'd think that he'd been trying to pull it out in clumps. As a lawyer he was one of the good ones. Hopefully that would mean something, but she wouldn't like to bet on it.

She slid into her chair, her hand on the microphone switch while she waited for Owen to take the seat next to her.

'Recommencing the interview with Hannah Thomas, Andrew

189

Parrish, Detective Owen Bates and DI Gabriella Darin. The time is 3.47 p.m. So, to repeat the last question, please can you tell me about Stephen Lee?'

'Before my client answers,' Andy Parrish said, his hands firmly on his lap and nowhere near his hair. 'How is this in any way relevant to what my client is currently going through?'

'We don't know that it is. What we do know is that your client has received a recent message of a disturbing nature. She also had her house burgled in such a way as to cause her the maximum distress and that's not even mentioning the events of last Saturday. It would be lax of us not to try and find out why, even if it does necessitate searching through her past for a possible explanation.'

'In effect, you're just rummaging around trying to find something to help you. Not very professional, I would have thought.'

Gaby gritted her teeth, any nice thoughts she'd ever had of Andy Parrish flying out of the window. While he might be a nice man, she'd forgotten for a second what a competent lawyer he was. Did he seriously believe that she relished having to delve into Hannah's past in light of what she must be going through or indeed that she didn't have far better uses for her time? Gaby lowered her voice, moderating her tone as she struggled to contain her rapidly building temper.

'We're trying to seek the truth, Mr Parrish, and, as far as we know, the death of Stephen Lee appears to be one of the few adverse events that's happened in Miss Thomas's life that might be relevant.'

'And the other adverse events?'

'Excuse me?'

'You intimated that there was more than one adverse event. My client and I would like to know what those are?'

At that moment Gaby hated Andy Parrish with a blistering intensity, which didn't prevent her from making a mental note to call on his services if she was ever in need of a lawyer, God

190

forbid – although the only crime she was planning to commit at the moment included him as the victim.

'You're making this unnecessarily difficult, Mr Parrish. The other event, that we know of, is what happened to Miss Thomas's parents and brother, but as that was clearly an accident outside of anyone's control there'll be no need to address it further, unless your client knows something that we don't?'

She watched them exchange glances before deciding to repeat the question for a third time.

'I see that's not the case. So, to get back to Stephen Lee?'

'I don't know why you need me to tell you. It's well documented,' Hannah said, her voice carefully controlled. Too controlled if the sight of her fingers biting into her palms was anything to go by.

'That's as may be, but we'd still like to hear your side of the story.'

'There's not a great deal to tell.' Hannah heaved in a sigh, as if she realised she wasn't going to manage to wriggle out of the question. 'At any one time the Beddows had a couple of students on placement. I was one of them. We were there to observe, only that, but that's not what happened.' She unclenched her fists and, lifting her glass, took a deep sip of water, taking far more care than was necessary to place it back on the table. 'There was a culture of laxity on the unit, something that was highlighted in the final report.'

'What do you mean exactly?' Owen said, shuffling in his chair.

Hannah lifted her hand only to let it flop back down against her knee. 'The nurses preferred to spend time in the staff room than out on the floor monitoring the patients. We, by that I mean the students, and a handful of healthcare assistants, were left unsupervised for long periods of time to provide the care. They only turned up for the medicine rounds and doctors' visits.'

'Okay so you were pretty much left on your own. What about Stephen Lee?'

'He was there the first day I arrived. To be honest, it was a surprise to find someone who looked and acted so normal on the unit. If you didn't know that he was an in-patient, you'd have mistaken him for a visitor. He wasn't on a special watch or anything like some of them.' She lifted her head from where she'd been staring at the table. 'I thought that he was nice.'

'And the evening in question?'

'The last job we had to do was to offer a bedtime drink. The nurse in charge allocated one of us to go into the kitchen to boil milk for hot chocolate and to fill the teapot. One of the rules was that patients weren't allowed in the kitchen but that evening he followed me and I didn't see the harm then.'

'The doors were all key-coded?'

'Yes. Security had to be tight because of the high-observation nature of the unit. It was on the top floor so even the fire doors were electronically controlled in addition to being alarmed. They'd open during the morning fire drill but only then, unless there was a fire obviously.'

'So, how do you explain accessing the roof if the fire doors weren't manually controlled?'

'That's the thing. Stephen was clever. Too clever. There'd been a storm that afternoon. None of the televisions worked and the phones were down. He must have guessed about the fire doors being affected.'

'Okay. A criticism at the time was that you allowed him into the kitchen and therefore access to the fire escape and roof, but if you didn't realise that the door wasn't secure …?'

'Exactly. I liked him. I didn't think that there was any harm in him giving me a hand to prepare the drinks.'

'But somehow he ended up on the roof?'

'I thought he was joking. You know, kidding around. I tried to persuade him to come back into the kitchen, but he wouldn't. He was larking about. I still thought it was a big fat joke until he headed for the edge, his arms extending out from his body.

Dear God, he said he could fly,' she said, a glimmer of moisture pressing through her tightly closed eyelids. 'I grabbed his arm, but he was too quick for me.' She reached for her wrist, massaging what looked like a thick rope of scar tissue, tears starting to track down her cheeks and landing on the table. 'It felt like hours on that roof but in hindsight it was a minute, maybe two. It was all over by the time help had arrived. I tried to hold him, but I couldn't. I had to watch as he leant backwards, a big happy smile on his face before ...'

'Shush. It's all right, Hannah. I'm sure they get the picture.' Andy bundled a fistful of tissues into her hand. 'I think that's enough, don't you?' he said, shooting Gaby a look of pure dislike.

Gaby was only doing her job but at that precise moment she felt like one of the lowlifes she was trying to protect Hannah from. Someone had it in for her, but she was no further forward in discovering who or, perhaps more important, why. If she knew the why then surely she should be able to work out the who?

'Not quite, Mr Parrish. The only other thing we need to discuss, if you might remember, is the diamorphine,' she said, in an effort to maintain eye contact. 'As you know, Ian's tox screen has come back positive for the drug. I've just been speaking to the pathologist and he's come up with an interesting discovery. Needles leave a small puncture wound, mostly invisible to the naked eye but I asked him to look again. Ian had an earring at one point?'

'Yes.' Hannah looked up from where she'd been tearing her tissue to shreds. 'He stopped wearing it when he joined the force.'

'Perfectly understandable. Not the most sensible of jewellery items for coppers to wear.' Gaby managed a shadow of a smile. 'After being unable to find any signs of a puncture wound, Dr Mulholland examined Ian's pre-existing one. The lobe of Ian's ear showed signs of recent trauma where someone inserted a needle then angled it to pierce the flesh.'

'But surely he'd have felt that even if he'd been asleep?' Mr Parrish replied, leaning forward in his seat.

'Not if an anaesthetic gel had been applied first, the kind that nurses use before taking blood from uncooperative patients or at least that's what Dr Mulholland informed me – he found traces of such a gel on Ian's skin.'

'I don't know anything about that.' Hannah looked ready to collapse under the weight of this new information and Gaby's unease escalated at the thought. She wasn't in the business of tearing apart the recently bereaved even if there was a huge question mark surrounding Hannah's partner's and son's death – she certainly wasn't about to tell her that Hunter had suffocated. One step too far.

'Detective, you do need to get to the point. Either you're accusing my client of at best complicity in their deaths when she has a perfectly good alibi or …'

Gaby sighed, well aware that Andy was right. A collection of circumstantial evidence that pointed in one direction was only a start. None of it would stand up in court by itself unless she had something to underpin it. She couldn't really believe Hannah was responsible, but the harsh truth was that somebody was.

Pushing back her chair, she managed a brief smile. 'The interview is terminated at 1600 hours.' She flicked off the switch of the microphone and, reaching into her pocket, pulled out a mobile, which she placed on the table. 'Thank you for the loan of your phone. If you receive any further messages please do get in touch at the earliest opportunity.'

'Is that it? Can I leave?' Hannah said, her expression one of surprise.

Gaby repeated her smile, one that didn't quite meet her eyes. 'Yes, you're free to go but you will need to stay in the area.' She qualified the sentence at the sight of Hannah's frown. 'In case we have any further questions that crop up.'

Chapter 42

Gaby

Wednesday 26 August, 4.05 p.m. St Asaph

'I wish I hadn't passed up on that doughnut now. When are we due to be interviewing the Strongs again?'

'Five minutes ago.'

'Really?'

'Yes. Really. I asked Clancy to offer them a tray of tea in interview room one,' he said, directing her to the stairs. 'I thought it prudent that they didn't bump into Hannah in the corridor.'

'Good thinking. There's no love lost between the brother and her.'

Owen waited for her to reach the top stair. 'You think that's significant?'

'Only in so far as he's the spit of his brother. It freaks her out as it does me,' she added, trying to catch her breath, her hand pressed into her side.

Dominic Strong was exactly as she remembered apart from the change of clothes. He hadn't bothered to shave, but then again he was meant to be on his holidays. The dad was long and thin with a grey tinge to his skin and a rasp to his breathing – probably related.

'Apologies for keeping you both waiting,' she said, slipping into her chair beside Owen and switching on the microphone in a repeat of the last interview. 'As you know, I'm DI Gaby Darin, this is Detective Owen Bates. You're probably wondering why you're here and, to reassure you, it's only a formality to ensure all those boxes are ticked.' She had a few lines scribbled on her pad and this is where she started, her pencil between her fingers as she ticked off the first item.

'Can you tell me about the last time you saw Ian, Mr Strong?'

He pushed his mug away. 'We went out for a drink, all three of us,' he said, nodding his head at his son. 'Dominic only arrived about a week ago and I'm so thankful he did.'

'Where did you go?'

'The Dog and Bark, the only pub within walking distance of the house. We went home after for a nightcap. He left about one but my memory is hazy as I was a bit woozy at the time.'

'I take it he got a taxi back,' Owen said, his elbows on the table.

'No. Why would he?' Mr Strong's jaw tightened. 'Ian was completely teetotal, which would make his blood alcohol level zero. Sometimes I questioned if he was even my son.'

Owen quirked his eyebrow at Gaby, a look that was intercepted by Dominic.

'I can see you're surprised but my brother was heavily into his sport and keeping fit. He used to drink but gave up about five years ago, said sport was the only stimulant he needed.'

'Okay, let's move on a bit,' Gaby said, glancing down at the next question on her list. The issue of his abstinence was something that they'd have to revisit but there were other questions that needed addressing first. 'How did Ian seem when you saw him? Happy? Sad? Or just his usual self?'

'Well, Dominic hadn't seen him for a bit, but he was a bit

pissed off, if I'm honest.' He coughed into his hand. 'Sorry. I didn't mean to swear; it just slipped out.'

'No apology necessary, Mr Strong.' Gaby smiled. 'Can you elaborate? I know working for the police can be trying at times but …'

'No. It wasn't that. He loved his job. He'd have joined up years ago if he hadn't cocked up his GCSEs. No, it was Hannah and the boy. Ian wanted to get married and make it formal like, but she wasn't having any of it. He just couldn't understand why not. He had a steady job after all and wasn't the type to knock her around. Wouldn't hurt a fly, our Ian. As soft as butter.'

'Far too soft, Dad,' Dominic interrupted. 'He let everyone walk all over him.'

'Even Hannah?' Owen asked.

'That I can't answer. I haven't been back in over a year so never got the chance to meet her before Sunday,' he said, his voice sharp.

The interview was meandering along better than Gaby could have hoped but she still had the most difficult questions left to ask.

'I've already had the opportunity to speak to your son, Mr Strong, albeit informally about Ian's death and he's adamant that he wouldn't have considered suicide. Is that something you'd agree with?'

She watched his mouth form into words as he searched for an answer. But instead of tackling it straightaway, he lifted his mug and, holding it between both hands, drained it before returning it to the table.

'I would never have thought that he would. He seemed so happy and full of life. Apart from the blip with Hannah – and she must have had her reasons – he didn't seem to have a care in the world. He loved her and he was growing to love Hunter. It was there in the way he never shut up about the pair of them. They were a family or as good as. There's nothing. No reason that I can think of and it's not as if we haven't spent the last four days talking about it.'

'Okay, thank you.' An awkward silence descended as she glanced at the next item on her pad, the one she was dreading. But the truth was, everything that had gone before was an appetiser leading up to this point. She already knew their thoughts on Hannah and that Ian would never have committed suicide. There was only one question left – the issue of Dominic's finances was one she'd prefer to keep to herself until Marie found the time to do some more digging.

'You said that Ian was health-conscious? Perhaps even fanatical if his abstinence from alcohol is to be taken into account. Is that a correct summation?'

They both nodded but, in Dominic's case, the nod was marred by a look of suspicion.

'We've checked his initial assessment when he applied for the police – we have to be very thorough as I'm sure you can imagine. He admitted to one instance of cannabis use as a teen.'

'Is that a question or a statement, Detective?'

'A bit of both.'

'He was only being honest. Ian wasn't a drug user if that's what you're trying to intimate. Yes, like a lot of other young people, he was offered drugs. I was offered them too. There's only …' Dominic paused, his jawline tightening. 'There *was* only a year between us so we attended the same parties and festivals and were offered the same drugs. Yes, I remember sharing a spliff with him at one such event but it was a one-off, not least because we spent the remainder of the party throwing up next to the bins.'

'So, what would you say if I was to inform you that your brother was shot full of diamorphine?'

Dominic went rigid. His face flushed a deep dark red and his hands flexed as if he was imagining Gaby's neck between his fingers. The only thing stopping him, a light touch on his arm and his dad's words.

'What's diamorphine, son?'

'It's another word for heroin, Dad, and no! There is no way you can ever make me believe that he would have taken it willingly. No way at all.'

Chapter 43

Hannah

Wednesday 26 August, 5.15 p.m. St Asaph

Hannah didn't want to go back home but she didn't feel that she had a choice. She knew both Milly and the Strongs would be happy to put her up as would Jon and Carmel, but it wasn't as if they were family. What she needed was the comfort of familiarity. To be allowed to grieve but without the awkwardness of having to make small talk with people she barely knew.

Mr Parrish was all concern and sympathy. The mild-mannered man had done more in the half-hour than a host of fair-weather friends could ever do. But then presumably he'd been in this position before on numerous occasions, she reasoned, a bitterness creeping in and slapping away any thought of thanks. He was doing his job and, like most people, would want nothing more than to drop her off at the earliest opportunity so that she could be someone else's responsibility.

Instead of asking him to take her home, she made him pull over at the bus stop opposite Conwy Castle. He tried to argue but she just smiled, adamant, her hand on the side of the door. She loved her own company. The only person she'd never minded intruding on her solitude was Hunter and, in a funny sort of way, it was the one thing that had made her relationship with Ian work. He was so busy with his own life that she was still able to fit in time for herself without feeling guilty that she wasn't making more of an effort with him.

The quay was still busy but, with the continued warmth in the air and the days steam-rolling ahead to when the children would have to be back at school, that was hardly surprising. She found a spare bench and sat back, her attention on the seagulls hanging around for titbits of food.

There was lots she could be thinking about. Trying to work out what had happened. Trying to remember more about the controlled drug check with Georgie. But it was all a haze, the terror of the weekend pushing all thought of the mundane back into a corner of her mind that she couldn't reach. The one thing she couldn't believe was Georgie's involvement in the theft from Daffodils and, as she knew that it hadn't been her, it had to be someone else. But that's where logic deserted her.

The issue of the keys to the house was also puzzling. Someone had entered the house twice now, on both occasions leaving no sign of a forced entry. There were only three sets of keys. Hers, the set she'd left with Jon for emergencies and Ian's, which were yet to be found. But it wasn't only the break-in and the keys that caused her the most concern because, of course, there'd also been things left as well as taken during the burglary. Everyone thought that Ian had been a user. The latest news headlines screamed out the fact from their front pages. But no matter how many newspaper articles she read to the contrary, she would never believe that of Ian.

Hannah didn't know how long she sat there, her thoughts going round and round in never-ending circles. She didn't know how long she'd have lingered if he hadn't interrupted her, the hard slats of the bench digging deep grooves into the back of her legs as the sun slid across the sky and the shadows lengthened.

'This is where you've got to. I've been looking all over.'

She closed her eyes, recognising the voice straightaway.

'I thought we could pick up fish and chips on the way and have them back at my dad's. He's expecting us. I think we both need a break from cooking after the grilling we had from that detective,' Dominic went on, dropping beside her on the bench.

She managed a smile. 'That bad?'

'The worst. I don't know how she sleeps at night.'

'She probably doesn't.'

'If you want to stop off at the house to pick up your toothbrush and a change of clothing, that's not a problem,' he continued, as if the detective was the very last thing he wanted to discuss.

'Why are you being so nice all of a sudden? I never asked you—'

'And you don't have to. It's what Ian would have wanted.' He rose to his feet, his shoes making a crunching noise on the gravel. 'I know I've been a jerk, but the way Ian kept banging on about you refusing to marry him, I got this impression that you were just stringing him along. You know, looking for a free ride until something or someone better came on the scene.' He held his hands up when she started to rise from the bench, her face mutinous. 'I know. You don't have to tell me that I've misjudged you. Let's start again. After all, we're all the family you've got currently whether you like it or not – and think about my dad. It will upset him if you don't accept his offer to put you up until …'

'Until what?'

He shrugged. 'Until you're able to look after yourself. And before you start having a go, when was the last time you ate anything of any substance – or are you going to lie and tell me that you've eaten today?'

Hannah remembered the tea they brought her at the station and the couple of digestive biscuits and felt a blush starting to build. But she wasn't his responsibility, far from it. She couldn't let him take control of her life, no matter how much she wanted someone else to be in charge of the reins for a while, someone who would do a far better job than she seemed to be doing.

She suddenly felt the energy seep out of her as if someone had punctured her skin like a balloon. There was no will left. No fight. No determination. She'd go with him because she didn't have the strength to raise an objection to his plan. There was nothing to object to. He only had the very best of intentions in addition to being a fellow healthcare professional. A doctor, for God's sake. Her skin blanched, all trace of her earlier blush erased. A highly intelligent, well-educated man who'd see the truth in an instant if he ever went searching in the right direction.

Chapter 44

Gaby

Thursday 27 August, 8.30 a.m. St Asaph

'Detective Darin, the chief inspector would like a word. He asked me to tell you as soon as you got in.'

'Thank you, Clancy.' Gaby held her hand out for her post, offering the middle-aged desk sergeant a wide smile in return.

It wasn't his fault that she always felt like a recalcitrant schoolgirl whenever Sherlock demanded her presence in his office. For some reason, he always called upon the desk sergeant to do his dirty work instead of sending an email or, God forbid, picking up the telephone.

'Take a seat, Darin,' were his first words – always a bad sign.

She dropped into the chair, carefully positioned in front of his desk, the early morning sun streaming through the window causing her eyes to smart. When DCI Sherlock was in a good mood he left her standing, her hands folded in front of her. But he also dispatched with formalities and called her Gaby, a strange dichotomy but one she'd had to learn to accept as yet another of his little quirks.

'An update please?'

He also never said two words when one would do the job perfectly well, just as she had no need to ask which crime he was referring to. While he always took an active interest in ongoing cases, the death of one of his officers was obviously going to take precedence.

'It seems to have come to a bit of a standstill, sir. We've had the report from the CSIs but there's no evidence one way or the other to indicate a motive for what happened. The autopsy report on both Strong and the child make for interesting reading. On the face of it, it looks like Strong killed himself after being unable to revive his girlfriend's son. However, it now seems as if someone injected diamorphine into his earlobe first and that's unlikely to be him. There is also the issue of the burglary and the fact of the boy's missing belongings, which doesn't make sense on any level.'

'What about the theft of controlled drugs from that nursing home, which subsequently ended up in Thomas's house?' He folded his arms in front of him and rested them on the desk, his eyes sharp behind his wire-framed glasses. 'I had thought you'd be looking to arrest the mother for theft of a Class-A drug with an intent to supply, not to mention this new evidence you've presented about its administration, but what do I know! I'm only in charge of the department.' He leant back against his black swivel chair, his gaze never leaving her face. 'I've just been speaking to Jason Moore and he confirms that Thomas's fingerprints have been found on the ampules but not Strong's.'

'That's as may be, sir, but as she was involved in the checking of the controlled drugs at Daffodils we'd expect her fingerprints to be all over them.'

'Why not Strong's? After all, he was the one found pickled in the stuff.'

'Because he didn't administer the drugs,' she replied, trying to maintain a sense of calm.

'Darin, I don't give a flying fuck what you do but I need an arrest for this drug business,' he snapped, in a rare outbreak of swearing. In fact, Gaby couldn't remember an occasion when he'd resorted to using the F word in her presence. She knew he was getting pressure from CS Winters but not quite how much until that exact moment. 'It's bad enough that you can't give me a definitive on what happened to one of my officers.'

'Yes, sir. I mean, no, sir.'

He removed his glasses and, folding the arms placed them carefully on the desk before reaching up and pressing the bridge of his nose between his thumb and forefinger. 'Don't make me regret your meteoric climb up the ladder, Darin,' he said after a moment's pause. 'I want this Thomas woman arrested immediately for possession of a Class-A drug with the intent to supply.'

'But—'

'No buts.'

Gaby cringed at the thought of her recent appointment to detective inspector being whipped out from under her feet because she wasn't about to give in to his demands, not without ironclad evidence. Everything pointed to a completely different scenario; the only problem was she couldn't come up with a set of circumstances that made sense.

'I'm sorry, sir, but I can't agree. Do you honestly think that Thomas would have left her son in the company of a drug user in light of his diabetes? By all accounts, she was overprotective as it was. Users, as we know, are unpredictable, something she'd be aware of as a registered nurse. And in addition, her home was broken into. Who's to say that the disturbance of her son's items wasn't a ruse while the perpetrator planted the drugs?'

'But to what end, Darin? There has to be a motive.'

That's where Gaby ran out of steam, because there was no motive that she could think of. None that made any sense. Even her questioning about the suicide of Stephen Lee was more about dotting the i's and crossing the t's than any thought that his death could in any way be linked.

'Give me twenty-four hours, sir. If I can't come up with anything constructive by then …'

Gaby walked into the incident room and headed straight for the coffee machine, wrinkling her nose at the smell of stewed coffee, a smell she should be getting used to by now. With her mug in her hand, she walked over to the second whiteboard to remind herself of the key points because, no matter what she thought, she'd made Sherlock a promise, one she didn't intend breaking.

Her eyes landed on the comment about Y Mwyar Duon. There had to be something there, something they'd missed. If Hannah was involved that meant she must have disguised her level of inebriation and left the hotel in the middle of the night.

Gaby placed her untouched mug on the nearest desk, having lost all interest in the lukewarm drink, her gaze now shifting between Malachy and Jax: the only detectives present. She'd like nothing better than a trip to Ruthin but, with her jam-packed schedule, she couldn't afford the time.

'Mal, what are you up to?' she asked, concentrating on his face and not on his screen in case he thought that she didn't trust him. She knew he'd have more sense than to mess about on YouTube in the office.

'Following up on Hannah Thomas, ma'am. I decided to give it another look now we know a little more about her.'

'But still no internet presence?'

'No.' He flicked her a glance, his dark brown eyes narrowing. 'But I can't say I'm surprised. The media gave her a complete going-over at the time of Lee's death. Hounding would be a better way to describe it. Remember this was six years ago so not that long after the phone hacking scandal, which should have made a difference to their behaviour but didn't. She was pigeonholed as the villain of the piece and appeared on the front of all the nationals on almost a daily basis.'

'I don't remember …'

'No. Well neither do I but then I don't make a habit of reading the kind of newspapers we're talking about,' he said, tilting his head in the direction of the folded-up *Times* newspaper peeking out the side pocket of his leather satchel.

'Fair point.' She preferred the *Guardian* but wasn't about to bring it up. 'So, what have you found then?'

'Nothing of any interest.' He rubbed his hand across his face, his square-cut nails scrupulously clean. 'Certainly nothing now Hardiman is dead,' he said, focusing on a pile of printouts. 'Breast cancer, diagnosed within months of her losing her job.'

'No one deserves that sort of luck, no matter what sort of a person they are,' Gaby said. 'So, what about another trip to that hotel in Ruthin? I can't help feeling there's still something we're missing. I know you interviewed the barman and saw the room but there's still a niggle.'

'Sorry for interrupting, ma'am, but I wouldn't mind going this time; that is if Mal doesn't mind?'

Gaby switched her gaze to Jax who'd obviously been listening in to the conversation.

'I was thinking of heading out that way with Georgie for a meal later – something to take her mind off things,' he continued, managing to maintain eye contact and control his stutter. 'I could try and catch up with the night porter while we're there, if you're okay with me leaving the visit until later? I'm happy to do it in my own time.'

She raised her eyebrows at his enthusiasm but didn't have the heart to refuse. 'If Mal agrees, it's fine by me. You can definitely add it onto your special duty sheet – it will help towards the cost of the meal – and remember to keep a note of your mileage. We can't run to dinner at Y Mwyar Duon but, to the best of my knowledge, you're far from a registered charity.'

She looked over her shoulder at Owen's empty desk. 'Any idea where Bates is?'

'Oh, yes. Sorry, ma'am. He phoned in, something about a dentist's appointment. He's been up half the night with toothache.'

'That will teach him, wolfing down those doughnuts yesterday,' Gaby said, less than sympathetic. 'What about Marie and Diane? Remind me what they're up to.'

Chapter 45

Marie

Thursday 27 August, 9 a.m. St Asaph

Diane and Marie were becoming firm friends, drawn together by the breakdown of their marriages. There were other similarities. They were both blonde but, in Diane's case, due to a monthly visit to the hairdresser. They'd both joined the police force straight from school and were now using their careers as a way to cope with the cracks in their personal lives. But that's where the similarities ended.

'This is only your second interview, right?' Marie said, picking up her notepad and mobile, which she quickly turned to mute before waiting for Diane to do the same.

'Yes.'

'Okay, so you know the form. I'll lead but if there's anything you want to ask just do it. Come on, we don't want to leave them too long. It will only get them thinking.'

*

'What's this all about then?'

Mr Lee had barely waited for the door to close on interview room two before turning on Marie, his belligerent tone matching his facial expression exactly. Mrs Lee ignored him, something she'd probably been doing for most of her married life. Instead she concentrated on settling in her chair, her handbag clutched tightly on her lap.

'If you'd like to take a seat, Mr Lee, we'll tell you,' Marie said, her voice holding a degree of authority that was impossible to ignore. 'Thank you for travelling out of your way today. As I said on the telephone earlier …' She paused briefly, her attention now on Mrs Lee and where she was fiddling with the zip on her bag. 'It's in relation to your son.'

'Our son is dead. He's been dead nigh on six years so I can't think of what your interest is after all this time.' Mr Lee sat down, his large body spilling over the side of his chair, a distinct smell of stale sweat as good an advert as any for the use of anti-perspirants.

'I'm sorry to have to bring up such a difficult topic after this length of time but—'

'But that's not going to stop you, eh? What about his poor ole mum? Can't you see what it's doing to her?' he said, poking his wife in the ribs, an action that made her wince.

Marie had come across his sort many a time on the beat, usually late at night with a belly full of beer in their stomach and a fight on their minds. There was no way to win him over. No easy way to ask the list of questions staring up at her from her notebook. She had thought Gaby was being kind asking her to lead on the interview – she was quickly changing her mind on that score. But instead of pandering to his oversized ego, she decided to get to the point.

'Tell me about your son, Mr Lee. What kind of a man was he?'

He opened his mouth to speak only for his wife to interrupt.

'The sooner we get this over with the sooner we can leave, Herbert,' she said in a soft breathy voice. 'Our son was troubled from a young age, Officer. Bullied at school, he dropped out after his GCSEs and never managed to find paid employment after. He got in with the wrong crowd and it went from bad to worse. I … we tried our best but …' She sighed, a tragic sound coming right from the depth of her lungs. 'We weren't surprised by his death, not really. It had been coming on for quite a while.'

'And what about how it happened? What about the Beddows?'

'Herbert wanted to sue but there would have been little point. Yes, they were in the wrong to let it happen but if it hadn't been that roof, it would have been another one.'

Marie caught Mr Lee's eye, the slight sheen of moisture on his lower lids shifting something inside and she started to regret her thoughts of only moments before. There was nothing worse than burying a child, no matter their age. She'd assumed that the wife was weak and undermined by her bullish husband but that wasn't the case. His wife was the one holding it together, albeit by the slenderest of threads.

There was nothing left on her pad; Gaby's instructions the vaguest she'd ever been given. *To get a feel for the couple and go for the throat, but only if indicated.* She shut her notebook with a snap only to shift her head at the sound of Diane clearing her throat.

'So, you've had no dealings with either Hilary Hardiman or Hannah Thomas, the two nurses involved in his death? The media went to town on both of them so it's not as if you wouldn't have had cause or indeed the opportunity,' Diane said, staring across at Mrs Lee, her look one of steely determination.

After a moment's pause, Mrs Lee lunged to her feet and started to batter her husband over the head with her bag. 'You stupid, stupid man,' she screamed over and over again. 'I told you they'd find out.'

'How the hell did you know?'

Back in the incident room, Marie grabbed a chocolate bar from her top drawer and split it in two. She watched while Diane stuffed it into her mouth whole.

'I didn't. It was just something about the way the wife was clutching her bag for dear life. I knew she'd lost her son, but it was six years ago and not her fault. Yes, anyone would feel nervous being called into the local nick for a chat, but she wasn't nervous. She was more than nervous. She was scared stiff and with no obvious cause unless one of them had done something.'

'But to have sent death threats through the post to Hannah. Ones that she never reported. Why?'

'Why the Lees sent them or why she didn't report it?'

'Both.'

'Grief makes people do funny things, Marie,' Diane said, filling the coffee maker and pressing the little red button on the side. 'As to why Hannah didn't report it, perhaps she felt they were only what she deserved. While she might have been a student and, by nature of her poor supervision, not ultimately responsible, that wouldn't have changed how she felt about the whole thing. After all, she didn't get any closure, did she? She had no family to turn to and certainly no sign of a public apology or a retraction notice from the media for dragging her name through the mud.'

'As if!'

'Exactly. The only thanks she got was to be allowed to finish her degree and by that time she had a baby to worry about.'

Marie grimaced. She needed more chocolate and in large quantities, but coffee would have to do if she wasn't about to explode with all the junk food she'd been eating recently. Sliding behind her desk, she booted up her laptop and launched a new search.

'What are you up to?' Diane placed a mug of coffee beside her and, leaning against the nearest wall, started taking tiny sips from her hot drink.

'Seeing if Hilary Hardiman …' She slammed her fist down on the desk, her eyes glued to the screen. 'I just bloody knew it. Listen to this. Between the first of August and the twenty-first of September, 2015, Hardiman received ten threats through the post of increasing levels of violence. They stopped abruptly almost as quickly as they'd started.'

'Probably because Mrs Lee got wind of them,' Marie said, her voice dry.

'Exactly. There was no trace evidence and no DNA but that's hardly surprising with half the world watching *Midsomer Murders* while the rest watch *NCIS*. So the likelihood is that Hannah would have received the exact same but chose to do nothing about it. I don't know about you, but I find that both illuminating and disturbing,' she said, pushing away from the desk and grabbing her purse. 'My turn. Milk or dark? Please don't say white. I can't abide the stuff.'

Chapter 46

Hannah

Thursday 27 August, 4 p.m. Llandudno

Hannah didn't know what to do with herself. She'd left the Strongs' house after lunch on some excuse or other and had been moping around Llandudno ever since. Conwy was too small, too restrictive. A place where she couldn't hide among the narrow winding streets for fear of being recognised. She could deal with many things but sympathy wasn't one of them. She couldn't even drop into work now an investigation was under way. While they hadn't gone so far as to suspend her, it was there in the corner of Gloria's eye and the way she'd refused to answer her questions. They thought her guilty and, the worst of it was, she couldn't blame them. If she'd been presented with the same situation she'd have drawn the same conclusion – erroneous as it may be.

Walking into the chemist, she picked up a bottle of her favourite brand of shampoo and stared down at the label, her thoughts in freefall. How many innocent people were in jail simply because they couldn't fight against the twists of fate that life flung at them? Probably far too many to count.

Hannah returned the shampoo to the shelf, righting the bottle so that it faced front. She'd bought a couple only last week on a buy-one-get-one-half-price promotion and didn't have the room, or the inclination to waste money on non-essentials now that her future was less than certain. Strolling up and down the aisles of the chemist was something to do, something to help the time drift along until evening. She still had to come to a decision as to where she was going to spend the night because the idea of going home, with all the memories it held, was something she couldn't face. Not now and perhaps not ever.

Her stomach rumbled, a sharp reminder that she hadn't eaten anything since the mug of soup and bread roll that Dominic had forced her to swallow under his watchful gaze. He was nothing like his brother. Oh, he was uncomfortably similar in looks, even down to his height, but he was harder and more determined, which was odd because as a doctor, surely he'd have had to learn to tailor his bedside manner to meet the expectations of all those women under his care. Obstetrics and gynaecology wasn't a field she was particularly interested in. However, as a mum, she'd had first-hand experience of the type of medic it attracted and, up to now, she'd seen little evidence that Dominic had any of the attributes required.

With her hands empty, she headed for the door and, turning left, made her way out of the shopping centre and past the library to Take a Break Café, situated near the corner of Gloddaeth Avenue. It was late enough in the afternoon for the lunchtime trade to have joined the thronging masses filling the beach along the North Shore and, apart from a handful of desultory customers, she had the cool interior to herself. She pulled out her phone and placed it on the table in front of her but, instead of switching it on, she turned to the menu, trying to decide what to eat. The soup and roll had filled a hole but she still felt a lingering hunger gnaw

215

her insides. She finally decided on a Belgian waffle, well aware that it wasn't the kind of healthy option she normally went for. But she had far more to worry about than ensuring she got her ration of five a day. No doubt it would result in a rash of spots but again she didn't care.

The waffle was warm and dripping with toffee sauce, the large scoop of ice cream exactly what she needed with the temperature outside back up in the high twenties. With her plate clean, she lingered over her coffee, her fingers laced around the mug as she again tried to work out why this was happening. Her mind drifted round and round in circles, never managing to reach any sort of a resolution. There was no answer and certainly no one she could think of who would hate her that much, not now. If it had happened straight after Stephen had died, that would have been another thing, but why leave it so long?

She shivered despite the heat flowing in through the open doorway and warming the room. Stephen Lee was someone she'd hoped to forget over time, but she couldn't. Even when she'd managed to push his memory under all the other stuff taking space inside her head, he was still there – a dark and looming presence casting a shadow over everything good that had happened since his death. The worst of it was she only had herself to blame.

Hannah eased her hands away from the now-cold coffee, her fingers sore from where she'd been digging the tips into the pottery. If she'd been stronger and less easy to impress, he wouldn't have slithered through her defences. He'd manipulated her and, because she'd let him, he'd died.

'Sorry to disturb you but we're closing in five minutes. You can pay at the till.'

She pressed the heels of her hands under her eyes, allowing the images to fade and wither as the café again came back into focus. The rattle of crockery as the waitress headed behind the counter and into the kitchen. The smell of antibacterial cleaner hanging in the air as a youth started wiping down the tables. It was time to go and not a moment too soon as she choked back the persistent image of Stephen's face when all she wanted to do was think about Hunter.

She reached for her untouched phone only to have it ring in her hand and, staring at the screen, she let a sigh form at the sight of a name she recognised.

'Hi, Milly.'

'Hannah. I'm pleased I caught you. I was wondering what you were up to later? I was thinking of grabbing a pizza and watching something on the telly. Nothing exciting but …'

'That sounds perfect as long as it's not too much trouble,' she said, jumping at the lifeline in the spirit it was offered. She paused long enough to pull out her purse from the top of her bag and remove her debit card. It would also be an ideal opportunity to apologise for her behaviour the last time they'd met. Milly was well-meaning and certainly didn't deserve her head being snapped off, despite the difficult circumstances. 'I've been staying at Ian's dad's but I can't keep imposing.'

'Not at the house?'

'No, not yet.' Hannah decided to change the subject. The less she thought about the house the better. 'I take it you have a few days off?'

'Not back until Saturday. Why don't you stay? It will save on taxi fares. You shouldn't be alone just yet.'

Hannah wondered if Milly had heard about the missing drugs, only to suppress the thought as unworthy. The home wouldn't want it bandied about until they had proof one way or the other and, as a healthcare assistant as opposed to a qualified nurse, there would have been no need for her to be informed.

'Thank you, then. I'll be over shortly. And, Milly, I really do appreciate it.'

It was a repeat of Saturday night with regards to the amount of alcohol that was consumed. It was also the thing Hannah needed to help shift things into perspective despite guilt staring at her from every corner. But life went on, as Milly kept repeating, and she had to run with it, one step at a time. It was all about firsts. She'd managed the first day without her son. It would soon be the first week, the first month. The first Christmas. His sixth birthday.

Hannah swallowed the lump that was clogging the back of her throat. She was well aware that she'd only be able to get through this by banishing such thoughts. Easier said than done.

'And you have no idea who could be doing this to you?' Milly said, returning from the kitchen with another bottle of wine.

'Not a clue but the police seem to be in agreement that it's unlikely that Ian took his own life even after ...' She cleared her throat. 'After what happened to Hunter. There's the drugs for a start,' she said. At Milly's quizzical look, she proceeded to tell her all about the missing ampules, deciding she had to confide in someone.

'Mmm. Well, it's obvious someone must have planted them during the break-in but who? I can't see how it would tie in unless it's someone who knows your every movement. What about those nosy neighbours next door?'

'Jon and Carmel?' Hannah shook her head. 'They're as good as gold really. She's too tied up childminding the grandkids, and Jon ... well, he's a sweetheart.'

'That's not what you said at the weekend, even before all this happened,' Milly said. 'I seem to remember something about you recommending he join Nosy Parkers Anonymous.'

'I know what I said.' Hannah felt weary of it all, the effects of the alcohol attacking her system like a sledgehammer. 'But I can't really believe that he'd be involved. They've been so kind since it happened.'

'You could say the same about me,' Milly said, lifting up the remote and searching through the music channels. 'What about Ian's brother then? You said he's a doctor, which is even better.

218

He'd know what to do with the morphine if you say that Ian wasn't a dopehead.'

'Far from it,' Hannah said, wincing at the term. 'He wouldn't even take a paracetamol for a headache.' She lifted her glass to her lips as she mulled over the idea of Dominic being the instigator of her misfortune. As a doctor, he'd be in the ideal position to interfere with Hunter's insulin pump then dose Ian up with drugs. Hannah blinked, remembering something she'd forgotten: her mobile phone. He'd taken it away when he'd left the room only to return it when he'd brought in the charger – she'd thought it most odd at the time but in the upset caused by the text message, she'd forgotten all about it.

Chapter 47

Jax

Thursday 27 August, 7 p.m. Ruthin

Unbeknownst to Georgie, Jax had been squirrelling away the odd fiver or two into what he called his rainy-day fund. There wasn't much in it, hardly anything, but with a steady job and a girlfriend to share the bills, he decided that a trip to Ruthin was as good a reason as any to splash out on a decent meal for once. Yes, he should really add it to their meagre savings for a deposit on a house but, for once he chose not to be sensible. A career in the police force had taught him many things – not least that the unexpected often lay around the very next corner and most of it was far from pleasant. He couldn't help being affected by what had happened to Hannah or the fact that Ian was a policeman. Statistically Jax was well aware that he was more likely to get run over by a bus than he was to be injured in the course of his job, but statistics didn't count where feelings were concerned. He also wanted to take Georgie's mind off what had happened at Daffodils. They both knew she was innocent of any wrongdoing but that wasn't enough to remove the nasty taste from his mouth or the worried frown off her forehead. Just as the police force was his life, nursing was hers.

'But we can't afford it.'

'Would you shush for a minute and listen,' he said, pulling into the car park reserved for residents situated at the side of the building. 'I have a few quid put away, not much but there's my birthday money from my grandparents …'

'Jax Williams, if you think I'm going to let you use that on treating me to a slap-up meal.' She clenched the strap of her seatbelt, her eyes flashing fire across the small space between them. 'I thought we were having a drink in the bar?'

'As if I'd drive all this way for a pint! It's my choice what I spend the money on and if I choose to spend it on us sharing a meal then so be it. Come on now, don't be a Miss Grumpy Pants. Darin is paying for the fuel and letting me mark the time up as overtime so, in a way, the meal is paying for itself.'

Georgie heaved her shoulders but he could tell that she was giving way. The idea of a cosy candlelit meal was far too tempting after the few days they'd had.

The bar was crowded with standing room only, so they decided to take their drinks into the conservatory restaurant at the back. There'd be time enough to investigate the bar area after their meal. He considered the tables, half wondering where Hannah had been sitting but he was wary of asking the waitress in front of Georgie now that she was relaxing into her large glass of gin. It was the first time he'd seen her unwind since he'd picked her up from her shift at the Annex and taken her for breakfast in Rhos-on-Sea. The only thing spoiling it was his glass of low-alcohol lager instead of the pint of Heineken he craved but he was happy to forgo the extra stimulant with the possibility of cracking the case hanging over him like a worm dangling on the end of a hook.

While laid-back to a fault, Jax was also fiercely ambitious, not least because of the accompanying pay hike that would help towards a deposit for a house. It would be back to bread and margarine tomorrow. Perhaps without the margarine, he thought with a frown, an image of the vegan brand Georgie had recently started to buy popping up somewhere in the space between his ears as he listened to her debating the benefits of a tofu burger over a medley of pan-fried vegetables. He snapped the menu closed, determined to stick to his guns. Yes, she'd be disappointed in his choice of sirloin steak with all the trimmings but not as disappointed as he'd be if he had to munch through a plate of vegetables for his dinner.

Plates cleared, he directed her into the bar and the wooden settle beside the fireplace, the same seat that Hannah and Milly had sat in – was it only five days ago? It felt far longer.

'The same again?' he said, nodding at her wineglass. 'Or what about a nightcap?'

'A nightcap sounds a lovely idea.'

'Your usual or something different?'

'Why don't you surprise me?'

Jax strolled to the bar, deciding not to draw the barman into a conversation about the case. He'd read Mal's notes and there was nothing left to ask. Within minutes, he'd returned to the table with a black coffee in one hand and a tall glass in the other.

'Ooh I haven't had an Irish coffee in years.'

'I thought it was time for you to reacquaint yourself with the taste. It's something that we could easily make at home too,' he carried on, trying not to groan at the price he'd just paid.

She settled back on the bench, her nose wrinkling.

'Is something the matter?'

Jax had only been with Georgie a little over three months, but he was well acquainted with her powerful sense of smell, something she blamed on all her years as a nurse.

'I'm not sure.' She lifted her chin, meeting his gaze full on. 'Knowing you, there's a reason we're sitting here?' she said, tilting her head towards the large squishy leather sofa on the other side of the room and then back to the hard wooden bench albeit scattered with deep raspberry-coloured cushions.

He blushed right up to his ears. 'You know me so well.'

'No. But I'm learning,' she said, with the shadow of a smile. 'So, I take it this is where Hannah and Milly had their night out on Saturday – and is this where they sat?'

'I'm dating a mind reader!' He watched as she glanced towards the fireplace which, as it was the height of summer, housed a selection of artificial plants instead of an additional heat source. 'What are you up to?'

She held up a hand to silence him.

'Shush. I'm thinking.'

Instead of doing what he expected, which was for her to relax into the seat and pick up her drink, she dropped to her knees and started fiddling about with the plants. He knew better than to question her, a lesson he'd learnt from working with Marie. She'd tell him when she was ready and not a moment sooner.

'Unless I'm very much mistaken, someone has been feeding this poor plant a cocktail or two,' she finally said, resting back on her heels, her fingers lifted to her nose. 'It wouldn't be so bad if it was real,' she went on, removing the plant from its pot and tipping it to reveal a surplus of muddy brown liquid in the bottom.

Jax pulled a frown. While she might be right, it would be impossible to prove who had used the container as a handy method of drinks disposal.

On the way out, he left Georgie sitting in reception and went to have a word with the night porter, who was able to confirm everything that Malachy had said.

'And this suspected prowler then. Can you show me exactly what happened?'

'Certainly, sir.' The porter grabbed his torch from behind the desk and headed out into the night. 'I was hanging around reception, manning the phones, when the call came through. A complaint from the newlyweds on the second floor about a prowler outside their room. I ran upstairs, initially thinking that it was in the corridor but they came out of the room and pointed at the window.' He walked around the side of the building, his arm extended in the direction of the second floor. 'But there was nothing to see and the car park was as quiet as a graveyard.'

Jax stayed where he was long after the porter had returned back inside, his attention on the second and third-floor windows and the location of the fire escape, which bordered both.

Chapter 48

Gaby

Friday 28 August, 8.30 a.m. St Asaph

Gaby was guilt-ridden and the worst of it was there was nothing she could do to alleviate even a smidgeon of the way she was feeling. Today was meant to be her day off. The day she'd pencilled in months ago when Amy had surprised her by asking her to be her chief bridesmaid. She'd planned on meeting her for lunch and an afternoon of pampering before an early supper around at her house. Amy was staying the night and that was still the plan but as for the rest …

Gaby had chosen to give up her day off with the threat of Hannah's arrest still hanging over her head, not that there'd ever been much choice about it. The hope was that the case would shift into a position where she actually knew where it was going by the end of the day. That was the hope – she wanted nothing to spoil tomorrow.

Instead of heading down to the incident room, she made her way up to the next floor and to her office, closing the door behind her with a sharp click. Having to work on her day off was one thing but ensuring that she made the best use of the time, without the constant interruptions normally found in the incident room, was something completely different. That's where Owen found her twenty minutes later, two take-out coffees in his hands and a bag from the local bakery tucked under his arm.

'Knowing you as I do, I'll bet you skipped breakfast,' he said, offering her first choice of the pastries.

Instead of her usual refusal, she pulled out a croissant and sank her teeth into the still-warm, flaky pastry with barely a murmur of thanks.

'How did you know I'd be here?' she said between mouthfuls.

'Shall we say an informed guess? With the case hotting up, where else were you going to be?'

'With Amy, supporting her on her last day as a single woman.'

'But with her mother and sisters here, surely it will be a bit crowded?' Owen said, removing the lid from his drink, the smell of rich coffee beans making him smile.

'You know as well as I do, she doesn't really get on with her mother or her sisters for that matter. They hated that she went into the police force straight from school instead of the university degree they were planning.'

'All I can say is that she's the best FLO I've ever worked with,' he said, blowing on his drink before taking a small sip.

'I doubt her family even know what the term means.' They both fell silent, sipping on their drinks and, in Gaby's case, licking her forefinger and picking up the flakes from her demolished croissant. 'I'm planning on leaving about four if you could cover for me? I hate to ask but …'

'No problem. I know you'd do the same for me. In fact, you have done on numerous occasions in the past.'

'I forgot to ask how the toothache is?'

'All gone. They've sorted me out with a new filling,' he said, opening his mouth and pointing to the troublesome molar at the back. 'So, what are your plans for this morning? There doesn't seem to be a great deal happening?'

'The only thing happening is Sherlock wanting to arrest Hannah ASAP, which is the main reason I decided to give up my day off with the wedding tomorrow,' she said, examining her nails. 'If Sherlock knew the sacrifice I'm making ...'

'He'd work you even harder.'

'He could try.' She pushed away from her desk, her cup in one hand, her phone in the other. 'Come on, let's round up the troops and get this over and done with.'

Walking into the incident room, Gaby's first thought was that Jax looked the worse for wear, the top button of his shirt undone and his brown tie not quite the artful knot he usually went for. Marie and Diane were standing by the coffee machine deep in conversation while Mal was hunched behind his computer screen tapping away at a rate of knots.

'Morning, everyone, take a seat. We're going to try and keep this briefing brief,' she added, a smile barely touching her lips. 'We all know it's meant to be my day off so I do plan on leaving early. Please don't do anything to scupper those plans or Amy will give me what for.' She took up her usual position by the run of whiteboards, a blue pen in her hand. 'There's a few things to catch up on with Owen skiving off yesterday,' she said, throwing a smile across the room at the sight of his scowl. 'First up, we had an interesting interview with Strong's brother and father who reiterated that, in their opinion, there was no way Ian would have taken his own life. As a teetotal fitness fanatic who, apart from one youthful dabble, was vehemently against the whole drug scene, I can see where they're coming from.'

'Which only supports that we have to discount the diamorphine as being self-administered,' Owen said, folding his arms across his chest. 'But it's no surprise, is it? There are too many untied loose ends, like Hunter's suffocation and Ian not calling an ambulance out, for it to be anything other than murder.'

'Something that we've never been able to discount and certainly not in light of the burglary. So, if we're saying they were murdered, we're back to that old potato of motive and opportunity,' she said, scrubbing the third whiteboard clean with the duster from the shelf below before drawing a line straight down the middle. 'Who have we got that had both?'

'Well Hannah has to be at the top, doesn't she?' Owen said, standing to his feet and making for his usual position by the window. 'The motive could be anything from madness to being sick to death of having to manage Hunter's illness or even a row with her fiancé.'

'And the opportunity?'

'Actually her alibi has more holes in it than a moth-infested jumper, ma'am,' Jax said, taking a deep sip from his water bottle.

'Explain?'

'As you know, I took Georgie over to Ruthin last night and she noted something suspicious at the hotel. You remember the fireplace they were sitting beside, Mal? The nearest artificial plant pot had a severe case of alcoholic poisoning. While we can't be certain it was Hannah, it does seem strange that someone would do something like that, especially at the prices they were charging,' he said, pulling a face. 'There's also that comment Mal made about the prowler in the small hours, ma'am. We assumed it was nothing, and with no CCTV it's impossible to prove, but what if it was Hannah returning via the fire escape?'

'Or it could have been her friend,' Diane said, smoothing her bob behind her ears.

Gaby turned to her. 'You'll have to expand on that a little before I add her to the board.'

'All I'm saying is that they were both there together. Who's to say which one of them ditched their drink or indeed that it was either of them?'

'Okay, so Milly Buttle had the opportunity but what about the motive?'

The room sank into silence.

Gaby scrawled Milly's name underneath Hannah's but with a big question mark beside it.

'Actually, Diane might be on to something,' Owen said, from his position resting against the radiator. 'Remember she also works at the same nursing home where the drugs went missing – drugs that were subsequently found inside Ian Strong.'

'Which is all very well but Buttle isn't a qualified nurse,' Jax said. 'There's only one set of keys and they're held by the nurse in charge at all times. I remember only last month when Georgie took the drug keys home by mistake. I never thought she'd hear the end of it.'

'Thanks for that, Jax. Okay, we'll still include Buttle until we speak to the home again. Right, let's move on.' Gaby scanned the room. 'Who else would have wanted to murder Hunter and Ian and then make it look as if Hannah was the culprit?'

'What about Ian's brother?' Malachy said, folding back the cuffs of his pale blue shirt. 'We don't really know what their relationship was but he's a doctor and therefore in the know about insulin pumps. Just supposing Hannah had taken the drugs and Ian was a user, stranger things have happened. Dominic could have been outraged to hear that his brother was a junkie. There's also that question mark surrounding his posh riverside residence.'

'Very good, Mal, and we only know what him and his father have already told us.' She wrote Dominic's name on the board with a tick beside it for opportunity. 'Don't forget he also drugged Hannah, albeit to help her sleep – or at least that's what the excuse was.'

'Wasn't she staying with him when she received that threatening text message too?' Mal said, clearly on a roll. 'What better way to ensure you're around to see the results of the damage you've caused than to offer to put your victim up for the night?'

'Malachy Devine, I've said it before and I'll say it again. I'm very glad that you're on the right side of the law.'

'Yes, ma'am,' he said, his broad grin exposing most of his teeth.

'Who else?'

'The truth is we don't know,' Owen said, stroking his beard. 'Someone from her past like Stephen Lee but he's dead, as is Hilary Hardiman. But there could be someone we don't know about, someone that she's upset. She inherited from her parents at the expense of her brother, who also died.'

'And who was only fifteen at the time,' Marie piped up.

'Okay, well I think that we can discount anything to do with the brother and her parents then.' Gaby recapped the marker and set it down on the table. 'To clarify, what we're saying is that it could have been anyone but the only person who had both motive and opportunity is Hannah.'

'That we know about,' Owen interrupted.

Gaby rolled her eyes. 'The question is: do we have enough to charge her? Sherlock thinks so but, if he's wrong, the media will tear us to shreds. Remember it won't be his neck in the noose if the shit hits the fan.'

She paused, her attention on her ringing mobile.

'Sorry for interrupting, ma'am, but it's important.'

'What is it, Clancy?'

'I've just had Mr Strong on the phone in a bit of a state. He'd arranged to meet Miss Thomas in Llandudno first thing this morning. They had a nine o'clock appointment with the undertaker. He went to check her house but the next-door neighbour, a Mr Marquis, said that he hadn't seen her since Wednesday morning. Also, her mobile is switched off.'

'Thank you, Clancy. Give me his number, would you?' She reached for a pen, jotting it down on a scrap of paper before returning her phone to the desk and lifting her head.

'An interesting turn of events. Hannah appears to have disappeared despite me telling her not to leave the area. Either she's done a runner, been abducted or ...'

'Woken up late and forgotten to charge her phone,' Owen said, but with no trace of a grin.

'Yes, there is that. Right, what are you all doing still sitting here?' Gaby picked up her mobile and stuffed it in her jacket pocket. 'I have a very bad feeling about this. It's possibly nothing but recent events seem to point in a completely different direction. Malachy and Jax, I want you to arrange a search but keep it under your hat. Don't alert the media just yet. We'll look a right bunch of Charlies if she has overslept, which must be viewed as a strong possibility after the pressure she's been under. Search her home too. Visit the neighbours. Check in with the Strongs because there is always the possibility that Dominic is lying to us. There's also Hannah's friend to speak to.'

She turned to Marie. 'In the meantime, I'd like you and Diane to continue looking into Hannah's background and that of her family. Owen, you're with me.' Gaby made for the door. 'We're going to concentrate on the death threats sent by Stephen Lee's father and the impact they had on Hilary Hardiman and her family. We'll meet back here at one unless someone comes up with something beforehand.'

Chapter 49

Hannah

Friday 28 August, 11.45 a.m. Brookes Street

The first thing Hannah always did on wakening was to check her phone for the simple reason that she rarely wore a watch. Ian used to tease her about her obsession with the time, but she couldn't help it and, as obsessions went, there were far worse. Her dad had always been late for everything and, after a daily telling-off at school, the importance of good timekeeping had been ingrained, along with the importance of brushing her teeth and combing her hair.

After the bellyful of booze they'd put away, it was a surprise that she'd managed to remember to take her phone to bed. She couldn't say the same about her handbag or indeed her shoes, which she'd surrendered somewhere in the lounge. She didn't think that Milly would mind but she made a mental note to retrieve her belongings just as soon as she'd managed to lift her head off the pillow and cope with the blistering headache that had set up camp behind her left eye.

Pushing herself up onto her elbow, she reached for her phone only to realise that it was out of charge, a situation that dragged her right back to the Strongs' spare bedroom and the last time her phone was in the same sorry state. Then she'd been lucky enough to discover that Dominic had the same model. As far as she could remember, Milly's was an iPhone.

But instead of worrying about it, she picked up the glass of water that Milly must have left on the bedside table, and took a sip, the cool drink dissolving the dryness in her mouth as if by magic. Afterwards, she slid her feet out of bed and headed for the window. The view wasn't exciting. Just roofs interspersed with a hint of blue sky between the chimney pots. But something told her that it was later than she imagined, which was unusual because she rarely slept past half six, seven at the latest. A lifetime of early starts and parenting Hunter, who never stayed in bed later than six, had fine-tuned her body clock to snap awake whether it was a workday or the weekend.

She'd slept in her T-shirt, refusing the offer of borrowing something from Milly – there was only so much hospitality she could take. With a quick pull to rearrange the neck of her shirt, she got her jeans from where she must have left them on the end of the bed and made for the stairs, surprised at how quiet the house was. Milly was one of those people who was always on the go and noisy with it. At the care home it was a constant source of amusement to the residents and the staff alike who always knew when she was on duty because of her heavy footsteps and loud voice.

Hannah instinctively knew the house was empty, not that it bothered her. In fact, she relished the opportunity of getting her head together with a mug of tea before having to make small talk. She liked Milly well enough but there was only so much useless chatter she could cope with.

The sight of a note on the kitchen worktop with the words: *I had to go out, help yourself to bread and milk*, was welcome.

Far more welcome than the timer on the microwave, which said midday in luminous green.

'Shit.' A word that exploded from her mouth at regular intervals but never in front of Hunter. She'd made arrangements to meet the Strongs but it had slipped her mind until that exact moment and the worst of it was that she had no idea of Dominic's number. She'd often thought that she should carry around a charger for instances such as this but had never gotten round to it. She couldn't even ring the undertaker because she wasn't sure which one he'd contacted. The plan had been to meet them in front of the bandstand along the North Parade and take it from there. And even if Milly had a landline – she hadn't seen any sign of it last night – there was no point in trying to find out his home telephone number because they obviously weren't going to be there.

'Shit. Shit. Shit,' she repeated, the noise causing her headache to explode in a crescendo of pain. There was nothing she could do except apologise as soon as she'd sorted out her phone.

Ignoring both the kettle and the toaster, she hurried into the lounge in search of her handbag, which she found where she'd left it by the side of the sofa. But her shoes were a different matter entirely. She remembered slipping them off when she'd tucked her feet under her on the sofa but that's not where they were now. They also weren't in the hall or in any of the downstairs rooms, not that there were many apart from the lounge, kitchen and tiny bathroom. With her hand on the end of the banister, she tried to think of what she could have done with them. She was pretty sure she hadn't taken them up to bed but then she didn't really remember much about the evening.

The bedroom was one of those unused spaces with little more than a bed, an empty wardrobe and an MDF bedside table that had seen better days. After pulling open the wardrobe door and searching under the bed there was nowhere else that they could be. It wasn't as if they were expensive, none of her clothes or accessories had that moniker attached to them, but she couldn't very well leave the house in her bare feet.

Back on the landing, she eyed the closed door opposite, a small frown in place. She had no reason to think that Milly would have taken them, unless she'd thought that the plain white flip-flops were hers – perhaps not the most unusual of scenarios when Hannah considered that she'd picked them up in Primark for less than a fiver.

The bedroom was an exact replica of the one she'd just left, maybe a little bigger but with the same style of furnishings and a distinct lack of anything personal. Hannah didn't want to linger. Being found snooping would be the worst possible conclusion of what was proving to be a pretty disastrous morning. But the lack of personal possessions intrigued her. She could get the absence of photographs, particularly in light of Milly's recent break-up – it was a rare woman indeed who kept pictures of their ex on display. Okay, so she should really be looking for her shoes because the sooner she left the sooner she could rush home and sort out the issue with the phone charger. She'd already gathered that Dominic wasn't the most patient of men. Hannah dreaded to think what his reaction would be the next time she met him.

The wardrobe was as much of a puzzle as the missing shoes because, instead of the racks of trousers, shirts, dresses and other sundry items that she'd been expecting, there were only a couple of hangers suspended from the rail. There was no sign of her shoes. There was no sign of any shoes for that matter, she mused, closing the wardrobe and looking under the bed.

It almost felt as if Milly had packed up and done a runner. Not that Hannah could blame her. Not really. Not at all. It couldn't be much fun moving to a new town only to be dumped and have to start fending for yourself. But if that was the case then why had she taken Hannah's shoes?

She walked back down to the kitchen and, lifting the kettle, tested the weight to check the water level before switching it on.

She'd hang around for a bit. Milly was bound to turn up, and in the meantime she'd make a hot drink and take a couple of the painkillers she always kept in the bottom of her bag.

She stumbled backwards, the room starting to spin. A wave of nausea caused her to reach for the sink as her hangover decided to crank up a notch.

Chapter 50

Gaby

Friday 28 August, 1 p.m. St Asaph

It was one o'clock and still no sign of Hannah. Gaby was starting to get worried, not least because the thought of her evening with Amy was disappearing into the distance.

They were back in the incident room hovering over the platter of sandwiches like gannets at an all-you-can-eat picnic.

'Don't forget to make room for pudding,' Gaby said, angling her head in the direction of the tray of muffins she'd purloined from the staff canteen. 'Right then, let's get this show on the road. But bear in mind there's no need to panic because it's still not definite that Hannah is missing. She's just not where she was expected to be. First up, Mal and Jax, what have you come up with?'

'Nothing of any substance, ma'am,' Malachy said, covering his mouth with his hand while he finished swallowing the rest of his sandwich. 'We split up because that was the best use of our time. I went to her home but there was no answer. The next-door neighbour,' he said, glancing down at his notepad, 'a Mr Jon Marquis, was in. A nice enough man. Very eager to be of help. He showed me around the back of the property, accessed via a narrow lane, with the idea that she might have left the side gate open. She hadn't. Instead he let me into his back garden and I clambered over the fence. I had a good nosy, looked in all the windows, but there was no sign of life unless she was hiding upstairs.'

'Or lying injured or even worse, out of your line of sight?'

'There is that, of course, but I didn't have any reason to break down the front door. Mr Marquis used to have a key, but she's recently changed the locks.'

'Which isn't a surprise to anybody in this room, least of all me. Anything else?'

'I then went to that Daffodils place but they hadn't seen or heard of her since Wednesday. I asked about Milly but she's not due to work again until the weekend.'

'Righto. What about you, Jax? Please tell me that you've had more success than your colleague here?' she said, sending a fleeting smile across to Malachy to soften the impact of her words.

'Nothing startling, I'm afraid. I went to see the Strongs – they both appeared genuinely concerned about Hannah's whereabouts. After that, I checked on Milly Buttle but she's not answering her phone and there is no sign of her at her address. I asked the next-door neighbour. Apparently I'd just missed her.'

'Okay, thank you. Diane and Marie, what have you been up to?' Gaby said, perching on the edge of the nearest desk.

Marie spoke first. 'I decided to look into the Stephen Lee angle again. There's something about the whole set-up that concerns me.'

'How so?'

'Apart from the aeroplane accident that killed her family, there's nothing in Hannah's background other than Stephen Lee's death that could make somebody hate her,' she said, fiddling with the strap on her watch. 'To murder both her child and fiancé, then steal anything with any memory attached to the boy, must be one of the most despicable acts I've ever come across. Somebody is trying to dismantle everything that Hannah has ever known or loved. Her family. Her livelihood. Her memories. The next act must surely be to destroy her.'

'So, what did you discover?'

'I started with Lee's parents. They've never been in trouble with the law before – not even for a parking ticket – so for the father to have sent those threatening letters means that his son's death tipped him over the edge. I've checked into their financial situation and there's no trouble there, no sign of any irregularities.'

'What about Lee's siblings then? Retribution isn't always down to the parents, and I can imagine that even if they weren't close to their brother, his death must have hit them hard.'

'There's a sister around about the same age,' she said, rifling through a small pile of papers on her desk. 'Here it is, Nancy, born two years after Stephen, which would make her thirty-three now. The mother says she works in Spain.'

'Okay, let's see if we can't pin her exact location down. We also need a photo ASAP.' Gaby shifted her position to look across at Diane. 'Anything to add?'

'I've been following up on Hilary Hardiman even though she died over six months ago. It just seemed the right thing to do in light of the death threats she received. Yes, she was guilty of poor management, but no one could have foreseen what was going to happen, least of all her. She wasn't able to get another job in healthcare after being struck off the register so went from one menial paid job to another until her cancer made work untenable.' Diane glanced up briefly. 'I managed to get hold of her social security contributions. I've also been in touch with her GP but she wasn't very forthcoming – however, reading between the lines, it looks as if it was an aggressive tumour to have seen someone of her age off so quickly.'

'Probably aided and abetted by the stress she must have been under. How old was she?'

'Only thirty-five.'

'Tragic.' Gaby shook her head.

'Extremely. If she was still alive, I would have placed her clearly in the centre of all this. She must have hated Hannah with a passion and, before you ask, she never married or had children.'

'What about her family, Diane?'

'Older parents. One dead. One in a dementia care home in Abergele. No siblings.'

'Okay. Probably a red herring then so you might as well help Marie with trying to track down Lee's sister.'

Chapter 51

Hannah

Friday 28 August, 5 p.m. Fox Cottage

'At last, I thought you'd never wake up.'

Hannah struggled back to consciousness, her eyelids flickering as she tried to remove the dead weight that appeared to be pressing them closed. Something was wrong, very wrong, but she didn't appear to be in any fit state to work it out. She finally opened her eyes, the effort akin to running a marathon – not that she'd ever been fit enough to run for a bus let alone a mile and certainly not twenty-six of them.

She aimed for a smile only to remove it super quick when she realised that she wasn't in Milly's kitchen. The room was square and dark with no source of light apart from a single unshaded light bulb hanging from a thin filament in the centre of the ceiling and, despite the temperature outside, she was suddenly icy cold. Icy cold in addition to being scared witless.

'Where am I?' That sounded like something from a bad romance, but they were the only words she could think of.

'That's for me to know and you never to find out.'

Hannah struggled to sit only to realise that she couldn't and, looking down, it was easy to see why. Thin blue rope bound her ankles and, with a jerk of her hands, she had to assume that the same blue rope tied both of her wrists behind her back. She licked her lips, her mouth parchment-dry as if someone had drained all of her saliva and replaced it with sawdust. Suddenly she knew she'd been drugged. The water by her bed and maybe even something in the tea she'd made to try and calm her stomach. The milk had tasted funny.

'Milly, why are you doing this?'

'Milly, why are you doing this?' Milly repeated, her voice taking on a singsong quality. 'Did you really think that I'd let somebody like you ruin my life and then get away with it scot-free? If you think the deaths of that brat of yours and your lover were bad … I've barely started.'

Hannah stared up at her, unable to equate the loud and boisterous healthcare assistant with the woman standing in front of her with what looked like a pair of pliers hanging loosely from her fingers. The pliers worried her as did the maniacal expression in Milly's eyes, an expression that reminded her of the time she'd spent at the Beddows. Any thought that she might be able to talk Milly around flickered and died before the idea could even take hold. She'd lost Hunter and Ian because of this woman. She'd thought that the worst thing imaginable. Now she wasn't so sure.

But she still had to try and do something.

'So, you're going to what? Remove my fingernails one by one and not tell me the reason why?' she said, glaring up at her. 'I never thought you a coward. I have a right to know why.'

'You stupid cow. You have a right to zilch.' Milly lifted her foot and kicked her in the head.

Hannah's world went dark for the second time that day.

Chapter 52

Gaby

Friday 28 August, 5.30 p.m. St Asaph

'Gaby, just go.'

'I can't, Owen. I have to be here.'

He took a step forward and, reaching out his arm, picked up her jacket from where she'd hung it behind her chair.

'No, you don't. No one would expect it especially as you're not even meant to be working today,' he said, lifting up her bag for good measure. 'There's an all-ports bulletin out for Hannah and all of the news channels have been alerted. We have men, and women,' he added with a smile, 'tracking the movements of all the key parties.'

'Except for Milly Buttle.'

'As you say, except for Milly Buttle but it's a lead we're following up. Of far more importance is the news that I've phoned Amy and told her you're going to be a bit late but that you're on your way.' Leaning across her desk, he took the liberty of picking up both Gaby's phone and keys and popping them in the top of her bag. 'You know very well that I'm happy to cover for you for as long as it takes. You might have forgotten what very nearly happened to my wife and child, but I haven't and you certainly don't need me to remind you that Amy is your best friend. She needs you now. So go.'

'I was only doing my job.'

But Owen didn't bother to reply. He just stood there, clutching her handbag and jacket in his hand, a belligerent look on his face. She knew she was beaten.

'If you hear anything about Hannah's whereabouts, anything at all, you phone me. Is that clear, Detective?'

'Aye aye, sir!'

She went to slap his arm with the flat of her palm, but he sidestepped her with a smirk.

'You'll have to be quicker than that, Darin,' he said, strolling out of the office with a brief lift of his hand.

Gaby felt torn but Owen was right. Her first duty was to Amy and the truth was that Owen was perfectly capable of leading the team without her. He'd had to manage earlier on in the year when she'd been off sick for an extended period with a punctured spleen, the same case in which she'd rescued Amy from the hands of a serial killer.

But Gaby was conscientious to a fault. Before she switched off her laptop and picked up her bag, she sent a quick email to Sherlock. She trusted Owen with her life, he'd had to save it on more than one occasion, but she was damned if she was going to leave him without any means of support from senior management.

Chapter 53

Hannah

Friday 28 August, 9.50 p.m. Fox Cottage

'Up you get. Time to go outside.'

Hannah watched her grab a spade, from what she now realised was the garage.

'Here, let me help you.'

Milly bent down, loosening the binding to her feet before pulling on her bound arms until she was in the upright position. But she wasn't free. Far from it. The thick rope that circled her waist acted like a grown-up version of baby reins.

'Walk. Now. I won't tell you again.'

It was a moonless night, the rain that the weather forecasters had been promising for weeks finally arriving in a torrent and making the ground moist and slippery underfoot. Hannah didn't know where she was. She couldn't see more than a couple of feet in front of her from the light cast from the open garage door. It smelt like the country so she was probably in the middle of nowhere. With that thought, the smidgeon of hope still lurking that she might be rescued disappeared.

A sharp pull on the rope around her middle dragged her to a stop.

'Here we are. This will do nicely.'

A high-powered torch beamed in her face, destroying any night vision that she might have had. The grass under her feet was thinner and covered in what looked like pine needles, pinging a memory. At the start of the summer Ian had taken them to Gwydir Forest as a surprise. He'd even laid on a picnic and managed to borrow a tartan rug from somewhere in addition to crystal champagne flutes. It was the nine-month anniversary of their first date – not that Hannah could remember. He used to say she didn't have a romantic bone in her body, something she couldn't be bothered to argue about. On the flipside there were certain dates that she couldn't bear to think about. The plane crash. Her time spent at the Beddows. The date of Stephen's death.

She was dragged out of her musings by the feel of a knife slitting through the rope binding her wrists.

'Start digging.'

'What?'

'I said start digging.' Milly pointed to the spade.

'What am I meant to be digging?'

The words popped out of their own accord but she already knew the answer. It wasn't difficult to see where all this was heading. There was no escape. Not now. The tears that she'd been holding on to with an iron determination started to trickle forth.

'I was hoping you were going to ask that. Your grave.'

The tears mingled with the heavy raindrops, making her hand slip on the handle and her feet slide on the sodden ground. Hannah still had no idea who Milly really was or why she'd murdered Hunter and Ian. All of her questions had been greeted with a stony silence of contempt, which made all this seem a million times worse. No trial. Only a death sentence out of nowhere.

Chapter 54

Gaby

Friday 28 August, 10 p.m. Rhos-on-Sea

'I couldn't eat another thing.' Amy collapsed back into the sofa, tucking her pyjama-clad legs beneath her.

'Are you quite sure? I have Italian ice cream in the freezer. Vanilla and chocolate if you're interested?'

'You're a demon; that's what you are, Gaby Darin. A demon disguised as my best friend.'

'Well, I thought I'd make your final day as a single woman memorable not least because of the alcohol-free nature of our little soirée.'

Amy leant forward in her seat, her expression flipping from content to serious. 'You know you can have a drink, don't you? Just because I'm not allowed is no reason for you to …'

'Yes it is, and anyway I've never viewed it much fun drinking on my own. It's a shame I don't have the same reservation about eating chocolate.'

'You and me both! So, how's it going with the case then?' Amy said, picking up her glass of tomato juice and, with her head resting back against the sofa, closed her eyes.

'I have no idea.'

'Which is a huge, big fib, Miss Darin.' She snapped her eyes open. 'We can either talk about Rusty Mulholland, the case, or the fact that it's raining cats and dogs outside. Your choice although I suggest you don't choose the last one, or I might have to strangle you.'

'Amy, a little bit of rain never hurt a wedding and it's not as if you're even going to notice. And anyway, I predict wall-to-wall sunshine for tomorrow. I have a suggestion: what about we talk about you falling out with your mum and your sisters instead?'

Amy sighed. 'No let's not. I can't help it if they don't think I'm good enough or that my choice of partner is inferior.'

'Inferior? Tim?' Gaby snorted. 'He's well on his way to making his first million.'

'But it's not all about the money, as we very well know. He never went to uni for a start and neither did I.'

'Okay let's not talk about your family then or, as you're still yet to meet my mother, mine.'

'Which leaves Rusty …' Amy rubbed her hands together.

'So, the investigation it is,' Gaby said. 'What do you want to know?'

'Everything. First up, is Hannah guilty?'

'She's missing, Amy, which means that she's either done a runner, which I can't believe for an instant, or someone's taken her.'

'And you're here babysitting me when you should be out looking for her.' Amy placed her drink on the small table beside her. 'You know I'm happy to stay here by myself?'

'I know you are, sweetheart, but Owen is on the case. He almost booted me out of the office, which was some feat as it was actually my office we were in at the time,' Gaby said with a chuckle. 'He's promised to call if anything crops up and, in the meantime, are you sure you wouldn't like that ice cream?'

Chapter 55

Owen

Friday 28 August, 11.30 p.m. Brookes Street

'Buttle took it on a short-term rental two months ago,' Malachy said, staring out of the car window. 'The owner died and the son wanted some income while he awaited probate. He said he'd meet us here.'

Owen remained silent, his fingers tapping against the steering wheel as he peered out at the driving rain, his attention drawn to the headlights in the distance. He felt sorry for Amy, the way the weather had changed overnight, but he felt far sorrier for himself stuck in the car with Mal when he should be at home tucked up beside his wife.

'She seemed nice enough. New to the area and employed at one of those old people's homes.' Mr Piper handed his umbrella to Owen while he fiddled around with the front door key.

'What about the boyfriend?'

'Boyfriend? What boyfriend? The contract is only in her name,' he said, wiping his nose with a tissue. 'I do hope this business isn't going to affect the sale price?'

Owen maintained a tense silence, too busy looking around the hall to give the man more than a cursory look.

'Thank you very much for your assistance. We won't keep you and we'll ensure that we pull the door closed when we leave,' Malachy said, showing a degree of maturity that had Owen's lip quirk in amusement. Mr Piper had no option except to leave, slamming the door shut behind him.

The house had that unused stale smell that came from properties that have been left unoccupied – something that wasn't helped by the old-fashioned decor and furnishings. The swirly carpet and grey sofa were of a type popular in the Seventies and reminiscent of his grandmother's front room before she'd moved into sheltered housing. There were no ornaments. No pictures on the walls. Nothing of a personal nature. The kitchen was inhabited by old-style pine cupboards with chunky round handles. The fridge held a new pot of butter and a half a litre of milk.

Owen removed a pair of gloves from his pocket and, bending down, pulled out the carton and took a quick sniff, his nose wrinkling in distaste at the sour smell. There was a kettle and a toaster and a full pack of unopened sliced white bread beside the sink. Nothing else. The kitchen bin came next but held no surprises because it was completely empty.

Upstairs the story repeated itself. The two bedrooms contained double beds each with the minimum of duvet, sheet, pillow and pillowcases. The wardrobes and cupboards were bare. There wasn't even a toothbrush left beside the sink.

He heard Mal stomp up the stairs and met him in the small landing. 'I've had a quick recce out the back, guv. There's a small courtyard but it's also empty.' He shrugged. 'What next?'

'We need to double-check with the care home if there ever was a boyfriend, but I'd lay a fiver on that being a negative.'

Chapter 56

Hannah

Saturday 29 August, Midnight, Fox Cottage

'Look at the state of you. You're filthy – not that I suppose it matters.'

Hannah stood staring down at the hole she'd dug, her fingers red raw and bleeding, the muscles in her arms and back tense and stiff after the unwelcome exercise.

She didn't bother to answer. What would have been the point? She didn't even bother to think about what came next. If she was to hazard a guess, she'd say that it had something to do with the long, slim blade winking in the light cast by the torch. But who wanted to think about their death with their final resting place less than a pace away?

The only thing she wanted to know was why this was happening but, after numerous attempts, it looked as if Milly was going to deny her that last wish. The truth, a truth she'd just realised, was that life was nothing like the movies. There was no happy ever after. No last-minute reprieve where the criminal was foiled in the final act before the curtain fell. She was going to die all alone, cold, wet and miserable and with the likelihood of her body never being discovered. The only positive she could draw was that she'd soon be reunited with both her son and Ian. She felt sorry about Ian, sorrier than she'd ever expected. She'd never doubted his love, only her ability to return it. But in loving her he'd ended up signing his death warrant.

Hannah didn't resist when her wrists were retied behind her back. She knew she couldn't win against Milly and that any attempt to fight her would result in more pain and misery. She only turned when the arc of light swung away, leaving her in complete darkness.

'Sleep well. Sweet dreams. I'll leave you to think about why you're here. See you in the morning if the foxes don't get to you first.'

'Why are you doing this, Milly?' she cried, in one last vain attempt to understand. That was the thing killing her far more than the driving rain and ice-cold shivers chasing across her skin and invading her bones. The need to know.

'Why are you doing this?' Milly repeated, her voice a snarl of sound. 'Because you're a lying, cheating, good-for-nothing cow who deserves everything that's coming to you. If I could have made it worse for you, I would have.'

'What's worse than losing a child?'

'I wouldn't know … but watching Hilary racked with so much pain that she could barely lift her head off the pillow was bad enough.' Milly leant down, peering into Hannah's face in the dim light. 'Yes. That's right. Hilary Hardiman. The person you hung out to dry and all because you couldn't follow the rules.'

'You befriended me? You invited me to the hotel and got me drunk because of something that happened years ago? Un-fucking-believable. I was only a student. A piddly little third year who wasn't meant to be in a situation like that, one I couldn't handle.'

'I don't care!' Milly shouted her down. 'You should have taken responsibility for your own actions.'

But Hannah wasn't listening. Her mind was awash with images from the past and the face she had to blink away. The face of Stephen Lee.

'So, you took my keys that night, drove to my house and murdered them. That makes you the monster, not me.'

Milly didn't answer. Hannah had to watch her turn away, the sight of her receding back growing smaller before disappearing into the grey of the night.

She felt her knees buckle underneath her but, with a swing of her hips, narrowly avoided landing in the grave. There was time enough for that yet. She lay on her side, wriggling into as comfortable a position as she could manage, the tears starting to stream.

Hannah didn't see the clouds shift to reveal a bright waxing moon or a white-winged, snowy owl fly low over the trees, which were only a stone's throw away. But she heard its long low hoot, which was enough to remind her of Milly's parting comment. She could lie in the open and wait for the inevitable, the rain continuing to soak her to the bone, or she could try and do something about it.

With a part groan, part sigh she lifted her head and bent her knees, pushing and dragging herself along the ground, trying to withhold her cries and screams as the rough terrain, sharp twigs and stones tore at her clothes and shredded her skin. There was no thought of time under the canopy of trees, just as there was no plan in her head other than a need to seek protection from the prying eyes of the forest. She finally collapsed at the base of a large Norwegian spruce, its spreading branches offering a degree of cover from the relentless driving rain.

Chapter 57

Gaby

Saturday 29 August, Midnight, Rhos-on-Sea

'Sleep well. Sweet dreams.'

Gaby pulled the door shut of her spare bedroom, replete with a brand-new double bed, and headed back to the lounge. But instead of collecting the remaining dishes she pulled out her mobile and texted Owen.

In less time than it took for her to walk into the kitchen and switch on the kettle her mobile rang in her hand.

'I thought you'd be asleep by now.'

'Cut the small talk, Owen, and tell me what's going on.'

'Quite a bit actually,' he said, his voice taking on a smug tone. 'I've just come back from Buttle's house. It looks like she's been planning something for quite some time. The owner of the property rented it out for a song because of the short contract he was only prepared to offer.'

'So who is she and where is Hannah?'

There was a momentary pause. 'We have no idea.'

254

'I'm coming in,' Gaby said, switching off the kettle and heading into the hall.

'You can't. You need to be there for Amy.'

'She won't even know I've left the house as long as I'm back by about five.'

'And what about sleep? You have a starring role tomorrow and you're going to look like shit let alone feel it unless you get a modicum of sleep.'

'I'll think about that in the morning. Fill up the coffee machine, would you, it's going to be a long night.'

Walking into the incident room, Gaby could be forgiven for thinking that it was the middle of the day. All of the desks were occupied, her faithful team busily trying to work out what was going on.

She dumped her bag on the nearest desk grabbed a clean mug from the shelf and filled it to the brim with Owen's extra-strong black coffee before joining him by the window.

'So, all we have to do to find Hannah is to find the friend?' she said. 'In hindsight, it all makes a weird sort of sense. We thought that Hannah could have been faking her drunken state but, of course, as Diane pointed out, it would have been just as easy for this Buttle woman to pretend to be inebriated, borrow her keys and Bob's your uncle.' She caught Owen's eye. It was all very well having a name, address and even an image of the perpetrator but not when they had no idea as to the woman's motive.

'She had the opportunity and the connection with Hannah to set up the stay at Y Mwyar Duon.' Gaby snapped her fingers, turning to Jax. 'Phone the hotel and find out how the stay came about. Buttle spouted some nonsense to do with splitting up with her boyfriend, didn't she? Also find out how she paid. If they give you a hard time, put them on to me.' She turned back to Owen, noting the grey tone of his skin and the red rim to his eyes but she was in no position to do anything about it. 'The ideal would be if she'd put it on her credit card.'

It didn't take long for Jax to get back to her. 'She paid an initial fifty-pound deposit using cash, and the remainder of the bill after the stay, again in cash. Unusual but not unheard of.'

'Bloody hell! Have they never heard of money laundering?' Gaby raised her eyes heavenward, not expecting an answer to her question. 'What about the home then, Daffodils?'

Malachy stood and stretched, for once looking less than immaculate, his tie askew and the top couple of buttons of his shirt undone. 'I've just come off the phone to the owners, ma'am. Buttle joined them as a care assistant two months ago. They're always looking for staff. She's been mainly on permanent nights since she joined and seems to have fitted in well. They didn't know anything about a boyfriend.'

'That's all very well but as an unqualified member of staff surely she wouldn't have had access to the drug cupboard?' Gaby asked, trying to work it out.

'Unless they were as slack as the nurses at the Beddows,' Marie said, tearing into a bar of chocolate. 'After all, they do take breaks on nights. It would be interesting to find out where the drug keys are kept when the trained staff are having their supper. They would only need one of them to stuff them in a drawer ...'

'Not that any of them would ever admit to it,' Gaby said, picking up her mug and gulping it down in one, the bitter taste catching in the back of her throat.

'No.'

'What we need is a stroke of luck.' She strode over to the last whiteboard and, picking up a pen at random, started twirling it through her fingers. 'Let's have a recap. What do we know about Milly Buttle?'

'Recently moved to Llandudno. Lives in a dive and started working at the same nursing home as Hannah,' Malachy said.

'What else?'

'Not on any social media that I can find,' Diane added. 'I've also checked the Land Registry. She doesn't own any property.'

'What about her birth certificate?'

'That's me, ma'am,' Marie said, with a lift of her hand. 'Born thirty-one years ago to Jane and Peter Buttle. Originally from Scotland. She never married and, from what I can gather, is childless. I have their current address in Coventry and was about to ask whether you wanted me to send a policeman to their door?'

'Just do it.'

Stepping back, Gaby continued to study the three whiteboards, taking a moment to read back over all the notes. 'What is the link?' she said, tapping the end of the pen between her teeth, her eyes returning over and over again to the name Stephen Lee. She couldn't help thinking that the answer was staring straight at her, her gaze now resting on a photo of the Beddows.

'Mal, you're on nights, aren't you?'

'Yes, ma'am.'

'Okay, the rest of you go home. No arguments,' she said, turning back to face the room. 'There's not a huge amount we can do in the middle of the night. Mal, I'd like you to get on to Stephen Lee's parents. We need to find out if they've ever heard of Milly Buttle and, while you're doing that, I'll go over everything again until I find something.'

Gaby crawled into bed at 4 a.m. rueing the day she'd decided to take a job in law enforcement. The alarm woke her at seven.

Chapter 58

Hannah

Saturday 29 August, 1.30 a.m. Fox Cottage

The fox came under the cover of darkness as she knew it would. It was all Hannah could think about as she lay there, silent and straight, struggling not to move. That, and how to free herself from the ropes securing her hands and her feet. She'd always hated the nervous system but she could admire the way her brain managed to concentrate on one problem with a fervent necessity while working through another, her ears tuned to every creak and groan as the wind whistled through the branches above. The forest of trees had a rhythm of sound and she was quickly able to isolate the flap of a wing from the noise from something small and furry. But when the fox came, it wasn't the sound that alerted her. It was the smell. Up until then she'd never seen one up close and she'd certainly never had the opportunity to sniff it.

Did foxes attack humans? She'd heard reports about babies but surely not adults? It was a question she'd never asked before and one she didn't need to ask now because, as soon as she caught sight of him staring at her, a loud scream wrenched through the air: it took her a second to realise that the noise was coming from her own mouth. She watched as he scarpered back the way he'd come, her expression wide-eyed and frantic.

Hannah rolled onto her side, her knees bent towards her chin as she tried to make herself as small as possible. Sleep was drawing her into its net and, despite fears of the fox's return she was unable to keep her eyes open.

The rain eased towards dawn, but it was too late. The damage of eight hours of relentless rain while dressed in only a T-shirt and jeans had turned her chilled bones into a fever and her mind into a random litany of disjointed thoughts and images. Was it a blessing or a curse that her body decided to extinguish all non-essentials like images of Hunter and Ian as it diverted all essential blood flow to where it was urgently needed? Her brain. Her lungs. Her heart.

She didn't hear the rat scurrying across her path. She didn't see him pause to sniff the air for danger. She didn't see him stop and take a cautious bite, chewing and swallowing before beginning the process all over again.

Chapter 59

Gaby

Saturday 29 August, 11 a.m. Amy's bridal car

'But what if I'm never this happy again?'

'Honey, it's only pre-wedding nerves,' Gaby said, taking both of Amy's hands in hers. 'You have a life filled with love and laughter ahead of you.'

'I wish I could believe you.'

Amy looked pale and wan, instead of the gloriously happy bride she was meant to be. As their eyes met, Gaby was transported straight back to that Caernarfon farmhouse where they'd both nearly lost their lives. They knew more than most that happiness wasn't guaranteed, but fear of the future had destroyed many a copper's life. She wasn't about to let that happen to Amy.

'I can't make this feeling go away, sweetheart. All I can promise is that I'll always be there for you, Tim and the baby. Now wipe your eyes and blow your nose,' she said, looking out of the window at the sight of the church up ahead. 'We've a wedding to go to.'

'I thought you'd never get here,' Rusty whispered out of the corner of his mouth as she slid into the seat beside him.

'I had to ask the driver to go round the block a couple of times. She was having a fit of the habdabs.'

'You look lovely, by the way,' he said, linking his fingers through hers. 'Far too much make-up for my liking but still beautiful.'

Gaby couldn't very well thump him in church even if he was right but, after three hours' sleep, the extra thick foundation was to prevent her scaring the children. She tried to remove her hand, the only thing she could think of apart from elbowing him in the ribs, but he tightened his grip.

'Shush, don't be a nuisance,' he said, dipping his head to her ear. 'I like weddings, especially when they're not my own.'

She bit down hard on her lower lip in lieu of a reply, her attention on Amy and where she was repeating her vows.

Amy looked beautiful, her pale brown hair piled in ringlets. Her white satin dress was slim-fitting with a high neck and long narrow sleeves, lace panels adding a hint of detail and mystery. All brides were meant to look beautiful on their wedding day, but Amy outshone them all.

'Here.'

Gaby looked up, from where she'd been searching fruitlessly for a tissue, to find Rusty shoving a pile into her hand.

'Women always cry at weddings,' he elaborated, his voice barely a mumble.

Straight after the ceremony they were put into groups for photographs before being piled into minibuses to take them the short journey to Tim's parents' hotel.

With a brief sigh and an even briefer apology, Gaby pulled out her mobile from a concealed pocket in the side of her dress and, reading through her messages, started typing a quick reply. Rusty grunted but, for once, remained silent.

'Everything all right?'

She shook her head. 'For some reason Buttle's parents are

refusing to speak to us, which is a complete nuisance,' she whispered back. 'Their testimony has never been more important.'

'Why?'

'Owen texted me earlier. The Beddows has just confirmed that Buttle and Hardiman were employed at the unit at the same time as Hannah. He's working through the staff list as we speak but it's going to take a while to trace them all.'

'Funny that Buttle's parents are refusing to speak to the police. I thought perverting the course of justice was still a thing?'

'It is. Comes with a maximum sentence of life imprisonment.'

'They must have a bloody good reason then unless they're in some way ashamed.'

'I don't get you. Why the hell would they feel ashamed?'

'Well, you mentioned that boyfriend of Buttle's didn't exist … This is a bit of a long shot, but I wonder if Buttle and Hardiman were a couple? We both know motive is the key in this investigation – and what's stronger than avenging the woman you love?'

Gaby turned to face him, forgetting her annoyance of earlier.

'You're a bloody genius.'

'I know.'

She elbowed him in the side, suddenly remembering the make-up dig.

'Hey. What was that for?'

But she ignored him. Instead she returned to her phone and sent Owen a quick message.

Recheck the reports into Lee's death. Like Buttle, I think there was something about her parents refusing to speak to the police. Rusty has come up with a good point. See if anyone who knew them can confirm, or otherwise, that they were an item.

Tim's parents owned a boutique hotel along the West Shore with expansive gardens stretching as far as the Great Orme. More photos followed on the lawn, which had most of the female guests bemoaning the height of their heels. All apart from Gaby who slipped off her shoes, the feel of the lush green grass between her toes far preferable to the alternative.

'You'll end up with green feet,' Rusty said with a smirk.

But Gaby wasn't listening, she was far too engrossed in her phone.

'Cover for me, would you? I need to speak to Owen.'

'How the hell can I cover for you, Gaby?' he hissed, towering over her.

'Do your best,' she said, wandering behind a large palm tree.

Owen picked up straightaway, ignoring any of the usual formalities. 'You were bang on, Gaby. Hardiman's parents refused to be interviewed six years ago. It looks like they were estranged ever since she was in her late teens. As good as turfed her out of the house when she left to start her nurse training or so their neighbour tells me. He intimated it was something to do with her life choices but that's as far as he'd go. It's a shame her mother is in that dementia care home or I'd suggest sending someone over.'

'Owen, just do it even if it turns out to be a waste. In the meantime, find out where Hardiman used to live and send a team over. We can't delay on this. God knows what kind of a state Hannah is in or if she's even alive.'

Chapter 60

Milly

Saturday 29 August, 4 p.m. Fox Cottage

Milly swung her rucksack over her shoulders and headed down the path towards the wooded fields that bordered the property. She passed the grave but barely gave it a look before following the trail of disturbed ground where Hannah must have propelled herself backwards by the force of her heels digging into the soil. But Milly wasn't worried. She'd been expecting it. It would have been impossible for her to get very far. Milly's father had taught her well all those years ago when he'd taken her out on his twenty-four-foot schooner, although it had been Google she'd turned to in order to expand her repertoire of undoable knots. Hannah would have needed a knife and Milly had made sure that she wasn't anywhere near one. To come this far only for her victim to escape would be a waste of the last six months of preparation.

She heard her well before she saw her, the sound of her rasping cough interspersed with rapid shallow breaths like music to her ears.

Milly didn't consider herself a violent person. She could never have used the knife despite waving it around like a lunatic. Messing with an insulin pump so that nature took its course was one thing but stabbing a child, or an adult for that matter, wasn't in her make-up. She stood looking down at Hannah's dry flushed face, her gasping breaths telling her that her job was done. She'd avenged Hilary's death in the only way she knew how. The death certificate might have stated cancer as her cause of death but both Hilary and Milly knew differently. Up to her last dying breath Hilary had sworn that Hannah Thomas had been responsible for Stephen Lee's death, and everything that followed. Milly still believed that to be the case.

A car horn hooted, causing Milly to swivel on her heel and head back the way she'd come to the waiting taxi. She had a new passport. A new identity. A new bank account. The one thing she didn't need was to see the final gasping breath of air leaving Hannah Thomas's lungs.

Chapter 61

Gaby

Saturday 29 August, 6 p.m. The West Shore

'Gaby, you're like a cat on a hot tin roof.'

Amy had dragged Gaby to the ladies' as soon as the speeches were out of the way but instead of asking for her assistance with her dress, she backed up against the sink and folded her arms.

'If you think I'm going to tell you what's going on with the case, Amy Potter …'

'You mean Amy Dunne, don't you?'

'Whatever. You know what I mean.'

'Gaby, you're desperate to leave and I'm not going to do anything to stop you. There's a recess anyway for a couple of hours until the evening session starts. Why don't you ring Owen and find out what's going on? You won't be missed by anyone other than me and Rusty.'

'Gee thanks.'

Amy raised her eyebrows. 'You know what I mean,' she said, repeating Gaby's comment right back to her. 'I'll expect to see you then at about eight and try and bring Owen with you. It's bad enough that he couldn't make the meal.' Amy moved to the door only to pause at the sound of Gaby's voice.

'You really are the best kind of friend, Amy.'

'Rusty, I need a favour?'

'Okay,' he said, his tone cautious. 'I don't think I'm going to like what you're about to ask.'

Gaby offered him a thin smile. 'I need your car and, before you say anything, I haven't been drinking but you have.'

'If you think I'm letting you drive my Range Rover you've another think coming. You're barely tall enough to see over the steering wheel, and as for reaching the pedals.'

'Rusty …' she warned.

'No, Gaby. That's final.' He grabbed his jacket from behind his chair. 'I thought you were in a hurry?'

'And I thought you said I couldn't drive your car?'

'You can't unless I'm sitting in the passenger seat beside you. Where are we going? I'll navigate.'

'Of course you will.'

'Hilary Hardiman and Milly Buttle were definitely an item, or at least that's the impression Malachy got from Hardiman's mother,' Gaby said, waiting while Rusty fumbled with his seatbelt. 'The poor woman could barely string two words together but when she saw her daughter's photo she couldn't stop crying. It all got a bit much when he showed her Buttle's. The staff at the home had to sedate her in the end. The matron was a fountain of knowledge and filled in most of the gaps. Hilary was buying a house near Betws-y-Coed until she lost her job and defaulted on the mortgage. The bank repossessed the property. It's still on the market.'

Gaby headed along the A470 with a total disregard for the forty-mile-an-hour speed limit. 'Owen is going to meet us there along with the estate agent.'

*

267

Fox Cottage was a detached house with a wrap-around balcony and panoramic views of the surrounding forest. Recently modernised, it featured a circular driveway and a mature garden. There was no sign of life apart from an old Ford Focus that had seen better days and the occasional tweet from a bird in the trees that bordered the back of the property.

Gaby climbed out of the driving seat, her phone in her hand. 'Owen's about five minutes away. Come on, let's have a quick scout around the back.' She made for the Ford and, hand on the bonnet, wasn't surprised to find the metal cool to the touch just as she wasn't surprised to find the doors locked. Nothing about this investigation had been easy.

Strolling across the large garden, her shoes again dangling from her fingers, she could almost imagine that she was in paradise. The property was so different to her small seaside cottage but exactly the type of home she'd have bought if she could have afforded it. That is until she saw the grave up ahead, a large molehill of soil beside it.

Her first thought was that they were too late because what was the point of digging a grave only to leave it empty. Her second was to holler for Rusty at the top of her voice.

Instead of waiting for a reply, she started following the track into the forest where someone had either been pulled or dragged across the partially decomposed selection of leaves, twigs and bark. She only knew she was on the right track at the sight of a torn scrap of bloodstained material in the middle of the path. That was when she started to run, forgetting about her shoeless state and the way the forest floor was cutting into the soles of her feet.

Gaby thought her dead. After all she'd seen quite a few dead people during her time on the force. The still chest. The waxy pallor of her skin. The blood congealed on her hands. Her inability to find a pulse.

'Rusty,' she hollered again before rolling Hannah onto her

back and opening her airway before starting to breathe air into her quiet lungs.

'What is it, woman? You know I've—' He never got to finish the sentence. Instead he lifted her out of the way, shouting orders as he started examining Hannah's lifeless form.

After that … Gaby didn't remember much.

'Fancy seeing you in the emergency department, Dr Mulholland. I thought you only dealt with the dead ones?'

Rusty grunted, which Gaby was beginning to realise was his staple response for anything he couldn't be bothered to comment on.

'And dressed up to the nines too,' the young houseman carried on, seemingly oblivious to Rusty's mounting temper. If he'd known Rusty better, he'd also have known that it was impossible to get the better of the eminent pathologist. But Gaby, with the case heading for closure, took pity on him.

'If there's anyone free, I wouldn't mind them having a look at my feet, if it's not too much bother?' she said staring down at the dirty hem of her rose pink dress and the sorry state of her ankles peeking out underneath.

'And she'll need a tetanus jab while we're at it,' Rusty added, between his teeth.

'I had one recently.'

'I don't care if you had one yesterday. You're having another one.'

Gaby was learning when it was best to stay quiet but oftentimes didn't follow her own advice. She opened her mouth to retaliate, only to snap it closed at the sight of the young doctor staring between them with his jaw wide open.

'Yes, darling.'

They were allowed in to see Hannah but only for a second. Dressed in a hospital gown, she was attached to more tubes and wires than Gaby had ever seen. It was still touch and go as to whether they'd managed to get to her in time but at least she was now in the right place.

'Will she make it?'

'It's too early to say. Pneumonia is a contrary visitor – it's impossible to guess this early as to how she'll progress. There's also the blood loss from the wounds to her fingers. Rats are filthy creatures but luckily for her, there's no rabies to worry about.' Rusty placed his arm around her shoulder, pulling her to his side as they walked out of the intensive care unit.

Owen and Malachy were waiting for her at the entrance to the emergency department, which made her both happy and sad in equal measure.

'Get away, both of you. I'll see you at Amy's dance shortly.'

'You might want to rethink your choice of garment?' Owen said, his gaze on Gaby's dress, which would never be the same again. 'And where the hell are your shoes?'

Chapter 62

Gaby

Monday 31 August, 9 a.m. St Asaph

'Milly Buttle has disappeared off the face of the earth, ma'am.'

'And a good morning to you too, Owen,' Gaby said, restraining a smile. 'I do hope you enjoyed the rest of your weekend?'

After an indifferent night tossing and turning, Gaby felt less than her usual self. Her pillow had been too hard, her duvet too hot, her Egyptian cotton sheets too cold without the addition of the duvet … She'd finally climbed out of bed at 6.45 a.m. and, with the seasonally warm weather making a welcome reappearance, took her bowl of porridge and cup of tea into the garden to spend fifteen minutes sitting under the shade of her pear tree. Somehow, Gaby knew that it was going to be the best fifteen minutes she spent that day.

'Yes, I did thanks. Did you hear what I said? Milly Buttle—'

'Has disappeared off the face of the earth?' Gaby placed her handbag on the back of her chair along with her jacket before heading to the kettle and giving it her usual little shake. 'Not quite true though, is it? She's presumably got herself a new identity off the dark web and is setting herself up somewhere where we'll never find her.'

'How can you be so relaxed about it? She murdered two people and tried to murder a third.'

Gaby spooned coffee into two mugs and hovered by the kettle while she waited for it to boil.

'Because I can and because there's nothing anybody can do about it other than what we're doing already. We've alerted Interpol and her face is all over the newspapers, both nationally and internationally. She'll either turn up or she won't,' she said, pushing a mug towards him and returning to perch on the edge of her desk. 'Arresting her isn't going to bring Hunter and Ian back. The damage has already been done on that score. The one thing we do need to look at is Hannah's protection.'

'I've been thinking about that. Buttle obviously assumed that she was dead. When she finds out—'

'Exactly. I'm not sure what Hannah's going to think about a change in identity but it's something we're going to have to raise as soon as she's well enough. Buttle won't stop until Hannah is dead and, if she stays in Wales, she'll be a sitting target.'

'We don't even know why she did it – not really,' Owen said, picking up his drink and wandering over to the window.

'Oh, I think we have a bloody good idea. Milly obviously blamed Hannah for everything that happened to Hilary right down to the rapid advancement of her cancer and subsequent death. Getting a job and befriending Hannah would have been easy and we already know what must have happened at Y Mwyar Duon. The thing we're not sure about is if Hunter's problem with his insulin pump was a convenient but unfortunate accident. It's my guess Buttle dislodged the pump and administered the diamorphine to Ian soon after – just enough to dull his senses – before enticing him into Hunter's room. A loud bang would have done it. He must have panicked, tried to reset the pump and when he couldn't, phoned for an ambulance, but Milly cancelled the call before the station had a chance to pick up. It wouldn't have been that difficult to persuade him into the car – by then he'd have been almost unconscious anyway. He wouldn't have known what hit him. After, Milly took his keys, which was a silly thing to do but it allowed her the access she needed to clear out all of Hunter's processions.'

'But I still don't understand how either Hardiman or Buttle could think that Stephen Lee's death was Hannah's fault. As a third-year student, surely they'd know she wasn't to blame?'

'That's something we may never know.'

Chapter 63

Hannah

Two weeks later

'I want you to return to Australia with me. There's nothing left for you here. You can sell the house easily enough and get something over there. Start a new life. It's not as if you won't know anyone. My dad has decided that with Ian gone, there's no point in him staying in Wales by himself.'

Dominic had it all planned – everything worked out right down to the sale of her property. It was there in his smug expression and arrogant tone. After a week in ICU and a week on female medical recuperating, Hannah had enough energy to realise that she was going to have a fight on her hands if she wanted to avoid moving halfway across the world.

'And what if I don't want to leave Wales?'

'Why ever would you want to stay?' Dominic said, staring across at her from the safety of the chair by the window.

'Maybe because I don't deserve anything better,' she replied, avoiding his gaze, her thumb and forefinger plucking at the duvet cover.

'Balderdash. Coming across the martyr isn't going to win you any favours with me, I can assure you.'

'Who says anything about trying to win favours? This isn't about you. This is about me.'

'What do you mean?' he said, his voice softening. 'Make me understand and I'll go away.'

'All of this, it's my fault.' She lifted her hand briefly, surprised at how thin and pale it looked against the pink duvet cover. Only this morning they'd removed the final drip, the micropore tape still marked the spot. She was still on antibiotics but discharge had been mentioned, although an actual date not set.

Make me understand and I'll go away. Those were his exact words and perhaps it would be better if he did understand. She closed her eyes and rested back against the pillow. That way she wouldn't have to see his expression alter.

'This is all my fault,' she repeated. 'No, that's not quite right. I suppose ultimately Stephen was to blame, but as he's dead … He was nice. He was nice to me right from the start. It felt as if he wasn't a patient.' She opened her eyes briefly only to close them again, disconcerted by the way Dominic was leaning forward in his chair, his stare unwavering. 'You'll know that being a doctor. Some patients take on the sick role as soon as they test the mattress on their hospital bed while others feel more like a visitor passing through. I think he realised that I was hurting. It must have shown.'

Hannah laughed. It was a tense, ugly sound without a shred of humour. 'He chose his target and pulled me in using all the skills at his fingertips. It wasn't rape,' she added, almost as an after-thought, only to pause at the sound of Dominic's sharp indrawn breath. But she continued anyway. Now that she'd started, she'd see the story through to the end. 'He was too clever for that. In the first week he'd wrapped me around his little finger. I would

275

have done anything for him. The only person to show me any love and affection since the plane crash that had killed my family.' She turned to him then, her eyes flickering open. 'Did you know about my …?'

'Yes. Ian told me.'

She paused again but this time for longer, suddenly aware of how pale he was underneath his tan – not that she was interested in how he looked. She felt disconnected somehow from it all. It was as if she was reading about somebody else's life in a book.

'Oh good. I mean I don't have to …'

'I know what you meant,' he said, his voice gruff.

Hannah swallowed, trying to pick up the thread of the conversation. 'The night on the roof. I thought it was all a joke at first. He kissed me there in the kitchen, slipping the passkey from around my neck and racing to the fire door. *Come with me, Hannah. Come and kiss me under the stars*, he said. I followed. I had no choice. But I still thought it was a big laugh. He was running around the roof like a bird, his arms extended. *I'm free. At last I'm free.* He ran to the edge and that was the first inkling I had of what he intended.' She took a deep breath, her fingers instinctively massaging the scar on her left wrist just above the bandaging. 'I shouted. I screamed, lunging across the open space and grabbing onto his hand.'

She opened her eyes then but all she could see were the stars up ahead and the sight of Stephen's screwed-up face as he screeched at her, words that dominated her dreams and her nightmares. '*You were a pity fuck and a pretty poor one at that.*' On hearing those words she let go and watched as he flew through the air, his arms extended like the bird he was trying to be.

Hannah couldn't repeat that. Not here. Not now. Not ever.

She sat up in bed, and almost managed a smile, not quite. 'So you see, Dominic, it wouldn't be fair on you or your dad if I came with you.'

'I take it that Hunter was his son?'

It wasn't the response she'd expected. She'd forgotten for a minute just how clever he was.

'No. Hunter was my son. Only mine.'

Chapter 64

Hannah

Two months later. Brisbane

'That was the estate agent,' Hannah said, tapping out a quick reply on her phone. 'There's been a bit of interest in the property. Apparently it's what people are looking for.'

'I wish I could say the same about my dad's. He's barely had any viewings.' Dominic placed a glass in front of her. 'It's all he talks about, other than leaving the dogs in quarantine. You'd think I'm the worst son in the world for dragging him halfway across the world. You're sure you're happy with iced tea?' he went on, frowning at her drink. 'It's not the summer, you know.'

'I think you've forgotten what a real winter is, living here. When was the last time you had snow for instance?'

Hannah glanced out at the Brisbane River and the ferries passing under Story Bridge before picking up her drink, her eyes grazing her left hand and the missing fingertips – a constant reminder of what she'd been through. She could escape life in

Conwy and almost everything about her previous life. But she couldn't escape her memories.

'Touché, although we do get snow here, just not in this part.' He picked up his spoon and stirred his drink. 'So, once you've sold the house, that will be your last tie with the UK. Have you thought about what you're going to do?'

'Not really. It was very good of you to whisk me away, but I can't stay forever. There's visas and things,' she added, her voice fading to nothing.

'And DI Darin's offer of a new identity – or have you brushed that under the carpet along with everything else?' he said, the spoon between his thumb and forefinger.

'What are the chances that Milly will still be looking for me?'

'I'd say there's every chance, particularly if you go back to Wales.'

'But there's nothing for me here.'

'Charming!'

'You know what I mean. Look, I can't stay, all right.' She lowered her voice, well aware they were starting to draw looks from the other people who'd come to the riverside café with the sole purpose of admiring the view.

'Yes, you can. Easily. I'll be hearing any day about receiving my fellowship and when I do I intend to join Médecins Sans Frontières for a bit.' He lifted his head briefly before returning his attention to where he was drawing circles on the table with the tip of his spoon. 'You can stay in my house with my dad, although he doesn't need much minding.'

'Dominic, you live in a bloody palace. I'd never feel at home.'

'I can sell it, get something smaller. It's only money at the end of the day.'

'It's only money, he says.' Hannah blinked across at him. 'You have no idea how arrogant you sound.'

'I don't mean to. It's not my fault I took a punt and invested everything I had in Bitcoin when no one really knew what it was and I do have a mortgage, you know. In fact, selling up is quite a good idea,' he said, leaning back in his chair. 'I can clear the mortgage and buy something you and Dad will both like. You can get a job if you think it's charity.'

'They won't let me.'

'Yes, they will. There's a global shortage of nurses as you very well know and, with accommodation already sorted, they'd be stupid to turn you away,' he said, returning the spoon to the saucer. 'I'll also be doing the one thing I promised Ian, which was to take care of you if ever anything was to happen to him. It's a complete no-brainer as far as you're concerned, Hannah. A new family in a new country where she'll never be able to find you.'

Acknowledgements

As a writer I know of the time and effort it takes to produce a book but, as with most things, I couldn't do it without the help of others.

I always leave my family until last. I'm not sure why. Not today! It's been a busy year, outside of books, with the twins undergoing GCSE assessments and my son in the first year of university. Stressful all round so I couldn't have done this without their support and that of my husband, Alan. Fitting writing around the day job adds a particular layer of anxiety …

Also thanks to fellow writer, Valerie Keogh, who I view as an honorary family member. You help keep me sane!

This is my fifth book with HQ Digital and the team have, again, done a fantastic job of leading me in the right direction. Dushi Horti is all I could ever want in an editor. Audrey Linton is a great editorial assistant while Helena Newton and Michelle Bullock have done a brilliant job on the edits. Publishing during Covid has meant working from home for many in the industry but, as a writer, I haven't noticed any difference in the level of support I get, so thank you to everyone involved.

I have a small team of super fans, including Beverley, Michele, Lesley, Lynda, Maureen, Susan, Clare, Tracy, Hayley, Elaine, Terri, Madeleine, Amanda, Adele, Daniela and Pauline. Thank you for your continued support. Also thanks to the dedicated book reviewers and bloggers that have found my books. Your help has been invaluable.

While I'm a nurse I'm not an expert in diabetes but Dr Kate Allen is. Thank you for your help, Kate. I'm also not a detective. I have sought out help with the nuts and bolts of this book from people in the know but any mistakes are my own. Apologies in advance. I've done my best!

While most of the characters in this book are fictitious, there are four that aren't. Amy Potter, my colleague and a fantastic nurse – I have to say that as she's now my boss. Amy, I never imagined that I'd give you a husband and a baby when I asked your permission to use your name in *Silent Cry*, that very first book – thank you for being so good about it.

Jon Marquis is a friend and member of CHOG, a local network. I hope you like what I've done with you – you're nothing like your namesake – I wouldn't want to upset Christine or Julie!

Tracy Robinson, a Facebook friend. Thank you for letting me use your name, Tracy. I hope you like your character.

Amanda Perrott, thank you for giving me permission to use your brother, Mikey's, name.

The name of Steven Lee was chosen by Amanda Carlton over on UKCBC, a crime fiction group on Facebook. It's a combination of her husband and son's names. Thank you, Amanda. He turned out darker than I had originally planned. A very troubled young man.

Hunter's name was chosen by Maria Bernard over on Tattered Page Book Club. Thank you, Maria. The perfect name.

Take a Break Café, Llandudno, and Coast Café, Rhos-on-Sea, both exist. Thank you for letting me include you both for local flavour.

Apologies if I've left anyone out. The family. My publisher. My characters. The people that helped me. The cafés. The cats! I can't forget them. One is even now butting my arm seeking attention. Perry and Nighty.

Keep reading for an excerpt from _Lost Souls_ …

JENNY O'BRIEN

LOST
SOULS

A DETECTIVE GABY DARIN NOVEL

Chapter 1

Elodie

Friday 31 July, 1 p.m. Colwyn Bay

Elodie Fry was bored. It was only two weeks since school had broken up for summer but she had nothing to do and nobody to do it with.

The house was quiet, the only sound to be heard the distant hum of the hoover as her mum vacuumed the stairs. She could of course help but when she'd offered she'd had her head snapped off for her trouble, which was such a rare event that she'd retreated to the lounge in a huff with her library book. That was an hour ago. Her book was long since finished, her water bottle empty and there was nothing on the television that grabbed her attention.

She scrabbled to her feet, her skinny legs almost too long for her body. Her fair hair was still pulled back into the netted bun she had to wear to her ballet lessons, a look that was at war with her pink hoodie and scruffy jeans. She left the lounge and wandered into the kitchen, humming a little tune she'd made up in her head. Her mum's bag was slung around the back of the chair, her half-full mug of cold tea abandoned on the pine table. She could always start on her lunch but she wasn't in the mood for a sandwich. Her normally placid demeanour was disturbed by the bitter taste of annoyance at the way her mother had spoken to her.

While she didn't have a dad, she did have an amazing mum who worked all the hours to ensure that they had enough money to eke out over the month. There was never much left over for treats and a new school uniform was one of the corners that her mother had to cut in favour of second-hand. But she always managed to scrape enough money together for a pair of proper leather school shoes and a decent pair of trainers, even if they weren't as designer as Elodie would like. No, Elodie had a lot to be thankful for. Her lack of a dad was a niggle but there were far worse things than a snappy mum and no dad.

There was nothing in the kitchen that she wanted so, instead of dawdling, she twisted the key to the back door and headed out into the fenced garden, the warm burst of sun on her face causing her to break out into her signature cheeky smile. The garden wasn't big: barely a few metres of grass bordered by a small patio and with a large shed taking up the whole of one corner.

After a few walkovers and handstands she was bored again. Her gaze lingered on the shed. What she needed was a ball, something she could bang against the side of the house until her mother had finished whatever she was doing upstairs.

The shed opened easily under her touch, the bolt sliding back with a slight squeak. She held her breath and her fingers gripped the edge of the door. Her mother had told her on more than one occasion that she had no business going into places that didn't concern her, which meant that the shed was clearly out of bounds. But just like Eve and that apple, Elodie didn't heed the warning. She was still feeling aggrieved at being told off and it wasn't as if she intended to do any damage, she thought, taking in the neat line of old garden tools hanging from bright red hooks beside the freezer.

Continuing to hum her little tune, she rummaged along the shelves in vain for something to play with. There were no toys but the possibility of an ice cream had her walking towards the freezer, her mouth starting to water. The sound of the shed door banging against its hinges caused her to quicken her step. She wasn't doing anything wrong, not really. As she brushed a stray cobweb off her sweatshirt, the hairs on the back of her neck stood to attention, her failsafe warning system finally alerting her to the danger up ahead. She turned and stared, her fingers trembling, closely followed by her arm, her breath heaving as her lungs scrabbled around for enough oxygen to meet the sudden rampant demand placed on it by her galloping heart.

Life paused, then flashed before her in a rapidly blinking strip of images. She couldn't move when she knew she must. One second passed, then two, before her feet found the will to turn and run, the open door of the shed forgotten in her hurry to escape the very worst of nightmares.

Elodie pulled the straps of her rucksack tightly across her shoulders, taking the time to scan the room for any essentials that she might have forgotten. There'd be no coming back, not now. Her gaze dawdled on the pile of teddies that had grown exponentially over the course of her young life. She'd allowed herself only one, Ted, because he was small and she was able to tuck him down the side of her rucksack at the expense of a pair of socks. She'd also allowed herself a book, again only the one. But suddenly she felt an affinity with Harry Potter and his Philosopher's Stone, not that there could ever be a happy resolution to her own personal tale of woe. Unlike Harry there was no Dumbledore to guide her, or Hagrid to protect her from what was coming. She'd poked her nose where she shouldn't and fleeing the security of the only home she'd ever known was the one outcome left to her.

Wiping her sleeve across her eyes, she headed for the door, not bothering to close it behind her. Her mother would know soon enough that she wasn't in the one place she'd expect – bed. With her hand clenched around the banister, she avoided the creaky first and third stairs as she hurried to the bottom, fearful now that her mother might guess that something was up. She'd certainly questioned her at length over the weekend, but what could Ellie tell her? She wasn't prepared to lie and she'd never in a million years believe the truth. Ellie had spent the last two days trying to persuade herself that Friday had never happened, but it was no good. She only had to close her eyes and she was back in that shed …

The kitchen was next and this was the place that delayed her the most. She had a few quid, not much but enough for a start. However, she needed food – as much as she could carry but not too heavy to weigh her down. Tins of beans came first, luckily with a ring pull as she didn't fancy depriving her mum of the only can opener in the overflowing cutlery drawer. A spoon, a fork and a knife. She paused over the knife, an intense look of concentration pulling at her brow. She hadn't thought of a weapon but what was the likelihood that she might need one? Her hand fingered one of the wooden-handled set of six steak knives that her mother had picked up cheap at some car-boot or other. The knife got placed in the bottom of her bag as did the small wind-up torch that lived in the pot on the kitchen shelf. She also took some matches, bread, cheese and a few other cans before testing the weight of her rucksack and reluctantly pulling the drawstring and lifting it onto her shoulders.

Ellie was small for her age, but wiry. A life spent practising ballet had firmed her muscles and hardened her resolve. She could do this. She had to do this.

There was no note. She wouldn't have known what to write in any case. A solitary tear tracked down her cheek. Instead she picked up a pink Post-it Note and drew a heart before sticking it to the side of the kettle and heading for the door without a backward look.

Chapter 2

Gaby

Monday 3 August, 7.05 a.m. Rhos-on-Sea

'Darin speaking.'

Acting DI Gaby Darin glanced down at the screen of her mobile, a frown firmly in place. With Owen Bates, her DC, still on paternity leave until later today, she was the senior officer on the North Wales Major Incident Team and as such available 24/7 whether she liked it or not. She didn't mind covering but she wondered why they always phoned her when she was about to sit down to eat. Porridge was bad enough but cold it was a thick, unpalatable, paste-like gloop.

'Ma'am, it's Jax Williams. We have a runaway girl.'

Gaby leant back in her chair, breakfast forgotten, her mind full of another missing girl, a mystery they'd solved only a short time ago: twenty-four years too late. There couldn't be a second one surely – not so soon. But, hand resting on her brow, she knew she shouldn't be surprised at the news, only her reaction. Instead of the adrenalin that usually soared through her veins at the thought of a new case, all she could come up with was a deep sense of disappointment. It suddenly felt as if she was losing her identity with each successive crime, as if someone was taking a chisel and chipping away. Gaby Darin: acting DI. Not Gabriella: sister, friend, lover.

Last week had been a good week, the best week in ages. Her relationship with Rusty Mulholland, the resident pathologist, was continuing to blossom. Still only friends, she could see that changing to something more but only if she was allowed the opportunity of cultivating their growing rapport.

'Ma'am, are you there?'

With a huge effort, Gaby pulled herself together. It wasn't like her to wallow in self-pity and it certainly wasn't like her to daydream about red-headed pathologists with startling blue eyes and a temper that was on an even shorter fuse than her own. She was there to fulfil the role she was paid for. If she didn't like it, she could always … She shook the thought away. No. She couldn't!

'Yes, sorry, Williams. It must be a bad line,' she said, crossing her fingers behind her back as the easy lie slipped through her lips. She wasn't going to tell him the truth. 'Go on, you were saying?'

She grabbed her keys from the centre of the table and, heading into the hall, picked up her bag and jacket from the newel post, careful to avoid the mess that was currently her lounge. Painting the wood panelling that lined the bottom half of the room at the weekend wasn't the greatest of ideas but, with work being quiet, she'd optimistically thought that she'd be able to get it finished in the evenings after work, refusing to dwell on the image of cosy meals for three while she continued getting to know Rusty and his young son, Conor.

'We got the call about thirty minutes ago. Elodie Fry, age ten. Her mother went to wake her this morning only to find that her bed hadn't been s-s-slept in,' he stuttered, heaving air into his lungs. 'After phoning around and a quick search, she rang us. I'm heading over to interview her.'

'I'll meet you there – and, Jax, grab Amy. The sooner we get a FLO involved the better. It's times like this that family liaison officers come into their own.' She pushed against the front door to check the latch had caught, making a mental list, which she started to tick off in the maelstrom that was now her mind. 'And get Marie and Mal involved ASAP. They can get the search underway while we wait for Owen.'

'Did you want me to give him a ring too?'

Owen. Her fingers gripped her keys, the hard, cold metal biting into the soft flesh of her palm. How would he take another missing girl after the recent ordeal that his wife and unborn child had gone through? How would he stand up to the pressure when he'd nearly decided to throw his career away? There was only so much she could do to protect him on a case like this.

'No, let me contact him. You've enough to do. What's the address?'

Ystâd golygfa'r môr, or Sea View estate, was the largest housing development in Colwyn Bay. A mixture of social housing, the sprawling concrete jungle had a reputation that struck fear into the hearts of the coppers who had the misfortune to attend any of the frequent call-outs. But as with most of these estates the inhabitants got on with their own business, the few bad ones spoiling it for everyone.

Number 312 was a narrow, two-bedroomed house with distant views over the Welsh coast and bordered by a waste-land of tarmac littered with potholes and the odd dolls' pram along with the usual detritus of cola cans and sweet wrappings. But the house was different again. While small and cluttered, it was spotlessly clean. The sofa and recliner chair were arranged around a small TV, the mantelpiece over the three-bar electric fire displaying unframed photos, all of the same pretty blonde girl. But Gaby wasn't interested in the girl's appearance, not yet. All her attention was on the faded middle-aged woman currently leaning forward on the sofa, a long, low keening sound coming from her mouth.

Jax dipped his head to whisper in Gaby's ear. 'Ms Anita Fry, ma'am. She's been like that ever since we arrived. I've sent Mal and Marie a copy of the most recent photo for distribution and DS Potter is on her way.' He turned, adding over his shoulder, 'I thought I'd make her a cuppa. S-s-she looks as if she needs it.'

Gaby nodded in agreement, her gaze pinned to the woman in front of her. About forty, and dressed in jeans and a loose top the colour of an overripe avocado, Ms Fry had the complexion of someone who'd had several knocks over the years: her jawline saggy, her skin that pasty tone of too little time spent out of doors. Life was hard for some families, none harder than in this room.

As an experienced detective, it took a lot to engage Gaby's sympathies. She'd seen far too much of the human race to ever believe what was in front of her. She'd been lied to and conned in both her personal and professional life far too many times to take people on trust. But if anyone was going to engage her compassion it was this woman.

'Hello, Ms Fry. My name is DI Gaby Darin.' She dropped into the chair opposite, leaning forward, her clasped hands dangling between her legs, the line of her favourite navy Zara jacket bunching around her shoulders. 'I've already pulled a team of officers together to scour the neighbourhood but I need to ask you some questions that will help us. To begin with is there any reason you can think of that might have made Elodie decide to run away? And are there any friends or family she might have gone to stay with?'

'Ellie.'

'Excuse me?'

'No one calls her Elodie. It's Ellie and she's not like that. She'd have no reason to run away.' Ms Fry raised her head from where she'd been staring down at the floor, her eyes red-rimmed and her skin coated in dark shadows that long predated her missing child. 'We're a team, her and me. A tight little unit. She'd never have just upped and left like that. She'd have had no reason. Yes, money's tight but we still manage to get by.'

'What about school? Is she happy? Friends?'

'Happy enough. She likes it, would you believe? I don't know where she gets it from but she's clever too. There's even talk of trying for a scholarship next year at St Elian's College.'

'And friends?' Gaby reminded her softly. 'Anyone she might have gone to stay with?'

'But why would she? There'd be no need and certainly not in the middle of the night,' she said, her tone taking on the shrill note of someone on the edge. 'There's really no one apart from her best friend, Heather, and even then they don't see much of each other. Only in school and for the occasional playdate. Outside of her ballet lessons – she's mad on ballet – she spends the rest of the time either reading or out with me.'

'I believe you're a cleaner.' Gaby watched her stiffen.

'And what if I am? It's a good, honest job.'

Gaby spread her hands only to clasp them together again. 'It certainly is. An essential one,' she replied, relieved to see Anita visibly relaxing in front of her. An aggressive witness – and witness was what she had to view her as – was the very last thing she wanted. Time was precious. The most precious thing where a missing child was concerned. They needed clear, accurate information and they needed it fast – it was up to Gaby to get it. 'So, what about anyone else she might have decided to slope off to see? Any siblings? What about her father or even a boyfriend?'

'There's no one. No father. He was never on the scene. No siblings, and a boyfriend at ten? Come on. She's not interested in boys and, even if she was, there isn't the time in her day for her to go and chase them.' Her features hardened, frown lines forming deep tracks on either side of her mouth. 'And before you ask, I don't have a boyfriend either. They're far more trouble than they're worth.'

Gaby took a sneaky glance at the plain, black-strapped watch on her wrist, her mind on the investigation. The seconds were ticking by. No one knew more than her what little time they had left if there was to be a happy resolution. But she still had questions that needed to be answered.

'Tell me about yesterday then. Anything that you can think of to spark her running away?'

'I've already told that officer on the phone earlier. Yesterday was a normal day. Nothing happened. We got up. Ellie stayed in her room until lunchtime finishing up a crafting project and reading. After lunch we headed out to the beach for a walk. We came home, had tea and slobbed out in front of the TV. The exact same as every other Sunday.'

No, not the exact same or otherwise your daughter wouldn't be missing. But instead all she said was, 'And there was no trouble at school? No bullying?' Gaby rose to her feet and walked over to the mantelpiece to study the photos: the 'thin as sticks' limbs, and eyes that dominated the girl's heart-shaped face. 'She's very slight. No problems with depression? Eating all right?'

'Ellie eats like a horse, Detective. You probably can't believe it,' Anita said, tugging at the pool of flesh around her middle. 'But I used to be the same.'

Gaby smiled briefly. 'I can well imagine. So …'

But she didn't get to finish her sentence. Anita sprung to her feet, quite unaware of the look of desperation etched across her cheeks. Gaby knew what she was going to ask. Every single relative of a missing person asked the exact same question, their words layered with the same frantic tone. They were asking the one question they knew it was impossible to answer at this stage but still they asked it.

'Will you be able to find her?'

Dear Reader,

I hope you enjoyed *Buried Lies*, the fifth in my Detective Gaby Darin series. It's always hard to come up with unusual plots but I hope I've managed. Hannah's journey is a tragic one, her story not finished but I think she'll have a happy ending. Dominic, for all his faults, is very strong-minded and a capable adversary. She deserves happiness if anyone does.

If this is the first book you've read in the series, you're in for a treat as there are four more out, each a standalone. In order, these are *Silent Cry*, *Darkest Night*, *Fallen Angel* and *Lost Souls*.

I have just completed the next book in the series, which shifts the narrative ahead by six months so, instead of summer it is set in the depth of winter. It has a completely different feel but with still the same set of detectives, all apart from Diane who is busy completing her detective exams. I've been writing about them for so long now that they seem like family.

I love hearing from my readers via social media. I'm on Twitter and Instagram as Scribblerjb. I also have a Facebook page, Jenny O'Brien, Guernsey Writer, which is usually woefully out of date, but I do try to reply to everyone who gets in touch.

If you did enjoy *Buried Lies*, I'd appreciate a quick review over on Amazon or Goodreads as it helps new readers find Gaby and her team.

Very best wishes,

Jenny

Dear Reader,

We hope you enjoyed reading this book. If you did, we'd be so appreciative if you left a review. It really helps us and the author to bring more books like this to you.

Here at HQ Digital we are dedicated to publishing fiction that will keep you turning the pages into the early hours. Don't want to miss a thing? To find out more about our books, promotions, discover exclusive content and enter competitions you can keep in touch in the following ways:

JOIN OUR COMMUNITY:

Sign up to our new email newsletter:
http://smarturl.it/SignUpHQ

Read our new blog www.hqstories.co.uk

🐦 https://twitter.com/HQStories

📘 www.facebook.com/HQStories

BUDDING WRITER?

We're also looking for authors to join the HQ Digital family!
Find out more here:

https://www.hqstories.co.uk/want-to-write-for-us/

Thanks for reading, from the HQ Digital team

If you enjoyed *Buried Lies*, then why not try another utterly gripping crime thriller from HQ Digital?

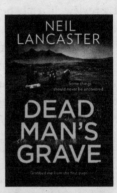